WILD TIMES WITH GRANITE

I0543058

Gail Varga

Hairinthwind Publishing

WILD TIMES WITH GRANITE

Copyright © 2016 Gail Varga
All rights reserved in all media. No part of this book may
be used or reproduced without written permission,
except in the case of brief quotations embodied in critical
texts or reviews.

This is a work of fiction. All names, characters, locales
and incidents are products of the author's imagination
and any resemblance to actual people, places or events is
coincidental or fictionalised.

Published by Hairinthewind Publishing 2016

Cover by Gail Varga

ISBN 978-0-9956203-1-5

In remembrance of my dear Csaba bacsi

Contents

1: Background to a Nugget   1
2: Backwards and Forwards: Happy Memories
and Screams for the Future   6
3: Love and Building Plans   15
4: Uncle Heap is Decrepit but not Daunted   24
5: A Steady Place   32
6: An Aside on Granite   45
7: Anticipation   50
8: Reality is Real Now According to Uncle Heap   67
9: The Wild Times   78
10: Dribbling with Great Uncle Lollo   87
11: Finding Out Things and Wondering Some
More   92
12: Building Begins   98
13: Bog Inheritance   102
14: Preparations, Goodbyes and a Nugget Gift   110
15: Big and Silent   120
16: The Red, Neo Carboard Era   128
17: Snoring Discovered   139
18: What I Did with my Pencil   148
19: A New View   154
20: Settling the Ownership of Smiles   167
21: Words Lead to Chocolate   173
22: I Become Truly Complicit for a Moment   182
23: Time Passes, Things Change   186
24: I am no longer Complicit in Shoddiness   195
25: Gratitude and Leavings   202
26: Alone with a Knife   208
27: I Learn About Normality   214
28: The Absorption of Doom   224
29: The Big Dipper   232

30: An Important Piece of White Paper   242
31: Crumbling   254
32: Finishing with Negativity   259
33: The View from My Window   265
(Today, Much Later, I Write an Extra Bit You May
Not Like, Sorry.)   271

About the Author   277

Acknowledgements   278

Chapter One: Background to a Nugget

The Wild Times had been raging for much longer than my little life. Generations of my people before me had been living under the burden of fear and had been driven to desperate measures to stay alive, often clinging to degradation rather than giving up. Unsuitable marriages were made in delusional attempts to change things for the better, but husbands in particular tended to die in accidents of one sort or another which only complicated things and left strings of loose-bowelled children squabbling at the queue for the outhouse.

Stealing was commonplace, and possibly vital, in my ancestry. Everyone did it as a means to eat and provide other basic necessities. I might not be here today if it wasn't for the stealing, so I have an especially fond feeling about the wealth of those acquisition opportunities. It is in me as well: a kind of innate instinct for when something is available, whether I need it or not. I am very proud of that skill and it has probably advanced my life hugely, if only by extremely subtle degrees. I am thankful to the world for giving up all those things that it doesn't miss anymore.

Although I have never stolen it, I have been led to understand that cardboard was one of the prized items to come home with in yesteryear amongst my people. Apparently it was very important as insulation during the worst bleak periods of weather: around bodies, to sleep on, over holes in walls, covering windows. The darkness of those windowless hovels must have been almost as bad as the Wild Times outside.

But despite the surprisingly good quality of the

1

cardboard back then, some of the family, sadly, were driven to desperate measures to cease to be alive. Imagine. The world was in turmoil. What else could you have expected but a little of this? Clearly it is not the same as someone curvaceous, loved, safe, living in a warm, bright house filled with windows and doors deciding to end it all. (I've heard of such curvaceous people: they never, ever look for these blunt, final answers.) Still, it wasn't easy, whatever rationale you applied. A few furniture throwing incidents bracketed the odd suicide, some tears.

I suppose the other relatives (who didn't kill themselves) coped in various ways, but I wouldn't say any of them were totally unaffected. It is difficult to remain unaffected by the sort of things that went on, to hold your head up, maintain equilibrium and relate to life in a straightforward way. Inevitably there was a little strangeness and some of them had to be restrained. Great Uncle Lollo was the most severe case in recent times. He strayed from the path early on in his youth, lost the ability to distinguish between path and not path and had to be tethered to a stake to stop him wandering into trouble or danger. I only saw him at the stake stage of course, which wasn't very pretty or dignified if you thought about it, but I suppose we had all become accustomed to it. Twenty-four hours a day he was strapped up in his little harness made of rough webbing, with a line attached right in the middle of his back where he couldn't fiddle with it. He had a separate shed home near the stake and simply went indoors, still tethered, if he wanted shelter or sleep. For me, he was a safe person to talk to, and I believe he understood some things in some ways, even if he couldn't explain them in words. I would tell him my hopes and dreams when I was a girl and he would become most enthusiastic, nodding and repeating, 'Nya, nya!' whilst holding his arms aloft as if in

2

thanks to some celestial force for the first sweet rain after the great dryness. If I spoke of my fears or troubles he simply hung his head and said, 'Mm, mm,' and suchlike, sometimes sniffing slightly. I have always wondered if he might have been happier than the rest of us, after giving up caring like he had. Mostly heedless of the Wild Times in his environs, he would wave his arms majestically around, conducting a symphony, if often unheard (the birds, the leaves, the clouds), smiling and working his gummy jaws at the same time. I had a lot of respect for Great Uncle Lollo.

Mother was different. I didn't have respect for Mother. Clearly suffering from her boggy journey through life, she passed through her plate smashing phase and simply went quiet and still, just rocking occasionally. It was strange though, there was something about her. How did she manage to keep going without appearing to move? How did she surreptitiously eat or defecate (I can't think of anything else that I definitely know she must have done)? They will always remain unanswered questions for me now, obviously. I had heard tell of her extraordinary intelligence, but that was impossible to confirm and equally impossible to imagine, although I will admit that she really was the ultimate talent amongst all the people I had ever met, or even heard about, when it came to hiding: as still as a rock, camouflaged in part by her very inertia, but un-seeably fast when fear of being seen gripped her. Anyway, it made me rather unwell to look at her, so mostly I did not.

Mother's other child, my much bigger sister Menith, was around too. We weren't what you'd call close, but there was a mutual toleration if not any deep understanding. Menith's life took a funny turn at the Wild Times Fair in the year that she began to go through her change phase to fat lumpiness. It was her defining moment. The fair itself was a great event. I have since learned of bunting and music and so on, but if this is what you associate with a country fair, put the image from your mind. Everyone had to bring what weapons they could for a start, just in case the Wild Times struck at the wrong moment. Similarly, bright colours were out, as were noise and commotion. The twenty or so visitors turned out in immaculately dull clothes, full and square-ish, swamping their shape. They enjoyed various permutations on the theme of whispering games whilst huddled in small groups in an open field high up on the hillside, twitching their eyes from side to side and nervously looking over their shoulders in case of the approach of anything unwanted. The big feature was the Wild Times Raffle. Small pieces of paper secretly passed from hand to hand while everyone looked the other way, and somehow my sister became known as the winner, if only unto her. The surprising thing that she won was to obsess her for the rest of her days (as far as I know): a lifetime's supply of nail varnish. That became Menith. She was always painting her nails after that, fingers and toes, rather boring and certainly useless I thought. She was very tetchy about getting it right though, lost as she was in the dizzying world of self-decoration most of the hours of most of her days.

The other person was Uncle Heap. He was the most extraordinary person I ever met, my hero, my teacher, my Uncle Heap. What big, veiny hands he had. What tatty, stained overalls he wore. What strange and beautiful secrets we shared.

Then of course, last of all, there was me, born a baby after the cardboard era but not within sight of bunting and music. I eyed the family without comment or participation mostly. I was just there.

Mother spoke to me once after I was about hip high. She said, 'You're doomed.'

I hoped that what she had really meant to say was,

'I'm doomed,' but I was botheringly uncertain (until I eventually found out for sure). She looked at me askance once or twice in the years that followed.

I had no idea of what I might be interested in. I had had a go at conducting with Great Uncle Lollo, but showed no aptitude for the music. Coloured fingernails and toenails were the most irrelevant things I could think of, and neither silence nor inertia grabbed me either. I sorely wanted for role models. What with mother rocking (or not rocking as was more usually the case), Menith seeing to her manicure or pedicure and Great Uncle Lollo conducting, it was left to dear Uncle Heap and me to stand watch against the Wild Times almost all day and night. In those hours on watch I learned a lot. It became apparent, under Uncle Heap's direction, that I had a fearsome growl to give when the Wild Times came too close (which was very often indeed). For many years this was most of what I knew about myself, this growl, but it was a good thing to know first, given the circumstances.

Amidst these growing growls, I like to think that some nugget of human normality was in me when I was born and when I was small (even smaller than I am now) and, furthermore, that I somehow spotted it and cached it smartly away, not totally knowing what it was, but sensing its importance and tucking it safely up in a deeply buried packet before anything odd happened to it. I must have forgotten about it as I grew up, but Uncle Heap suspected something when I started to smile and helped me look for it. Wise Uncle Heap. And that is the nugget of my story: what I have done with my nugget (so far).

Chapter Two: Backwards and Forwards: Happy Memories and Screams for the Future

From when I was a tiny little girl I remember some things that Mother did before she went quietsad. I think I remember them, but Uncle Heap has helped me to remember in some instances probably, either keeping the memory alive or nudging it from the sleepy place where memories sometimes go. He is usually reliable, in my opinion.

A nice thing that I remember is the garden. Mother used to grow things close to the house and take an interest in them growing. Some were flowers, (and therefore useless), and some were vegetables, the very idea of which set our saliva flowing. I don't think she ever believed she could make them grow and, unfortunately, the vegetables and flowers believed this too, so her flittery eyes were always nervous about our saliva. Uncle Heap guarded the small oblong beds of pale soil against all harm to give the plants the best possible chance. They had a kind of privileged existence, touched only by her. From the open window I once nervously watched her watering the lacy rows of young leaves with a fine-spouted watering can. She breathed heavily through her teeth and the black hair in her armpits leaked with the exertion. As I observed this activity her first grey head-hairs appeared whilst tending the carrots, the veins in her legs lumped varicose while she waited for the potatoes and her cheeks became heavy and fell from her face as she gave up on the sweet peas.

At some point her confidence popped. The unflourishingness of her patches embarrassed her and

6

she could no longer bear to be with them. In fact, she moved indoors, unable to mention or even look at the garden. It no longer existed for her. Another nice memory is here though, because now I remember her working at household chores, sometimes sewing buttons on, sometimes cleaning the plates (that later were her victims). Her loose cheeks wobbled in the dimness, but there was purpose in her. I hardly dare say it, but I believe I heard her humming a song once, a love song I fancy. Her mouth didn't move, but I felt the longing words behind the soft melody. Imagining what might have been at the back of that song makes me shiver today.

Poor Uncle Heap was left in confusion by the abandoned oblong garden beds. He shifted from foot to foot day after day and week after week. He could not tend them himself, of course, but he could see that the plants were withering. He valiantly guarded them, on and on, from the prowling Wild Times, but it eventually appeared that he was guarding only weeds. I saw panic rising in him as he paced about. My own fear rose, and I felt calamity closing in on us, tragedies lining up, retribution for our inability to safeguard these former treasures began to choke the air I breathed and my mind became fascinated by catastrophic scenarios.

Believe it or not, Menith (with her useless nails) came to our rescue. I stationed myself by the open window and pried my tincey eyes toward her as she wincingly looked over the garden. She was wearing her usual long brown skirt. She rocked back on her heels, her lacquered fingers spread on her lumpy hips, clenched her jaw and said, 'Hm,' with a rather sick expression of determination on her face, unique in her repertoire of facial expressions, seen neither before nor since, by me at least. She said 'Hm' quite a few times actually before she finally started on the flower beds, bending her face into new contortions of disgust, but not once did she flex her fingers. She kept them straight as straight and rigid as rigid, clasping the plant stems as if her hands were the beaks of birds, in an effort to protect her painted nails. She had brought scissors, and waved them around in the tall grasses and other more trailing things in search of real flowers. She did manage to find a couple of stringy stems that were definitely not weeds and she cut them awkwardly and laid them on the ground. Enough of that: the gesture had been made, and she moved to the vegetables. This was trickier I could see. Dirt. She crouched to pull carrots up by the leaves, took a half-wished clasp of them with her bird-beak fingers and lent her (not inconsiderable) weight backwards. Suddenly she let out a gasped, 'Ah!' and rolled onto her bottom, the leaves still in her hand, the carrot still in the ground. A thorough inspection of her nails, followed by more distortions of her otherwise recognisable face, much clumsy stabbing in the soil with the scissors and some more leaf pulling yielded several tiny carrots, smaller than my own smallest finger, a handful of potatoes, (some with worm-burrowed holes), and a scissor-hacked parsnip.

Uncle Heap's relief was great. He looked younger again at the dinner table. The matter of the garden had been closed because the harvest had been taken. Menith decked the table with the two stems of browned flowers and presented the food as best she could but Mother would not eat. She stood hugely in the corner facing the wall, clenching her fists. She looked so heavy, so solid that I was sure she could not fall over however much she rocked. I looked with my eyes but kept quiet, as usual, my secret thoughts brumming around my head. The potatoes were not what I had hoped for, but the carrots and parsnip were silently bursting coloured music in my mouth. The sun gave a beautiful light that evening and made the little slither of sea we could spy from our window go golden. I heard two friendly birds later. One said, 'Kerwit!' and the other replied, 'Whoo-whoo!' It had been a truly great day. In the morning I slipped out and told Great Uncle Lollo about the meal and the sun and the friendly birds and my dreams and he champed his gums together in appreciation.

I suppose it was a bit downhill from those great days and that was mainly due to Mother. She was less active and more quiet, except when she went the other way. Mostly she didn't notice me, but even from the shadows her tantrums were terrifying. She would shout, 'Hell and Damnation!' to no-one at all with a deep, slow vibration in her voice like the threat from a huge storm rolling over with the intent to kill. In these moments her jowls would wobble with the passion of her feeling as she gritted her teeth, baring them slightly, her body muscles tightening beneath her loose flesh and her facial and neck skin becoming blotchy in shades of red and purple. If I'm honest, she was not the most presentable person even on a good day. The skin hung loose around each plain feature on her round face, and even she seemed to shun her unshapely and solitary body. These outbursts however, seemed to degrade whatever looks she had to something more ugly than death (that's what I thought at least, and I'd seen plenty of dead things). At some subtle level these frightening moments marked the brief coming of the Wild Times right into our little home, such as it was, and they came through Mother. Unlike the fearsome things that were outdoors, there was no growling that Uncle Heap or I could do to make it run, fly, slither, slime, lurch, limp or fizzle away. She belonged to us. So, we just readjusted to this as an ordinary state, got on with things and ignored her as best we could. It seemed to be all we were able to do and we stuck with it. Uncle Heap made a monotony out of our response to the situation. We would bolt her in and let it pass, sometimes having to sleep with Great Uncle Lollo for several days. The banality of it all became glueily acceptable for me, frumpily mundane, but I quite liked the change of scene at Great Uncle Lollo's even if the quarters were cramped and I was battered by his floppy conducting in the night.

One day Mother's mood came by surprise and I was in the wrong place, which was unusual for me. I was on my shadowy way from the toilet, hugging the wall all the way to the door to go on watch with Uncle Heap. There was a sudden zhu-um-craash! and a plate cut the air and shattered on the wall not half an arm's length from my throat. I ducked as she reloaded, and was offered some hell and damnation as I scampered to the door. I popped out with a sudden racing in me, heedless of whether Uncle Heap or the Wild Times were as near or far as I might have wanted them to be. Fortunately Uncle Heap was close by. He was already rushing over when I emerged and he gently slipped the bolt across the door then put a hand on my shoulder to lead me to our watch blocks and to reassure me that everything was as it should be. The shattering hell and damnation staggered on in a syncopated counterpoint to Great Uncle Lollo's bird piece that he was conducting in the dusk, but he did seem to be in touch with the plate-crashing sounds, as though they were a necessary extra section to his orchestra for a certain part of the music. He only had one other opportunity to conduct such a piece before the plates and bowls ran out. The next time she fired off a few at the wall then threw the rest down at the floor in stacks of five or six at time in several cataclysmic climaxes. Along with the cursing, it was a noise that truly belonged to the era of the Wild Times and it was ironic that we watched outside for danger while it happened, trying to discern any unknown and potentially troublesome sound in the spaces between the din.

After that it wasn't just the plates that were gone, but all the hell and damnation went out of Mother. She was just quietsad after that and never needed to be bolted in again, which was much less bother. I played an important role here because I had 'discovered' two chairs at the Wild Times Fair one year, rickety things, and I clandestinely dragged them back home with a beating heart full of pride. It was on one of these rickety chairs that she remained quietsad for the rest of her days (as far as I know). I'm surprised the chair lasted.

Uncle Heap and I went over all these stories and many more when we were on watch together, especially on uneventful nights when the space in the air that was laced with our thin voices belonged to us in a different way. Apart from me talking to Great Uncle Lollo and him not talking back, my long night-talks with Uncle Heap were the only real talking that happened in my family at all, that I knew of. It was discreet though, very discreet. Above all, we spoke so lightly that any sound of approaching danger would filter through neatly into our alert brains right away. We were ninety-nine percent awake to the footfall of a malevolent visitor, their breathing, the beat of their wings, the drip of their saliva or even the smell of their threat, but still our chatter seemed utterly indulgent.

Indulgence was not something I had heard of back then, but I have now learned about chocolate and understand that indulgence is something both commonplace and dangerous that also has an exaggerated sense of allure. I don't think that the allure I felt towards our conversations was exaggerated though, because they were very interesting and meaningful and I learned a lot of what I know in those hours.

Even my knowledge of myself comes from Uncle Heap. For instance, it was him who reminded me of my quashed dream that had visited me when I was just old enough to remember things. It had been a single image dream of me lying peacefully asleep in the moonlight, and while I was serenely sleeping I was dreaming that I was peacefully asleep in the moonlight, and in my sleep in the dream within the dream, I was dreaming that I was peacefully asleep in the moonlight, and in my sleep in the dream within the dream within the dream, I was dreaming that I was peacefully asleep in the moonlight. And so on, until I thought I might be sleeping peacefully in the moonlight, which I was not.

He also helped me to keep alive the story of my spider. It lived under the board at the bottom of the wall far from the table in our living space. It was huge, as big as my face was then, and almost as big as Uncle Heap's favourite flowery breakfast plate that became a discus for Mother. Being quiet, as I was, it was easy for me to spend a lot of time in the shady spot where it would sometimes come and go. I watched its stiff articulations of delicately haired limbs, one at a time, as it was born from its hole each day. I could perceive the juicy thirst of its killer fangs, glinting. I could catch the muted sheen off its multi eyes that looked like tiny globes. I almost felt what it felt as it learned about the world through twitching its fuzzy bits. It didn't make extravagant webs or nests or such unkind sticky traps like other spiders I knew, but I could see the dusty remnants of something just inside its hole, and sometimes it would emerge wearing a bit of it by mistake. I reasoned that all the silk for spiders' webs must come directly or indirectly from their food, so my spider probably didn't make a web because it didn't get much to eat. I saw it foraging for something edible in the dust often. In retrospect I think it was a lot like my Uncle Heap in many ways: resourceful and persistent, somewhat hairy, not afraid of dirt and always acting in a slightly furtive or suspect way. I asked Uncle Heap's advice one day about feeding it and in the ensuing experiments found that it had no vegetarian inclination, but I once had success with a dead fly, which was another great day of my early life.

It wasn't that I was emotionally involved with the spider, but I had noticed its hopeful ways and felt its fragile, hairy life moving harmlessly through my world. When one day, still in the era of remaining plates, I awoke to some loud 'Hell and Damnation!', I had no reason to suspect that it was anything to do with my dear eight-legged friend. The drill was to grab a blanket and make cautiously for Great Uncle Lollo's cabin when mother started up. It didn't bother me doing this, and on this day I shook myself as far out of sleep as I could before nervously peeking out to see if the way to the door was clear. I could hear her heavy breathing and whispered curses, but I couldn't see Mother at first, so I set out along the shadowy wall with nothing at all like a thought in my head. Then, all of a terrible sudden, I did see her. I had never seen a naked person before, not even myself, and the horror of it was immense. She was white and hairless and formed in ways that I could not imagine to be true. The bits I knew- the veined legs and the wobbling flesh of her arms- were attached to something altogether alien and distressingly corpse-like. But worse than that, it was a moving corpse. She was bent over, wobbling greasily, holding a shoe in a slapping sort of hold and hissing death wishes on my spider, the only word of which I could clearly make out was a protracted '...ssssquasssssssshhhh...' Between the hissing I heard the rustle of my spider's feet across the wall (I knew the sound well).

She didn't notice when I became hysterical, but fortunately Uncle Heap heard me. He swept me out of the house, only glimpsing the murderous sight briefly, but just enough to recount it to me afterwards. I still clung to my saving blanket. I was screaming in shrill

13

peals, four or five rivers of tears streaming from each eye. I was shaking all over and my eyes had lost focus and started to go poppy. I was probably as alarmed by the sounds coming out of me as by the sight of this grizzly naked murder. I had only ever whispered or growled before and had now somehow lost control, a new and alarming noise spontaneously emerging from inside me unexpectedly. Uncle Heap bound me up in my saving blanket with his big hands to stop me shaking so much and left me in Great Uncle Lollo's cabin whilst he went to bolt Mother in. Menith had already arrived in the cabin and she was frightened by my screaming, so she unwrapped me and I promptly ran away flailing my arms. The collar of my dress was wet from tears by now, as was my hair. My nose was red and my eyes swollen. Somehow I managed to trip over Great Uncle Lollo's tether. I fell down on my head and he fell down on his back, pinning me to the ground with his solid torso across my legs. When Menith and Uncle Heap found us I was silent and only small parts of me remained that were not bruised, but Great Uncle Lollo's symphony was still under his careful direction.

Long after, when Uncle Heap told me about the screaming I looked for it again, and I have to say it added to my growling repertoire and was handy once or twice when a particularly fast-moving thing approached us out of the Wild Times. Funny how these things work. And that's what happened anyway. That's what Uncle Heap told me when we were out on watch together one night, very late, when I was a slightly bigger small girl. I like the story.

Chapter Three: Love and Building Plans

'Listen!' Uncle Heap would whisper in the darkness, hunching his shoulders slightly, cocking his head and pausing his hands in mid-gesture, listening with his ears, his fingers. His eyes got wider too, as if the sound could get in more easily like that.

I too adopted a frozen stance and would make a bold and mad conjecture as to what he had heard. 'It's still in the bushes Uncle Heap! It just stepped on some leaves by accident!'

Our faint voices became increasingly whisperish after we heard a sound, until we were just mouthing words. But talking wasn't that important. These things had all happened before and we knew what we would do. We orientated our noses in the direction of the coming trouble, and our bodies followed in a slow motion synchronicity that didn't disturb the air. We always had our slingshots with us, and we usually picked up our clubs too, but these were last resort things that rarely were used to do any more than frighten. Depending on what we had heard, our response was different. Sometimes we had to wait agonising seconds until the danger came close enough for us to scare it off, sometimes we fired a warning shot close to it, sometimes we rattled a stick in a metal bucket, but most times Uncle Heap would tap my shoulder three times (the signal), and I would growl my growliest growl. It was good enough to be effective alone since my lungs got strong, but if it was a big danger or a pack of prowlers he would growl with me something like this:

Me: 'GRRRRRRRRRRRR!!!!!'   Breathe.

'GRRRRRRRRRRRRRR!!!!! Breathe.

    Uncle Heap: 'GRRRRRRRRRRRRRRRRR!!!' Breathe

    Me: 'GRRRRRR!!'

    Uncle Heap: 'DZI-I-I-IP! DZI-I-I-IP! DZI-I-I-IP! DZI-IP!' Breathe. 'GRRRRRRRRR'

    Me: 'RRRRRRRRRR!!!!' Breathe, breathe. 'WAH-OO-WAH-OO-WAH-OO-WAH!!'

    Uncle Heap: 'RRRRRRRR!' Breathe. 'GRRRRRRRR-OW! OW! OW! OW! OW!'

    Me: Breathe. 'KEE-KEE-KEE-KEE-KEE-KEE! KEE-KEE-KEE!' Breathe, breathe...

    Uncle Heap: Breathe. 'GRRRRRRRRR...'

And so on, making as great a cacophony as possible. We didn't go on for too long, because if we did our threat became banal and unthreatening. We heard the danger retreat and stopped immediately, back to our listening statue poses until finally we relaxed and sat down again on the wooden watch blocks.

    'Well...?' whispered Uncle Heap.

    'You were just starting on about how a sudden noise had killed your grandmother's second husband when we heard a sudden noise in the bushes,' I whispered back.

    'Well... a different sudden noise.' He rested his hand on mine, just as I liked him to, and I studied the pattern of the veins on the back of it in the moonlight. He told his stories in a stilted Uncle Heap code, gave the information in tiny scraps but, after many repetitions over many watch block sessions, I could usually piece together more or less what had happened. 'Frube was deaf,' he continued. 'A lot of problems in the Wild Times. He shut his eyes at the wrong time when the insect came.' He snapped his hands together suddenly next to my ear. 'And that was the end of him.'

    So this was the story about how Uncle Heap's grandmother, Ninnie, had married a not deaf Frube who later became deaf and therefore a Wild Times liability. Their several children had gone hungry for uncounted ages in order to pay an ear doctor man to cure him and thereby save the family. This went well, until the day after the treatment when a terrified and able-to-hear Frube sat like a fencepost at the kitchen table with small pieces of cloth hanging from his ears, his hands shaking, his eyes frightened and an impatient, impoverished and hungry Ninnie angrily clanking pans around him. The worst came when Frube, tired of course, shut his eyes just at the wrong moment. Some safe summer insect buzzed into the kitchen and Ninnie squashed it, clack!, as it flew right by his ear.

'But what happened as he died Uncle Heap? Did he collapse?' I said this by way of suggestion that he tell me the best bit of the drama that I had heard so many times before, just as he liked to.

'Yes! You collapse when your heart explodes! His mouth foamed in colour! His eyes rolled! His body lurched! He kicked Ninnie! He messed his pants!' The climax was coming. 'He died!'

I realised that she couldn't have been very pleased with him, partly because they only had an outside toilet so who would accompany the smaller children there was an immediate problem.

'Poor Ninnie,' I sympathised.

'Well...'

I could just make out the little breeze lifting Uncle Heap's thin beard from his chin. He shaved the rest of his face, but not his chin. I thought that real men had beards, so felt proud of my Uncle Heap, especially while he held my hand.

We let our thoughts wander comfortably while the trees played with the wind. We couldn't hear the sea on this particular night, but sometimes we could: crashing and relentless and utterly unknown. When our little triangle of blue that we could see from our house turned something like white from being churned up by wind and weather, there was always a solid noise coming from over the faraway cliffs. I'd never been there, but Uncle Heap said he had, once, as a young man, ventured so far as the cliffs, the drop that only birds could survive, and then he had turned back. He told that story on stormy days. Today was quiet.

'...Frube did better than Crimpin.'

'What, Ninnie's first husband? Your grandpa?'

'Mm.'

'I thought he died from eating something bad.' It was true, I did think that.

'Well... She killed them bo-' Uncle Heap stopped sharply. 'Listen!' He removed his hand from mine, and we both listened with our ears, hands and eyes. Uncle Heap made a wiggling motion with his arm through the air and pointed below the house. I responded straight away and pulled out my slingshot which danced a blow in that direction. There was no sound after that, and I looked forward to the morning when I could carefully go and see if I had hit something. It wasn't impossible that I had killed something edible even. If we were dubious about something's edibility we usually tried it out on Great Uncle Lollo because he had a very strong stomach.

'Good,' whispered Uncle Heap after a suitable listening moment or two. 'She killed them both.' He paused again.

'How sad Uncle Heap,' I said dreamily.

'She got the mixture wrong. He was extra hungry. It took him a week to die after it solidified inside him.' He let that idea settle. 'Ninnie tried massage but it was a rock.' He rolled the 'r' to let me know exactly how rock-like it was. 'His body went black.' He trailed off, his energy now flagging for the dying part.

I pictured this sad lump of hunger lodged in

Crimpin's grave long after his bones had gone. 'Poor Ninnie,' I repeated.

'Well...' breathed out Uncle Heap, with a resigned blankness.

I always felt strongly from Uncle Heap that he had loved and lost. He was my love expert. His tragic stories were told with a dead flat compassion and I knew why: he had loved his wife very much. I never met her, but he told me how delicate she was, how elegant and how neat her handwriting was. I think the Wild Times must have been much too much for such a porcelain lady, but it wasn't that that killed her at such a fresh young age. No, Uncle Heap always said that she was 'killed by suicide', as if it was an illness that had visited her and left her dead. I didn't fully see the paradox in his point of view until I was much older and had heard the story many times but, needless to say, I never questioned him about it. The story of her death was one of the more flexible ones. On some days he told of how she had laid herself down by a poison fumerole (a tiny hole in the grassy beauty of an idyllic place where stinky and deadly gasses escaped from the deep evil inside the Wild Earth), and she never stood again. She had put her best dress on and looked so pretty there amongst the flowers. On different sorts of days he was absolutely clear that she had become confused when a lively moth got caught in her ear and bashed herself to death on the head with a rock. There was a hint of almost accidental whichever story he chose, but otherwise the tale was never consistent. This didn't bother me though, I believed it was all true and, most importantly, I knew that he had loved.

For this reason I decided to tell him about my snail. To admit to having a pet snail was as good as saying that I loved something, which was not something we did as a family because it was much too risky in those days. I told him about how I had stolen some of Menith's nail varnish and painted my snail's shell in a spotted spiral pattern to suit her, how I kept her little tub home fresh with (also stolen) leaves from the garden, how magical her stringy black poo was, how I talked to her and called her by name: Curlywurly, how she morphed in and out of form with strange, sticky appendages. I was terribly nervous that something bad would befall me because of Curlywurly.

'Well...' reiterated Uncle Heap.

He waited too long and I felt very small, even smaller than I was, and I started to shake a bit and chatter my teeth.

'Well...' he continued, 'some things are worth great risk. This snail thing means great potential for you.'

Then something happened to my face. It did it by itself and was rather frightening both during and after, especially after. I had never been so complimented in my short life and I felt my ears shift backwards on my head, my eyes widen, my lips tighten and the corners of my mouth head up somewhere into my cheeks. I smiled for the first time. I cried too, but that had happened before. Uncle Heap eyed me with curiosity and, I saw, a little pride. My guilt was washing over me in a steadily increasing flood and I didn't know what to do, but my face kept smiling without me. Then Uncle Heap rested his hand on mine, just as I liked him to.

We sat there for a long time, him resting his hand and me getting over my smiling guilt. Heavy clouds had started to come over the sky so the moonlight was flicker-flashing between them when he pulled out his knife. I had seen it once before. I knew this was a special moment.

'With this knife you can do anything,' he suggested tantalisingly.

The stories about the knife rushed through my head: gut-spilt killings and flesh-torn skinnings and mucus-hung birthings and over-ripe burials and mouth-leaking feasts. Creation and destruction alike had come from this tool.

He began to show it to me slowly in the moonlight like a dream: all the slim fold-out blades, the minute scissors, the spike, the file... it was all unbelievable. I didn't know where he was leading with this, but I was sure now that he had been waiting for me to smile, it was a sign, and that, yes, you could do anything with my Uncle Heap's knife. My guilt tottered and shambled around and my fascination swelled and grew fretful. I was only a small and, as yet, frail child, and all this was too much.

'With this knife you could build anything,' Uncle Heap continued mysteriously as he folded in-out, out-in, one marvellous tool after another.

Build, build, build... Build what? My mind went jiggarty. My hand reached out to touch the knife, but he drew it away and I asked my hand to come back.

'With this knife you could build a safe safe house against the Wild Times,' Uncle Heap quietly stated, deliberately and slowly, not moving and staring straight at me.

A safe safe house? Weren't our house and Great Uncle Lollo's house as safe as houses came, patrolled by fearless, growling warriors like me and Uncle Heap? I now remembered the stories about cutting the trees and shaping the timber and building the houses with this very shiny knife that now glinted in the night before my goggly eyes. It was true. It was a house-building knife. The houses were rather thin-walled and cool in winter I admit, but we slept, all of us I believe. What was Uncle Heap driving at?

'With this knife you could build a high house of stone that would keep you far from all lusting evil.' He only needed to say 'lusting evil' and the sky crackled out the first of the lightning from the dark clouds that had been sweeping in.

A stone house! Now that was ambitious. Uncle Heap had divulged his secret. I was puny by comparison with that secret.

'The house is for you. You will have the knife for it,' he said flatly.

My spirit quavered and I knew I would have to grow into the idea (physically I mean), but I accepted it at once because Uncle Heap's conviction was absolute, his word was truth. So this was what was in store for pathetic little me. My wiry muscles on my stringy limbs tightened into determination right then and there, and I became tough, like turning on a switch.

'Thank you Uncle Heap,' I whispered confidently from the back of my throat.

In the days, weeks and months that followed there were many dark, thunderous days that the Wild Times sent, and many terrible dangers fretted around our home, clawing to get in. Between helping Uncle Heap to keep us safe, I was quietly absorbed in the first important thought I had ever had in my head. My scrappish young body began to unfurl as I skulked in the dark corners of our house, as my stone house thoughts took shape. I could tolerate anything now that I knew my future was great and that I was strong enough to be the main person in it.

I told Great Uncle Lollo about it first. Of course with him it was easy to go to any lengths of details, so I did. He was impressed.

'Nya, Nya,' he repeated over and over again.

Weeks later I found the right moment to talk to Menith. I thought it was the right moment anyway, but I might have been wrong. Her nail varnish brush paused in mid-air as she listened intently with a frowning face. She looked at me for the first time in years and I made it short because I felt uncomfortable.

'Can't you see I'm in the middle of this coat?' she snapped. 'You've ruined the purple now, and look at my brush!' This was the sum of her response. I'd forgotten the sound of her voice.

Mother was next on the list, and eventually I whispered something about my plans in her cold ear as she sat (as was her custom) by the west facing window, her body more still than the tumultuous land outside. I thought I did see some recognition flicker across her face as I spoke. Maybe her eyes widened a little, one hand jittered briefly. I wasn't sure what had passed through her. Was it fear of rock, or fear of the Wild Times, or fear of change maybe? It could equally have been a sort of inert joy at the news that I planned to leave.

Chapter Four: Uncle Heap is Decrepit but not Daunted

Some things change quickly over time and some things hardly change at all. That's how it seemed to me as I left my girlhood. The coming of that first smile was a big change and it happened in a blink, but the leaving of the guilt was not fluent in any way. That guilt clogged me up from time to time for years, even more so because I found myself smiling unwittingly on several other occasions. Uncle Heap was constant in his approval of the smiles but, despite fully understanding the law of Uncle Heap, my mind fought the idea of smiling strongly, even when I was with him. Deep down I knew that smiling during the Wild Times was a bad thing, a social madness. To smile was to build yourself a tower of unrelatedness, to reach toward a kind of loneliness that could only spiral out of control towards some infinitely torturous hermitude. Smiling was so dangerous! I could feel the danger when the smile happened. It was all so obvious: it could only be the precursor to some disaster, some repercussion, and each time that I smiled by accident I waited for the trauma to follow. Fortunately none of the traumas were too bad: a large warring troop passed between us and the coast (the stench was awful and we hid indoors but they showed no interest in burning us); Menith had an infection under her left thumbnail and the nail fell off, taking months to grow back (she cried a lot and I apologised for my part); a large slithering thing got into the house while I was distracted (smiling) and slipped between Mother's static legs at least once before Menith battered it with the other chair; and, worst of all, the birds didn't come to sing for three weeks and the skies remained a poisonous black, dropping thick, acrid ash (Great Uncle Lollo was deranged with grief, straining constantly at his tether and whining, his arms limp by his sides, his orchestra departed).

Anyway, I slowly turned from being a bigger small girl to being a very small big girl. The difference was more in principle and I was just my usual kind of puny. Menith had got a bit bigger though I suppose. She had been pretty big for as long as I could remember, but now she seemed to be creeping towards a further and greater lumpiness. I noticed this from a distance more than up close, and I noticed it silently. Her exquisite nail painting skills left nothing to refine, so she sort of changed slowly around her nails, which remained pristine. Her eyes became smaller as they disappeared into her puffed face and she breathed noisily with a clenched jaw whenever she was concentrating on nail painting. When her knees accidentally showed from beneath her brown skirt I could see flaking skin and the dimples of fattiness. I didn't like to think what was between there and her armpits, who would? But I couldn't help but wonder a bit anyway. Crowning all was her hair which still retained a certain glossy standard all by itself, despite her neglect of it in favour of her twenty, dear, coloured nails. It was long and dark and wavy and had a presence about it which was quite inspiring such that you could almost be distracted from the frightening suggestion of the lumpiness beneath the skirt.

Great Uncle Lollo had developed his conducting considerably. As he began to approach his old age, his hands had learned different languages and his conducting was more delicate, enigmatic you might say, and brought out the songs of the birds and the clouds and the land in flavours of sound that befitted an elderly man who lived on the end of a tether and had mostly done nothing except conduct. I liked it best when he lifted his arms high and danced his fingers down toward the earth, lifting the dry leaves in a rustling ostinato to the dry skies above. It was so beautiful. I admired him more and more and he was very settled, on the whole. I talked to him as much as ever, and he was still responsive and encouraging to me, but his response became decorated increasingly by his dribbling, which was profuse in a way it hadn't been before. He had dropped the last of his teeth over a short period of time, so that probably didn't help. His toothlessness and his now floppy old face made him look terribly sad when he was simply relaxing, but I knew better. Even his body's response to gravity, how it had sunk from his shoulders to his pelvis, did not convince me that the quality of his happiness was any less, although it did seem to necessitate a waddling shuffle when he moved around on his tether which looked less than comfortable. I hoped he understood that I thought well of him.

For his part, Uncle Heap became quite decrepit as I got to be less girlish. It was as though his power departed from him and left only this decrepitude, which had always been in the background. Where his power went was a funny thing, because it seemed to come to me. He grew feebler as I grew tougher, and I think this turnaround was a lot to do with the way that he talked us into it.

'Listen!' He would whisper in his usual pose of over-dressed alarm. And I would dutifully bend my concentration toward our impending doom as it approached, soft-footed. 'You see!'

'Ah, but I think it's only a small one Uncle Heap,' I would return. 'It doesn't sound like it's in such a bad mood either.'

'Yes!' he would declare. 'You see! You are growing bigger than the Wild Times. They are shrinking before you.'

'Well...' I would imitate his usual response to anything that had a difficult answer.

We would set about our growling (or whatever needed to be done) and Uncle Heap's exaggerated seriousness would make me feel extremely important and brave. When all was safe again he would pant faintly.

'You see! For me it was a monster. Lucky you were here to save me.'

His beard was still a great matter of pride, but it definitely got wispier and whiter, as did the shy hairs that peeked out from his shirted chest in times of exertion. His shy, black hairiness of former days (which I had considered to be somewhat like my spider's), now was white and had thinned. His skin thinned too. It crumpled and never uncrumpled, lying like a shroud over his muscles. He shrank to be a slightly hunched figure and the belt that had sufficed to carry his slingshot for longer than I had been alive was drawn in by another hole, and then another. The veins on the back of his veiny hands stood out more than ever, and made a new purplish colour.

Of course I see all this in retrospect only, because my Uncle Heap was so much mine, and I was so much his, that whether his power resided in me or in him was difficult to tell for a long time. Maybe it was something that belonged to neither of us but merely resided somewhere between us. We had talked about building the stone house for so long that I felt like I couldn't think thoughts about it without him being there. The secret words like Granite or build or knife or life could not be spelled in my imagination without Uncle Heap sitting by me and letting me know that I was actually able to spell such soaring concepts.

'Well...' he started up again, with long pauses between the quiet words. 'Must be, you are getting ready.'

I heard Great Uncle Lollo shuffling outside his cabin, probably emptying his bladder, and I had a brief thought about how things seem to go in the world of strangeness and danger and fresh air and stuffy houses and night skies with flying stars and frosty endings to the dark hours that claw at your insides and faraway near things like other people and the cliffs and the birds in flight and the next day after this one and suchlike (I know a lot more things now than then), and I felt emboldened into believing that, one day, I could be safe against all the terrible perils that momently threatened my existence and that I, as yet, lived in constant subjugation to.

'You are bigger than the Wild Times, now that you're big,' he whispered.

And I believed him, so long as he sat there. I felt like I had a special kind of bigness that came in small special packages.

'You are impossible to break,' he whispered.

He stressed the word 'impossible' and a rippling steeliness clanged through me between my brain and my fingertips and toes which would repel all forces.

'You are too tough and stringy to be palatable to the wickedness,' he whispered.

And I tasted at once the bitterness of the flavour of me that would protect me from ever becoming an appetiser for any bad thing.

'You are stone,' he whispered flatly.

I wondered about this. It didn't sound altogether good at first, but I peered out into the darkness and there my imagination rested with the Granite that lay still and relaxed, afraid of nothing, owning its own space on the land over millennia and right through this frightening era in which we lived.

The world is funny and to this day I still try to work out what is really going on. At the time Uncle Heap was saying all this to me, I think what he was really trying to say was, 'I love you,' because love immortalises the loved one, so I've heard. He had immortalised the wife he loved with his stories, but maybe he didn't know the word because he had had a different kind of life. I understand the word and I can tell you now that I definitely loved Uncle Heap because I always felt bad when he felt bad and good when he felt good because we were co-stars in the same story. For me, Uncle Heap was super-heroic, invincible and bathed in an aura of bounce-ability that would protect him from all harm. He would always think of something or move out of the way just in time or be more fearsome than anything. In short, something about him would always save him, whatever the odds, not like the relatives I'd heard of who had strange accidents. They had neither luck nor love, but Uncle Heap had at least one of those two things at a time I think.

'Well...' His whispery voice started to become somewhat croaky around the time he started to look decrepit. 'You've got something that will always keep you safe. You've got determination.'

It became a fact as soon as he said it. He was not daunted at all, ever, not once. He simply saw his personal kind of success coming through my funny little body rather than his own as time went by. He again got his words a bit wrong to describe it though, I believe. It wasn't determination I had, it was Uncle Heap I had, and all his whispered sustenance.

He did more than this too: he dedicated many days to showing me all the features of his life-wielding knife. He never allowed me to touch it but it exuded its sacred power which sent shivers through me, so it touched me in another way I suppose. I dreamed about it at night and saw each miraculous appendage slip in and out, shining coolly. I could feel the nearness of his knife whenever I was close to it. I could sense its willingness and, by and by, I learned a lot from watching with my fixed eyes as Uncle Heap made several useful things for our home. None of them were big things, not by knife standards, but they represented a variety which demonstrated the versatility of talents that it possessed.

The first was a new slingshot which Uncle Heap made for himself, silently. The guts of a dead furry thing were given new life in this springy weapon and it proved its worth just days after completion when we had a minor surprise near the back wall which faced onto the open moor.

The second was a loom extension which was a bad weather project. It unsettled us both to be indoors for too long but the concentration with which Uncle Heap and the knife worked was a balm to our lurking inquietude and the loom extension turned out brilliantly. Now we could make bigger squares of fabric whenever we came across suitable materials (but that rarely happened, obviously).

The third was an elegant flagpole with a rag flag, (and later many rag flags, feathers, leaves, grasses and, the crowning glory, a plastic bottle we found once, blown in from a plastic bottle land, far away). Uncle Heap believed it would deter at least the low-danger feathered flying things. It worked, but my own opinion is that it had the drawback of attracting furry flying things somewhat. We didn't talk about that and the flagpole was a splendid thing that I was very proud of nonetheless. He whittled it with great speed, and the pole, at least four times as high as me, shaped itself with alacrity.

Fourth was a supple hat with beads of bone dangling all around the broad brim. I coveted this hat wildly, especially after he let me try it on once. Although it didn't save Uncle Heap's eyes in the end, the feeling it gave was of great security (even though it was swampily big for me). The craftsmanship of every aspect was extremely fine. Painstaking hours had been eked out of patient days sitting outside the north wall facing Uncle Lollo's shed hooking long, thin leaves dryly through themselves to make the weave or sawing and filing lengths of delicate, well cleaned tibia and threading them on their dangles.

The last thing I remember Uncle Heap and his knife making around then was the sorely needed new well. We had been having a lot of trouble de-poisoning the water from the old well after it was rudely and inconveniently fouled by a toxic thing falling in. So he cut and sunk a new one deep, deep, but still not so far from the house that we would fear being estranged from safety when fetching a bucket. He said he knew where the water was but I think that was just bravado and a touch of a lucky guess because the first water was thick and brown and useless, and only cleared much later. He made the well wider than the old one and lined it with small Granite stones that he took from somewhere close by and fashioned carefully into beautiful curving shapes that fitted together to make beautiful inside well walls. I was his eyes and ears for creeping nastiness as he worked, and it suited me to have another job because, in truth, I found it difficult to watch him work at this: it seemed rather frightening, the Granite and the knife and the depth and the necessity. I manage to give half an eye to the splendid knife goings-on, but my stomach was getting churny at the thought of some day being responsible for such a tool.

When he finished the well, he hadn't spoken for quite a while. He said only one quavering thing before another long word silence set in, and it was this: 'Time for building plans to start.'

I gulped.

Chapter Five: A Steady Place

After the first of my gulps there were a lot in the following days, but they gradually got quieter until I was just gulping meditatively in my head. My fantasies oscillated between believing that the time hadn't really come for building plans to start (i.e. Uncle Heap didn't really mean what he had said (unlikely)) and that, if the time had come, I was a mighty, knife-wielding warrior for whom frightening things like stone building projects in Wild Times environs would be as easy as brushing my teeth on a hot day when teeth were most likely to rot.

Uncle Heap interrupted my gulping meditation on watch one night with the frugal words, 'Tomorrow we will go and look for the place.'

I guess he saw my wide eyes flinching in the starlight or heard my stomach glugging, because he looked at me later in the night and said, 'You can wear the hat,' which was very kind and reassuring of him.

The annual Wild Times Fair was the only thing that had taken me beyond the gate before, and there were many eyes keeping watch at those times (I still felt frightened though). I had rarely even reached the fence to be honest, but here I was, just me, Uncle Heap, two slingshots with various ammunition, two clubs (one spiked), a metal bucket with a stick, a self-possessed knife of magical appendages, a bone-beaded hat and a lot of potential growls setting out through the early morning breeziness of the day to the far beyond nether edge of moorland which I had wondered about all my life.

In my giddy weakness I looked back from the fence through my fringe of bone beads and I saw Menith busily painting her nails outside the door, very busily, looking more erect than usual. Uncle Heap had told her that we were going, and left her in sole charge. My mouth opened involuntarily as I saw her looking so familiar yet so distant and I let out a slight gloop. It wasn't me she heard but I suppose she thought she heard something at the same time because I saw her leave her brush hand quivering mildly in the air while she craned her neck and flashed her tiny, fat-sunken eyes from side to side in a random way. There was nothing there of course, she was just flitterous at her assumed responsibility, but once the hand had paused for too long, the nail varnish on it dried too much, and I knew things would go downhill.

As I put foot in front of foot through the tufty green, I felt my tingly back, high up near my shoulders, was more present than it had ever been before and that I had a sense of all-round-ness hitherto unknown to me which this windblown exposure had brought to light. I shuffled slowly, clanging my bucket a bit by accident, swishing my head from side to side, looking listening, looking listening. I had to hold Uncle Heap's hand because I couldn't see much with the swampy hat on, but I felt safe enough at one point to notice my enjoyment at the bone beads swinging, all this way then all that, like a dance around my head. I didn't mention it.

What I could see pretty well was the ground as it moved under me. I imagined myself walking on the spot while the whole rutted Earth slid by under my feet, and then (in my head at least) I became that clean-toothed and mighty knife-wielding warrior.

And it was beautiful and changing, what the Earth showed as it moved under me while I correspondingly shuffled my feet. Being the right time of year, the flowers were in full flow. They sprung up, even through the ground which was burned, tiny stellar colours of perfection. The familiar blooms and grasses that grew

33

near to our house and Great Uncle Lollo's cabin were sometimes repeated within my bead-bordered panorama: the blue ones with the radiating stripes if you looked closely, and the yellow ones with lots of petals whose leaves Curlywurly had favoured. There were others though that I had not seen before: pink tufty ones on wiry stems that grew out of cushions of tiny leaves, which were soft in a springy way and hard in a prickly way. I was glad I had put on my full-foot shoes.

There were, obviously, the other kind of plants, the ones that scratched and clawed and trapped you, poisoned you with milky acids that ate into your skin and climbed over you and stuck to you in a smothering way, but Uncle Heap guided me niftily away from them, waving a silent hand of dismissal. These made me feel that I was also happy to have thought to put on protective long leggings for the sake of my ankles. The leggings also had an unforeseen use when I began to realise that all these strange, wonderful or evil plants hosted a similar variety of insects and crawling things. Nestled in the green scrub were some quite fast black biting things, one or two flutterers which I was dubious about, and I'm sure there were many other things hiding, sneakily planning nastiness, because I could sense their furtive scurryings.

After much tiring travelling, switching our bodies this way and that and sometimes walking back to back to be best aware of our surroundings, we reached the lee of the stunted tree that I had occasionally noticed when talking with Great Uncle Lollo. It had the crack of an ancient lightning strike down its seaward side and was leaning exaggeratedly inland, the upper leaves and branches forming a twistedly woven shelter over a bare patch of scorched earth. The few grasses that clung around its base were sprinkled with dew whose droplets looked shiny and perfect next to the ravaged bark and burned things that were around. We paused here and Uncle Heap made me gasp when he let go of my hand and lifted the hat from my head without warning.

He bent down and said, 'Half way,' whilst he looked straight into my eyes.

I nodded quickly, looking straight back into his eyes so that he would know I was not afraid of dying and in the hope that he would put the hat back. The cover from the dew tree was not nearly as comforting as the supple hat.

There was a vast tract of open space between us and our house, the fragile building itself being the only protection we could seek nearby apart from the weapons we carried. I tried to hide my shaking, but I think it was mostly on the inside, so that was all right. Uncle Heap took up my hand again, and it was in this way that I felt him flinch as he noticed some strings of great juicy purple flowers hanging alluringly down long stems that curled around the dew tree's trunk. Each blossom dripped something clear and thick from its hairy insides. I was spellbound by their enticing invitation and reached out to touch them with a kind of licksome feeling running through my tongue. Maybe I had stood there a long time looking at them and wanting them, or maybe I had started for them straight away, I don't know, but what I do remember is Uncle Heap yanking me back with a terrible force that hurt my shoulder and made all the bone beads go whichaways at once. I suppose there are tricky things that it is useful to know about, and those purple things were one such thing that I did not know about. As I recall their magnetic qualities today, it brings to mind again the dangers I have heard so much about concerning chocolate. We are always learning, hopefully.

As we went forward again under the open sky I felt a new nausea as I thought of it, so vast above me and so full of unknown things. The sun was risen now and I could smell some badness in the air, meaning that things would be falling soon. I wondered if we would make it to wherever we were going, whether we would make it back, what it would feel like to end that way, how long I would be conscious before I lost consciousness, would I melt? Uncle Heap would obviously think of something and would be fine, but would he be able to save me? My head started to sprint, and my shuffle through the tuftiness became more urgent, which spurred Uncle Heap on to the same. I saw pass below me black, black burned earth with strange contortions of charcoal stems which rose out of it like the fingers on withered and begging hands that wanted to be lifted out of a fatal, dark pit. It blackened my shoes and leggings as I crunched and pushed through it. Then things became greener and softer again abruptly, now interspersed with Granite whose smooth shapes belied its roughness. I felt very unsure of this Granite and to me it seemed ready to tear my knees to shreds should I stumble. But I didn't stumble, at all, and I held tight to Uncle Heap.

My poor brain and my poor body were all but exhausted from the tension and the arduous travelling when Uncle Heap gave another, more gentle yank on me. I needed no persuasion to stop. My empty stomach suddenly filled with an ocean of boiling liquid that rose to make contact with the base of my neck, making me very top-heavy. The pressure of this swift uprising nearly made my eyes leave my head, and for a moment I thought they had. I wasn't sure if my eyeballs were hanging down out of my face or flying up on the huge wind which was screaming up up up, vertically up the cliff, over my face and up to some higher wherever. We had reached the infamous edge.

Uncle Heap held both of my arms firmly from behind so that I could move neither forward nor backward. The bone beads were blowing in any mad direction (some of them went up!) and I had a heart-stopping glimpse of an unimaginable down-ness, through flying birds and wet air onto water which revealed nothing but an enigmatic, heaving surface which struggled against itself and gave occasional hints of killer rocks just beneath. I was feeling less than steady already, as you can imagine, when Uncle Heap did a second hat trick without warning. I screamed a big scream, a scream like I had discovered during the naked spider murder, because the near and far sky seemed like a sudden, incinerating enemy to my bare head. In all this huge up-ness and down-ness, space itself seemed to be reeling, and things that I formerly thought to be solid and fixed were moving around in a spinning, loose-stomached way. I threw myself on the ground out of Uncle Heap's grip, clattering my bucket horribly and screamed again. But it was brief. I came to my senses right away and wondered what I might be lying on which could be perhaps worse than an incinerating sky.

Uncle Heap held me as I got up and put the hat back on my head saying, 'Better that you see,' in a matter of fact way. I did not look into his eyes.

We scrambled back over the smooth Granite shapes and greenishness at a highly motivated speed, clutching each other and clattering, one of us full of trust and the other full of knowledge, I hoped. Then we stopped again. I was still feeling unsteady but I instantly knew that the land was not twirling here and I felt this place have the good effect of de-spinning whatever was inside my skull.

'Here,' whispered Uncle Heap.

I scraped my gaze over the large, flat area, fringed with Granite and burned stuff: the building plot. It was slightly higher than the surrounding land, such that you might have called it a platform or stage, and it had a dusting of brave blue flowers (with the radiating stripes if you looked closely) decorating its centre among some short grass that looked over-eaten. To the north was a big patch of high scrub, all thick with yellow flowers. They really caught the taste buds with their sweet smell, but I knew them to be duplicitous and filled with blade-sharp scratching things, so the odour gave me some fresh nausea. To the west, where we had come from, the presence of the deadly drop cliffs was still strong. From this little distance I was able to first contemplate the juxtaposition of the Granite and the sea, the frontier of a slow battle over aeons which not even the Granite could win, but neither could it concede. To the south was a solitary, wind-bent tree, a fruiting type I believed, and then the smooth shape of the charred earth fell away to I don't know where, so far away that it made my imagination go gooey. It was pretty lucky that the fire had come to the building place really because it meant that I could see everything, eaten back to the ground, and also nothing much would have to be cleared to start building here.

I tipped back my head and looked Uncle Heap right in the eye, waved my bucket in a cavalier fashion and ventured to say, 'It's a great place Uncle Heap,' really meaning it.

The sky had been getting darker as we had journeyed and now it became really what I call 'ominous' (meaning deadly very, very soon). The first splotch fell on the supple hat. I was aware of its heavy landing, and it made a splotching sound that caught Uncle Heap's attention too. He looked from above the brim as I shuddered below the brim and the splotch went straight through it, landing at my feet with a little spray. We ran.

What contrast! Our cautious shufflings were a thing of the past. Our nervous examination of each new blade of grass was forgotten. Urgency had visited us, and wondering about what bad stuff might be near us didn't happen any more because we had found out the thing most worthy of note in our vicinity: a dark and deadly sky which was starting to evilly rain down on us. We ran ran ran, Uncle Heap gripping my hand painfully, although I was glad he had me so tightly when I tripped a bit on a burnt and twisted root exposed by some previous heavy rain and he gave me another strong yank to save me.

Because I am an organised sort of person I began counting straight away, as soon as things changed and we started running. There were four steps before I breathed. Then my breaths came in a random panting somewhat related to my random footfall over the rough ground. It went on forever, endless lung exertion and fear rushing, bottomless swirling of the unknown in time and space. In four pants there was the surprise stumble, then I think I took something more like a gasp before the last five random pants which brought us to the gate again. No stopping there. On we ran. My head was down and my ears were pounding with fear of being splotched or melted, but I perceived the comforting flap and swoosh of our elegant flagpole as we passed it. There were two breathless steps and then, at the final push, two more pants were hurriedly pressed through me and we were indoors in the familiarity of our house.

In short, the building place for the safe safe house was a minimum of six steps, eleven pants and a gasp away. I stored that information in my head alongside the memory of the terrible sense of exposure that had followed us out there. It sounded unimpressively close but, put it this way: when you make a journey swallowed by such a great yawn of exposure (as we had), six steps, eleven pants and a gasp is the longest journey imaginable and takes half a lifetime.

Obviously being indoors was a great relief. The supple hat was somewhat damaged but nothing worse had happened. However, we met a disaster when I shut the door behind us: Menith. She was lying curled up in the middle of the floor whimpering, twitching and holding her shaking hands out before her like frozen claws. Even I could see right away that her nail varnish was all awry and blodgy, some of it even on her finger tips. I usually didn't pay that much attention to her colour choice and painting style, but as I looked now, it was clear to me that she had been in the process of some elaborate pattern of green and gold on a red background on each minute canvas of fingernail. I couldn't tell what the design was supposed to be of course, because it had been reduced to blodginess, but I was sure that it could never have been achieved using the splayed brush which was on the floor next to the spilled gold bottle and the standing but open red bottle of nail varnish. I felt quite sorry for her and for a moment I almost forgot 1) the excitement and nervousness associated with finding my building place after so much travel through new lands, and 2) the fact that I had just narrowly escaped death by splotching, probably due to my proximity to the invincible, hand-gripping Uncle Heap.

I knew that Menith must keep her nail varnish remover in her nail varnish wardrobe, so I started quietly towards that goal, past mother by the window, who looked as statuesque as usual, past the dark and shady wall, past the bolt-able door and into Menith's quarters. As I made my way the splotches started to really fall heavily on our undulating metal roof. It started as an irregular dance of hard sounds which touched me like fake blows that I had to make a show of fakely dodging or getting knocked down by, then it built up into a wall of horror, just millimetres from my life, from which I was entirely separated. I felt very grateful for that roof of life and had a small celebratory mutter to myself because no-one could hear me now anyway. Amidst this din I sheepishly opened Menith's nail varnish cupboard for the first and only time. Cro-o-o-o-onk! One door opened and I had a full view of half of the collection. Wow. It wasn't quite as jaw-dropping as Uncle Heap's knife, but I was truly moved by this wonderful colouredness of tiny bottles, hundreds and thousands of them, reds mostly, but blues, purples, gold, silver, ones with spangly bits in and some white or clear, green, colours, colours, colours. I didn't think about colours much, and still don't today, but there they all were, many I had never even imagined before, all in neat, minute samples, placed in an orderly way with all the labels pointing outwards so that I could read the gold-rimmed letters that said Luxury Nail Lacquer in a slanty way. They were placed on very neatly constructed shelves just the same width apart as the height of the bottles, and they stretched from the floor to way above my head. The perfection of it was what impressed me the most I suppose: perfection in our little home, hidden in a cupboard, distilled in weeny bottles. Maybe I could be drawn in by the varnish obsession? I hoped not, but I was dizzyingly still as I took it all in, a bit like the spinning wooden apple that Uncle Heap made for mesmerising things (and me). I knew that if the bottles wobbled and fell they could break my toothpick bones due to their sheer and shiny numbers. But thankfully it was not them who wobbled but me, and then I was able to pull myself out of my trance and realise that there was no nail varnish remover there. How puzzling. Cro-o-o-o-onk! I opened the second door and saw more of the same, in rows joined to the ones I had already seen, neat as anything, waiting for me to drop saliva over them in my amazement or sustain mortal injury under their attack, but there, right at the bottom, were two similarly neat rows of Nail Varnish Remover in smoky pink plastic bottles the size of my hand. Phew. I reached out to take one bottle, breathing hard like Menith usually did, slowly, slowly sliding it from its neighbourly home, then watched, goggle-eyed, as the identical bottle behind it slid forward to take its place in the line. Funny.

Anyway, it all happened in an enormous din of poison precipitation and, in the end, I can only presume that Menith sorted her life out because I saw her the day after I had left the nail varnish remover next to her and she was just the same as ever before: her nails were perfect and she was avoiding my eyes as avidly as usual.

The noise went on all night and I became accustomed to it like a six-fingered child must cease to notice the extra-ness of herself. Because I had escaped them, I felt like those splotches were meant for me and were acid in their resentment of my skipping to safety. They inspired me to high thoughts about powerful things because they made me feel powerful and escape-ful. Most of my high thoughts were weighty thoughts, about Granite. My journeying adventure with Uncle Heap had shown me a glimpse of the massivity of Granite. I had seen small pieces before, but just stones near the house. Now I had walked over a whole landscape, six steps, eleven pants, a gasp and more wide, sensed the underlying boss in the situation, peered over the teetering drop of Granite-ness into the far-down-below of the bottom of everything that a mind could hold without dying. The perilous wavering that had happened above the pitiless semi-submerged Granite boulders far down, peeking through the toiling waters and drawing my top-heavy body towards them, heavily revisited me and I began to think about Granite as my building material. How frightening it would be. How safe in these Wild Times.

The next day I began a Granite obsession that would last for a long while. I began to look closely at each small piece I came across and pick apart its sharp constituents in my mind. I turned small gritty stones over in different lights and weathers and quiveringly examined them, heart to heart. I slowly grew into the understanding that my house, if ever it came to be, would definitely be built of Granite and, although this was a very terrifying thing indeed for me, I ceased to see any other possibility. I still knew nothing of how houses were built, and therefore had nothing to base my certainties on, but nevertheless, certain they were, young or old, soon or late, me or Uncle Heap, poison rain or nourishing sun.

Whatever my certainty about Granite as my building material, I sometimes doubted my own ability to be so audacious as to build this house at all, to be safe, to create myself as a new kind of person, be happy, move away, cast off the cardboard past of my ancestors. Like the moon coming up, some days my plan would shine, but it always went down too, and sometimes it wouldn't been seen for long stretches as it was eclipsed by the glare of some awesomely solid silence or some terminally heavy sadness. The words of mother that I thought I'd shaken off came back again and again. 'You're doomed' haunted me like an ailing shadow and I wondered and wondered afresh what she could have meant, how powerful she really was and where did her power come from. Should I be afraid? Should I feel weak, like her doom suggested, or should I feel strong like Uncle Heap said? On the worst days I felt the glooming of her upon me, and I struggled not to be bent slowly by her dark forewarning. Sadly, I often did bend, despairingly, into a bent stick of wavering inertia, cowering under her doom-laden cloud. I did not trust my own words or actions or judgement at these times, because something made me feel that maybe I was the shadow, not her. And those words, actions or judgements of mine (that I could not trust) I knew were unreliable both now and in the future, and I knew how they all could turn against me, betray me and trick me and lay me down in a hopelessness of life or even death, but I did not really know why. There was no point in building. (I smile now as I remember this, and I laugh a little, but there is some naughty malevolence in my laugh.)

Chapter Six: An Aside on Granite

Here is a good place to digress and tell you everything I know about Granite, and I should, because it plays such a mountainous role in just about everything important. It would be thoughtless of me to ignore such vital information. My house was to be built out of its limitless supremacy and built on its mysterious mass. All that immense and enduring stability that was present in the depths of the landscape (and scattered on top of it too) had qualities that were to be shared by my house, the house for puny, squidgy me.

It is obvious that it is called Granite because *it* is full of all those *grain*-like crystals, but I questioned where it could have come from or what things came together to make its aggressive splendour manifest. I wondered if Granite had made a choice to be that way, or had something yet more omnipotent made a recipe for it. Being such a perfect answer to the terrible Wild Times, surely its express purpose was for building my house? I tried to consider what it might feel like to own such a mighty presence as this rock did. Vast ideas whirred in my head like: is Granite dynamic on a time scale I cannot relate to, or static and in slow decay? My brain swelled, and my pride swelled that I was brave enough to hold such thoughts but, to go further than this, my many other questions would have found no factual answer but for a happy coincidence near to the beginning of my Granite obsession, which I will now describe.

Of the limited paper that we had in my home, most had already been used once and saved for a second life. I assumed that at least some had been stolen from somewhere outside the Wild Times by my ancestors (like the cardboard), because I simply could not imagine where else it came from (although I admit that 'stolen from somewhere' did not create a very clear picture either). Our pencils made thick, scratchy lines, so anything with small print or pictures did not distract from our writing or drawing. We didn't write or draw often. Given the lack of rightful reading material available to me (none), after Uncle Heap had taught me to read I took a natural, if covert interest in whatever might be written on the used paper. A vast and almost bottomless supply of attention-grabbing stuff was there, from which I learned about many kinds of apparently normal things. There were secret delights for me like pages thirty-four to sixty-four of The Pruner's Handbook, which dealt chiefly with what it called 'grafting'; a very thick slice of the small-lettered Music Through History, printed on thin paper for economy, which helped me to understand and describe Great Uncle Lollo's profession, although not with nearly such subtle beauty as the music itself; or the exciting closing pages of Adventure on Distant Seas, illustrated by neat pictures of boats that looked very small on the turbulent waters that they rode.

One day I came across an eye-popping, single, huge page (388) of Gray's Scientific Encyclopaedia, folded in half, almost transparent and with tiny script cramming the space with intelligent information, not all of which I fully understood. So great was the grip on me by this wise text that I read it constantly for months in every moment that I was not battling with something life-threatening. Although the intensity of my study of this paper later slowed, I kept it as a treasure and still have it with me today, such vast tracts of time later. In it, many words seemed to have been put into the entry 'Igneous Rocks and Processes' just to dazzle the reader, like porphyritic, pegmatite, metamorphic aureole, orogenic, batholith, aplite, magma, felsic... and more. I was dazzled. I memorised the words and would mumble these magical sounds to myself in bed at night, sitting on the watch blocks alone or in the toilet, hoping to slip some spell of slithering insight into me. However, I reminded myself right at the beginning of reading, that part of Granite's authority is in its enigma, so I left myself small, just like that, and read on, accepting the scraps of comprehension it offered. To my happy astonishment, I found amongst these spangling words some impressions that made me think I was not alone in truly understanding Granite's fearfulness. In fact, I felt touched by a sense of my own beckoning normality and suddenly connected to an unknowable number of diverse people. We were joined by this powerful knowledge about Granite thumping in our chests, like a hero wanting to escape and be heard.

For a start, I had already agreed with myself that Granite was an extremely domineering kind of rock. I had always felt myself quake before it, and I now learned that the Gray's Scientific Encyclopaedia people agreed with me too, and went even further than me, because they described it as 'intrusive' as well. I had known for as long as I could remember that Granite does penetrate your life even when you don't want it to. It wheedles its way into your lumping fears and so on, but I now discovered that it also lives in confrontation with its own kind and intrudes other rocks. (It was a vast thing for me to begin to imagine, but I managed it.) Not only this, but the difficultness of Granite in general was expressed in the frustrations of Gray's Scientific Encyclopaedia writers themselves, who clearly fall prey to Granite's haunting power just as much as me, and are caught up in a battle inspired by its humbling force. Granite sits massively by without laughing once, while the word-wielding nobility pull each others' hair out over its contentious origin, no less: did it float or did it flow? (Granite never flows any more than it floats, so maybe there was vital information on the previous page (that I didn't have) to aid in the understanding of how Granite got here. That previous page haunted me.) After many hours of my brain frowning and my body going to sleep, I felt my understanding of the text was at least moving towards moderate.

The thrilling section 'Uses of Igneous Rocks' gave all kinds of pause for wide-eyed thought as well. I came to know that I was not the first to consider Granite when needing a formidable building material and, more surprising, its formidable qualities had not put potential builders off using it (not that it says in Gray's Scientific Encyclopaedia at least. I suspect all builders have shaken before its command throughout history, just like me). According to these writers and their followers (none of whom I have ever yet met, sadly), Granite, as a building material, has saved lives against murderous storms; it has saved the memory of lives in magnificent monuments; it has made lives worth living with roads and baths and buildings; it has preserved the deadness of dead people in graves (as I was later to find out personally); and Granite has even allowed the question, 'What is life?' to be asked wordfully in places of worship (where people have been enabled to enter the part of their souls where hushed awe and reverence swell in round songs and ring out) then answered wordlessly afterwards, perhaps. This is what page 388 said. I wondered how anyone could ever live or die without Granite, especially me, an aspiringly normal girl caught in the Wild Times.

In the end, everyone concerned (including me) seemed to agree that Granite was hard and tough and nearly always massive and, furthermore, that it is highly Dangerous! Its dangerousness radiates from it just like other rocks, except more so, much, much more so. I read that some people, who are really onto the truth about this terrifying stone, believe that using it in your home could be extremely hazardous. This sounded very exciting from my perilous position. The clever writers even invented a name for the fear that Granite radiates: Radon, and stressed that it could kill you. The grating, gouging crystals that could scar your brain just by thinking about them were no longer the only fearfulness that Granite possessed. The tearing sharpness of it, which would only be a short and uncomfortable preamble to a lengthy, swollen infection from its associated green slime, was no longer the whole story. The sense that your life was only spared at the whim of Granite's great crushing weight could all be described in a single word: Radon.

But not all of my swirl of knowledge and thoughts originated in the tiny words on the transparent page (388). Instead, reading this learned text made so many things I had already read or seen or imagined or questioned clang into a proper fitting place of conception. I knew with an unmovable certainty that Granite would be the material I needed, and perhaps even deserved. Mine would be a house worthy of such an elevated constituent, even in this wild urgency of building, surrounded as I was by the raging Wild Times. As I floated in my encyclopaedically-induced Granite reverie, I saw Granite pillars, thick, and softly concealed by benignly flowering vines and clambering leafery, constructed, just so, to draw the attention of the curious to the entranceways of magical gardens where a person (especially a small person) could remain forever at ease.

And it is a very good rock for climbing, to which I can also now attest.

Chapter Seven: Anticipation

Once a building site has been chosen and the certainty of frightening building established, you can imagine that there are some high-pitched feelings. I tried to keep the feelings down but they just screeched into all my quiet, blank, vacuous places (of which there were many). Sometimes they screamed for days or months at a time from a dark corner of my head where I couldn't even see them. But you can't listen to that screaming for ever and all the time, season after season after season, it would make you go mad I'm sure. My brain called the screaming all kinds of things, trying to disguise it as something I could live with. 'Excitement' was exhausting if not quite so distressing, 'coming to terms with things' merely led to a constipation of stress, and then my head fairly well settled on the finite concept embodied in the word 'anticipation'. The word seemed to curl around the throat of my screamer, and when it did so there would be some high-pitched coughing and a somewhat strangled hiss, but the screaming definitely relented, in a blue-tongued, eyeball popping way. It was great to have a rest, even if the anticipation lingered.

It did go on for a long, long time: anticipation went on and on. Then afterwards it went on. In this time I remember the blue flowers with the radiating stripes (if you looked closely), and the yellow ones with lots of petals (whose leaves Curlywurly had favoured) all dying and being reborn many times under the sky.

I remember days of darkness, intense storms that lasted for weeks, tossing our slither of ocean to white, forcing the far tree into further wizened subjugation, tearing at the wilful, stapled-down roof that our tiny house bore and stroking the grasses, such as they were, in a frantic passion. These tempests forced the sunshiny days a grave distance apart, which wasn't an entirely bad thing. Although the sunshine delighted Great Uncle Lollo, it made Uncle Heap nervous. Me, I didn't believe in sunshiny days really, so they always whizzed by before I noticed them much at all.

Several lightning strikes that came resulted twice in small fires which we could do little about, but they created nothing more than a mess in the end. One came when I was particularly disillusioned and I watched it with the fascination of a crazed fire artist, holding back my cackle. It took out some of the scrub, still laden with its sickening yellow blooms even in such a drought as there was. I sneered with a wavering lip at its instantaneous demise, gloated over its crumbling thorns and breathed in deeply, letting the smoky destruction enter me. At first I imagined the flames trying to leap after me and rob me of body parts that I often used and me springing deftly out of its wicked path. But superiority never was my strong point. My disillusionment rose up, grabbed me hard about the belly and shook the gloating out of me. Then all I could see was my stupid hopes burning up in a flash, the way stupid hopes go, being stupid and never to be realised, and I was limp and pathetic and overcome by the screams from that dark corner of my head again. Times and times. Change change change. More aniticipation.

I kept up my organisation though and made many calculations to measure the reality of our lives as the years passed. I didn't know what went on in secret of course, but I estimated that Menith used a total of seven hundred and sixty millilitres of nail varnish in twenty-three different colours, ninety-two brushes and two thousand six hundred and fifty millilitres of remover. She painted her ten fingernails three thousand eight hundred times and her ten toenails the same, spending something around two thousand, eight hundred and fifty hours doing it. Great Uncle Lollo rehearsed symphonies with seventy-two different orchestras, under different skies and different weathers, solving the mystery of our condition in a mysterious way, and spending one thousand, five hundred and ten hours doing it. As for me, I was breathing, as usual. I counted my breaths and reckoned that the tide of my breath was probably about three hundred millilitres. In all, I calculated that I had breathed at least eight hundred and fifty-two million two hundred and forty-nine thousand, six hundred litres of air whilst in a state of anticipation. This was conservative because, obviously, I would breath more rapidly when frightened, and both days and even sleepy nights could be gory. It seemed a horrendously bold and grabbing thing to take so much air from the world for myself, and I felt ashamed to be making this outrageous theft, but there was little I could do. At least I tried to do it without making much of a show. As a family, our air consumption shot shockingly off the scale which was available to me in my brain, somewhere beyond six billion litres, and that was only counting Mother as a non-breather. Of the four thousand, seven hundred and eighteen frustrations that I noted, only nine hundred and eighty-two brought me to tears. This represented just twelve percent of my tears, a further five percent being down to agonising doubts about my future, four percent due to the Wild Times and the rest I could only say were a gluey blankness which stalked in my bones and occasionally leapt up into my throat causing that familiar squeezing behind my eyes that meant my tears had to come out (or if not my eyeballs would come out instead I presume). Uncle Heap held my hand in his great veiny paws, just like I liked him to, in an amazing ninety-two percent of teary moments. This could have led me to hypothesise that he brought on the tears, I'm aware of that, but of course such a suggestion could only be flatly untrue. Despite so much time being taken up by all this, I still managed to have eight ideas, but none of them survived. Another noteworthy statistic is the number of smiles that took me, which escalated to a dizzying four occasions. When it wasn't happening, fear of the memory or the possibility of it often seized me, somewhat in the way that a bandage seizes body fluids, and the old words 'you're doomed' whispered in the loft of my brain as if they were being hissed malevolently through dry leaves in a big wind. I felt more and more determined to get this smiling business under control.

But the main feature of this time of anticipation was planning.

'What will the house be like Uncle Heap?' I often furtively asked when on watch.

And the response he gave evolved. In the early days he didn't give too much to let my imagination run away with, merely stating, 'Stone!' as if this told the whole, obvious picture. But time brought out all kinds of information and probabilities and problems and hopes. 'I think it will be very heavy,' or 'The top of it will be very heavy,' or 'We will need help,' and 'It will take a lot of cleverness to make it,' or 'It will glow pink in the sunrise,' or 'Plants will like to taste its minerals,' and 'The walls will be thick and cold,' or 'It will fit you perfectly,' or 'It may last forever,' or 'The Wild Times will hurt themselves on its walls,' and many other such illuminating illustrations of my future.

After some time I could spend hours together going over it with Uncle Heap. These were my luckiest days. This kept my spirit quiet, if not my mind. Slowly, I think I built up more of a picture, and probably so did he. My dreaminess floated me over, way over the faraway lands of scrub and the lone tree and burntness and open space with sky and smells, six steps, eleven pants and a gasp, over over and away, a mushroom cloud of 'you're doomed' hanging at my heels as I sped, breathing fast, as fast as I could to my building place. And I would try to articulate my dreaminess for him after I got used to it having me. I tried to say all I felt.

'Uncle Heap, I think I might be lonely in my safe safe house, even though the walls will be very beautiful... The walls will be beautiful, I know, but I wonder if the Wild Times will sound different from over there... Or maybe I won't hear them at all because my safe safe walls will be so thick... The wind might be very strong so close to the sea. Perhaps it will make whistling sounds through chinks in the rock... Will there be chinks in the rock do you suppose?... It will be warm in there, of course, cosy and warm... But what if it is cold? What then? Where can warmth come from in a stone house?... Will spiders come to live there do you think?... And snails in the cracks of things?... And it will smell friendly too, just like a real home where you can relax... It will be tall I suppose, not like this house, it will be tall and thin and proud... I'll be closer to the sun than ever before. That should keep me warm... '

'Well...' Uncle Heap would often trail off in his usual enigmatic way.

His assessment of my dreaminess was not always favourable and he reproached my fussy curiosity once or twice. This project was very important to him, and it felt catastrophic when we didn't agree about something related to it.

'Well... Nice, but we need a plan!' came the urgent whisper. 'We need labour! And stone! We need...' and he would pause for dramatic effect, 'we need to start!'

'Yes Uncle Heap.'

I would cower a little in the dimness of our talking

hours and let his mood sweep me down. It really did make me feel small, but another part of me knew that the funny thing about Uncle Heap was that, for all his bluster about getting on, his way of approaching things never seemed that straightforward to me. This kept a secret part of me in the naughty knowledge that he was fallible. He guessed at measurements that later were forgotten. He made lists of probable materials, none of which we had the faintest idea where or how we could obtain. He swelled the plan into prize-winning architecture when we knew of no competition. He looked for helpful information by searching through his old documents which were stored in small dusty boxes, but found only paper. He spent silent days with a creased brow, licking a blunt pencil over a precious piece of paper recovered from a dusty box, but never made one single mark on it.

My quavering smallness and his blustering speculations were finally eclipsed as our separate senses of anticipation came together in a big push.

Years before, Uncle Heap had very painfully taught me to write, as I have already mentioned. Writing was what (apparently) rendered our paper precious, but it was (somewhat ironically) the only thing that used our precious paper up. As it was all only theoretically useful (and he never told me the theory actually) I found it difficult to give myself over to the importance of it or even concentrate at all. Somehow he did eventually get the basics into me. Of course, there was writing's cousin reading to contend with as well. I did, much later in life, find a lot of those random reading excerpts and later even a book once but, at the time I began, reading also held an unfathomable practical place in my very practical life. (Let me point out that Uncle Heap never pointed out the precious readability of our paper. This I discovered in another clanging moment of beautiful realisation.)

Suddenly, sometime deep in the era of anticipation,

reading and writing became obvious, became the light to show our way, became my vehicle to goodness, became the means to progress and the only link that could bind my present to my future. The lateness with which I drew this conclusion was more to do with my blank brain than Uncle Heap's fallibility. As it turned out, the dusty piece of paper, which had been almost attracting the attentions of his damp, blunt pencil, turned out to be a letter from an unimaginable architect to his unimaginable client about an unimaginable building project, a long time ago, in an unimaginable world. So, now knowing that such experts existed, we began to compose a letter to send to such an architect who had their workplace in a way out and beyond world where there were no Wild Times. Surely such a person would understand safety in the most profound way. Surely this would be the person to make concrete plans for my safe safe house, the house that could herald the beginning of it all, the change of everything and the forever separation from dangerousness. I had never even dreamt of trying to contact a world beyond our pitiful lives. Rumours at the Wild Times Fair said it existed, but I had not believed until this moment. Now it became surely true for me, as my fantasy and my head filled in the details of this architect drawing man, down to the wrinkles around his friendly smile as he read my words.

Our first attempt went something like this:

Dear Sir or Lady Architect

I am a small person of small means but I have big plans (which my Uncle Heap put into me) to make a safe safe house to protect me from the Wild Times in which we live. Don't worry, I have found a building place near the wild ocean beyond the lone tree which will be great. What I need is a plan and I think this is your job, so good. Please contact me with the plan right away. It's Granite.

> *Yours*
> *The Daughter of the Silent Woman*

The more I read it over, the more I noticed that we had made no offer of what we might give in return for this architect's work, as an incentive. Having no idea what architect's needed or wanted, I decided that I would wait until this question was brought up by the important and distant architect, if ever (I didn't know what to expect). Instead, I decided to focus my persuasions on alluring details of my project and, after many revisions, we eventually came up with this:

> *Dear and Noble Architect*
>
> *I have long lived in admiration of your esteemed craft and my puny life has somehow led me to the door of your mighty profession. I am writing to beg your very important help in realising a life-changing building project which rests outside my humble abilities, partly because I am small and partly because I am barely a person. I trust that you live in comfort and safety and without cause for great worries, and I am sure that this is your due, but I must make you aware that I live in the worst of the Wild Times which press on me sorely, day and night, night and day. I have full intention to lift myself from this pit of fear and be a worriless individual who might enjoy things. I have no expectation to ever reach the starry heights of easeful life that are yours, but in order to reach toward an even minor amelioration of my tragedies, I have to solve the fearful issue of the Wild Times which flock around me. This is where you come in. I hope you will be interested in making your spotless conscience shine yet more by playing a role in changing the lowly life of one twig-like human*

being for the better.

This is what I need exactly:

1. Drawn plans for a house suitable for one person's residence (me, small, female) made from our local peerless stone, which makes such a profound answer to terror that one can hardly call it merely stone. This stone is aptly named Granite and is heavy beyond my imagining.

2. A design which will, above all, be safe, and after that be still safe. As I am sure you have heard, the Wild Times offer perils of all kinds, and strong walls, foundations and roof are all imperative.

3. The aforementioned Granite is of qualities which inspire piety in every normal person. Such as it is, it deserves to be crafted into an edifice of style and presence. Therefore, the design which I am requesting must be for a building of Granitic Grandeur.

4. Safety is really at the top of my list.

5. The sourcing and delivery of all materials, including that heavy heavy Granite.

6. Help. I need a lot of help to build this magnificent building. I believe that I may need at least two men, big, silent men who will lumber through great labours and not shrink or shirk, who can stand up before the mighty Granite which they will handle and demonstrate the beauty of the plans that you have furnished. They will be men who can bring this project to fruition without expressing fear, without uttering complaint and without changing or withering, in fact, men who will be, in character, much like the stone that will be both their master and their subject.

7. As a project this must prioritise my safety as a future home, ie, it must be thick, heavy, solid and unshakeable through any crisis that the Wild Times might come up with.

This is what I already have exactly:

1. A level-ish building site in a somewhat remote coastal place which is underlain by Granite and overlooked by a single tree which I believe will bear fruit and add a certain dignity to the property.

I trust that the above details are comprehensive enough for you to begin your work and I look forward to hearing news from you about your role in this exciting undertaking.

Yours
The Growling Girl

There was a sense of acceleration of wonderful life as we worked, and the feeling was of pure exhilaration when I had finished this first correspondence, scribing each careful letter of each considered word with a resolute hand. I could feel my eyes were shining and my mouth twitched slightly once or twice, but I managed to keep it under control. For the first time things seemed to be making sense in my life, there was a connection between the past and the present which could potentially alter the outcome of my future. I felt purposeful and like a player in the story at last. Uncle Heap looked several inches taller than I had ever seen him before and he held the small envelope lightly in his big, veiny hands (which were shaking a bit) casting his eyes between it and me for a long time. His love wrapped me in a light veil which made me feel floaty and secure, in a cloud-like way, dashing through enormous space and commanding the elements.

I wanted that moment to last forever, obviously, but unfortunately I soon got to thinking something and the thought just blurted out of me before the sweetness of the situation had been given a full chance to blossom.

'But how are we going to get the letter to the architect Uncle Heap?'

My heart crashed as my mouth said it, and time folded around me like a lead cloak. I have since heard of postal services and the like, but the Wild Times had drawn a line between its people who lived in company with its fears and limitations, and those that lived in the faraway lands outside its dominion. It is difficult to know now of course, but I wonder sometimes if that line was just drawn in my head because I had somehow agreed to believe in the Wild Times. But back then, as it seemed to me, communications were impossible and I could not imagine how my letter could be allowed to serve its purpose.

It took Uncle Heap more than a week to answer the problem. During that week all the inches that he had gained in height sank off him, his pallor was grey and he wandered around, always clutching the vital letter in his still shaking hand. He made such a striking sight that I even noticed Menith look up from her nail painting with a curious expression on her face, almost as though she cared. Great Uncle Lollo dribbled and scratched his lower back vigorously as he stared at Uncle Heap passing by. Me, I watched him guiltily, knowing that my stupidity had ruined everything, that I had trampled love and slain optimism in one pathetic and thoughtless blurt.

Then he saved us. I instantly knew that I should never have doubted him.

'Come!' he beckoned, waving me forward meaningfully with the envelope.

We jittered our awareness this way and that in a cautious way as we rounded the house, where Uncle Heap pointed my attention at what you might call a small cage, hastily put together from sticks lashed together with strong, long leaves. At first I thought it was fake: it didn't look like it had always been a bird, as though someone or something had sewn or glued bits on. It stood in haughty scruffiness, a little above the height of my knees. Its hooked beak was chipped and askew and its globby eyes rolled independently, were streaked with several colours and one was clouded by a cataract. Most parts of it were naked and stubbly, but clumps of mangy feathers hung from its wings and rear end, all a dirty nondescript colour, and it wore a thick black wig over its head. Its feet were fat and paw-like but with claws that curled back this way or that or even spiralled, each taking its own direction. It appeared to me that walking would be hard and possibly painful for this poor creature and certainly in whatever travelling it had done by foot, it had picked up some unsavoury souvenirs which still clung to these twisted talons. I wondered if this was the source of the pungent smell which was dissolving the delicate tubes inside my nose.

'Our postmaster,' Uncle Heap declared confidentially, 'brought back from retirement. Toobit Lonkins.'

I was having an unsteady moment and didn't immediately know what to say. It threw its head back and let out a vibrating croak and I saw its dry tongue quavering, so I tentatively replied with, 'Nice to meet you Mr Lonkins,' which elicited a further croak.

Uncle Heap was scowling (at me I think) when he started to untie the cage and arrange things. Toobit Lonkins stepped out into our yard space and flapped in an arthritic kind of way.

'He'll take the letter to the architect,' said Uncle Heap factually.

'Ah,' I whispered back, adjusting my mind rapidly to this new state of affairs.

'You keep watch while I prepare him,' came the instruction.

'Aha,' I returned, 'right away,' and I shuffled off to

our watch blocks trying to focus my attention on anything more probable than Toobit Lonkins.

It was hard, and I did try, but I couldn't help but spend half of my time glancing over toward Uncle Heap and Toobit Lonkins in the yard to see what was going on. The long and short of it is that Uncle Heap bent down and strapped on an aged chest bag to Toobit Lonkins and slipped the precious letter inside. He took the creature onto his lap and cupped its head in one hand, holding it against his whispering mouth. What Uncle Heap could have been saying to the bird I don't know, but it took a long time for him to say it and my mind went jiggarty wondering if birds (or Toobit Lonkins for that matter) really had ears to hear with beneath the feathers (or wigs as it may be) about their heads.

Eventually it was time for takeoff. Uncle Heap threw Toobit Lonkins into the air and he flapped feebly and fell to the ground just short of the prickly scrub. There was a pained croaking and they tried again without success. I felt my tears coming on, but Uncle Heap was undaunted as usual. Again and again he tried, and I noticed his strategy to make Toobit Lonkins try harder: with each subsequent launch Uncle Heap would toss him into the air closer to the prickly scrub until there was no surrender to early failure that could save Toobit Lonkins from a very painful drop. Unsurprisingly he flew, if shakily, and I watched the little blob that was Toobit dip and rise with strained effort until he was well inland and then, shortly, invisible.

Uncle Heap walked up to see me at the watch blocks. He nodded to me meaningfully and I said, 'Aha,' again and let my mouth hang open. My feelings zigzagged wildly and I wondered if this was the real beginning of my safe safe house or just the beginning of some spectacularly drawn out demolition of my dreams with Toobit Lonkins as the agent of slow destruction.

'You're doomed' wagged about in my brain, however I chased it off, but I did my best to keep my spirits up.

Toobit Lonkins became an important part of my life in the following months and I got to know him, as far as anyone could. I no longer have the letters which he subsequently brought back for me in reply to my masterpieces, but the first one took several weeks to arrive and went something like this:

Esteemed Customer

Thank you for your correspondence. Having dedicated my time and that of my entire team to an expert and in depth consideration of your proposal I am happy to inform you that I would be delighted to take you on as our client. A full quote for our services will be prepared at our soonest convenience.

Graciously Yours
pp Ervil Nitzo, Architect Extraordinaire

Good old Toobit! There was delight and excitement when this came. I further understood the importance of reading and writing and of Uncle Heap as a beneficent force, and I fully believed my house would come to me soon. Uncle Heap's pallor improved and the days sped by in a confident sweep of capability over the prowling Wild Times.

It couldn't last though, not until Ervil Nitzo, Architect Extraordinaire found time to send us a letter again anyway, and the letter did not arrive, even as patient time grew impatient. Uncle Heap went grumpy and grey coloured and I started to become quieter than ever before. We were not happy. One dark-sky-ed day, with Toobit pacing his cage out in the yard, we decided to take action.

'We have to write another letter,' whispered Uncle Heap.

And this was the result:

Elevated Architect

I am on my knees with gratitude for your acceptance of my humdrum project into the glittering world of your architectural practice. What I really need now are the plans. And the help. And the materials. I am right here waiting for them whenever they come. In fact, I am so much in anticipation of them that I may expire soon without them. I do hope your soonest convenience is soon and I would urge you to hurry before you might have my expiration on your hands. I trust that you are well, happy and not too overworked to fit us in very very soon. Please send me a projection of likely events. Please.

Yours in oozing anticipation
The Girl for the Safe Safe House

The 'very very' was Uncle Heap's idea, as was the expiration bit (although it was almost true). We felt much better when Toobit had taken off with our latest letter and we settled down to wait for a reply with steely hearts and nerves.

It wasn't until weeks later that Toobit came scratching the sky with his distinctive, tired flight pattern and delivered the reply for which he had waited so long at the architect's office. As I said before, I no longer have Ervil Nitzo's replies, but I assure you that the second one went something like this:

Esteemed Customer

Thank you for your correspondence.   Having

dedicated my time and that of my entire team to an expert and in depth consideration of your proposal I am happy to inform you that I would be delighted to take you on as our client. A full quote for our services will be prepared at our soonest convenience.

> *Graciously Yours*
> *pp Ervil Nitzo, Architect Extraordinaire*

That was when Uncle Heap really started to dig his heels in.

'Write another!' he said slowly through his teeth, with a voice that made me think he was trying to frighten me.

I noticed that Toobit was looking tired, so I slipped him some extra food that evening. I thanked him for all his hard work and he croaked as he swallowed. Before the sun had gone that night he had left again with this letter in his chest bag:

> *For the attention of Ervil Nitzo in person*

> *Dear Sir*

> *You have now received two letters from me in which I have urged you to render your professional help to my vital building project. You have offered twice in writing a quote for your services which has not been forthcoming. For the sake of my own state of health I must know when we will get underway with the aforementioned heavy stone and also for the sake of my health this date must be very very SOON. I don't believe that you are so far away and I do not want you or me to have blood on our hands as a result of any delay. I would be reassured if you would respond at once.*

Yours
The Not Quite Yet Expired Girl

Uncle Heap wanted the letter to be much nastier, but there was time for that later. Dear Toobit came winging back in a definitely shorter period of time with another identical letter and so the rounds began. Back and forth went these letters and Toobit started to look in pretty good shape from all the exercise. I was eventually persuaded to include some fantastical threats like, 'the insects are under my control' and, 'my mother will send doom upon you of the highest order' and lurid insults like, 'you careless fellow' and, 'you numpty' which at last brought back this response:

Esteemed Customer

Shut up at once!

Graciously Yours
pp Ervil Nitzo, Architect Extraordinaire

It was the breakthrough we'd been waiting for. By this time we called him Nitzo Pits-oh. At last we knew he had truly and personally noticed us and we were onto something. Unfortunately it was only two letters later that we were met with the heavy silence of no response at all. Then something even heavier happened.

Chapter Eight: Reality is Real Now According to Uncle Heap

I was starting my watch just before dawn one rather damp morning. Everything was as it often was: quiet, with a squelchy, lurking feeling. I was toying with my club and considering the possibility of giving it fresh spikes as the old ones were getting rather blunt from overuse. The leather strap which held it around my wrist was shiny and worn but remained strong, and the wood was solid too, unharmed by any of the blows I had had to deal with it. The spikes were something else though. I felt concerned, and I determined to put it to Uncle Heap later that he might surrender some of our precious ironmongery to repair this valuable weapon which had saved us so often. I had a mighty feeling that it might be hard to repair because, looking over the club, it was clearly not 'of us'. In other words, the wood, the now dull spikes, and the leather strap were all fashioned by someone else, before some member of my family 'obtained' it. It was a great club.

Pretty much nothing else was in my mind at this time. Menith was still doing her sleeping goddess impression with her hands draped romantically across her pillow. Uncle Heap was shuffling around but not near me, and nor did I know where he was. Mother was as mother always was: a glass statue constantly threatening to shatter in her ringing world. Great Uncle Lollo had emerged once to urinate at the extreme edge of his territory and then followed his tether, hand over hand, back to his bed in the gloom without once opening his eyes. He never rose early. I was on my normal auto-alert for smells, sounds and sights, and the light from over the never-explored land of mysteries to the east was showing quickly. I had spent so much time watching that I knew just about every blade of grass, every barren pebble, every withered root, the scar left by every lightning bolt, and every footprint left by a malevolent visitor that the eye could discern. Given this, obviously it took not much light at all before I noticed the dramatic change out beyond the lone tree to the west.

'Ah!' The shock came out loudly and I had no time to compose a whisper. My own shock shocked me, and I reined myself in before I let any other unbidden sound leave my head. 'Uncle Heap!' I whispered urgently. 'Uncle Heap! Uncle Heap! Uncle Heap!... Uncle Heap! Uncle Heap! Uncle Heap!' I was beside myself with whispering, and scampered off around the yard on my twiggy legs in a state of great agitation, not exactly heedless of my watch, but neither applying my concentration as much as was normal or proper. 'Uncle Heap! Uncle Heap! Uncle Heap!'

It didn't take long for him to hear me because Uncle Heap is always ready. He emerged suddenly from behind the scrub with a huge knife fitting in his hand and a readiness of questions on his face.

'It's here!' I whispered through my cupped hands to direct the full force of the news at him.

He ran to me in an elderly sort of way, picked up my hand that wasn't holding the stolen club with his hand that wasn't holding the knife and we glided niftily back to the watch blocks in the dimness. He pointed his sunrise eyes toward the west.

'Grrranite!' he exhaled through clenched teeth as he gripped my hand furiously. 'Yes! Reality is with us!'

Uncle Heap immediately began a jigging dance which belied his decrepit state, flinging his arms in the air and then letting each hand fall in turn as if it were dead whilst his legs alternately threw his balance in some opposing way. I raised my eyebrows in wonder at all this, as you can imagine. It didn't last long but it gave me a roundish feeling that it would be a great day.

As the sun came up over the land we saw, fully illuminated, the massive pile of mixed sized rocks that had arrived. I didn't question how it had got there any more than I questioned anything else in my Wild Times. It was a miracle, a marvel, something I could never have expected to see, and so big! The idea of my house had always been modest. In fact, it had always fitted inside my head. This pile of rock could not. It was mountainous. At last we knew that all our letter writing had come to something, the materials had arrived and no doubt the big, silent, labouring men would follow soon too. The reality of my house which Uncle Heap had borne alone so long in his tired old heart had finally become real in a solid and measurable way in the normal world outside of his funny soul. It was like birth. Maybe like the birth of land itself, come from the ocean or the sky. But for me it was not the realisation of an inner reality, but an unreality becoming real, which just showed me how little a girl I was to have not fully trusted that it would actually happen. My eyes leaked from the confusion. Anything was possible from now on. We could do it.

'We must go and see it!' Uncle Heap puffed.

'Nuh-now?' I jittered, feeling the immediacy of his command.

'Get ready!'

My fears and excitements and confusions all jumbled and scrambled together and all I could hear was a waterfall of change in my head relentlessly churning the pit of my stomach before flowing off to some unknowable place. Slosh, slosh it went, rather greenly, doing its best to erode the solid banks of my fortitude in a rushing whirl. I was just getting accustomed to this new tumult, stabilising myself rather than getting swept away, when everything changed again.

'Listen!' Uncle Heap whispered suddenly, killing my newborn waterfall in an instant.

He struck his listening pose, his eyes, fingers and ears alert to whatever was this new sound. I was snapped out of my whirling dream and back to the monotony of our lives in the Wild Times as we synchronously turned to the scratching sound in the scrub. Threats from here posed a difficult problem (that we often faced) because the scrub was excellent cover through which it was hard to harm an intruder. I let out an involuntary sigh of frustration and Uncle Heap shot me a rapid, withering look. He could never tolerate someone who would not deal with the matter in hand, and that was one of the reasons we got on so well almost all the time.

He tapped me once on the shoulder which, in this instance, meant 'go and get the slingshots'. I dutifully did this in ultra slow motion, whilst continuing to listen attentively. The snuffling told me that it was looking for something by smelling, and the smell that I smelled told me that it was a male. At smelly times like these I try to breathe as little as possible so I don't get sick at the wrong moment, but, well, I still have to breathe, and I did start feeling quite high in the throat and loose in the stomach almost right away. I came back as quickly as I could in slow motion, starting to retch. Uncle Heap saw the emergency, immediately shot off two stones into the scrub then ran at it, growling loudly, thrusting the blunt-spiked club into the foliage and thrashing around clumsily but with purpose and confidence while I started to empty my stomach (sadly) right next to our watch blocks. As the acid stuff came through my nose, my eyes wept and I simultaneously heard the scream of a clawed thing from Uncle Heap's direction. I managed to throw a feeble look his way just in time to see a flash of fur and a spurt of black blood as he swiped it.

Fortunately there was only one of them, and Uncle Heap was by my side almost right away. He did not allow himself to feel sorry for me because he knew he was supposed to be angry with me, but deep down I think he was sympathetic because he didn't say anything at all. He became like a statue for the ten minutes it took me to get to my feet again, and even then never mentioned my pathetic state but just went on with the plans for our outing as if nothing had happened, whilst I scooped up my vomity acid gloop from the ground.

'We'll need the bucket again. I'll tell Menith...'

I scooped my stuff.

'...it's a very long way. A lot of Granite to inspect. May have to...'

I scooped my horrible acid stuff.

'...we can make a guess about the whole...'

I scooped up the horrible former contents of my acid stomach, but eventually Uncle Heap gathered his thoughts enough to actually leave and I hastily made the best of what was left, threw some dust over it and started to gather the weapons. I think my internal waterfall had been largely spewed already because its return was modest, more trickling, like a swampy, thick kind of fear that glooped in an opaque sort of way. I felt weakened by it, but managed to collect our defences together without making a sound, steadying myself from my mind out.

The bewildered Menith was forced from her bed to be watchkeeper. She took on an air of slow panic with the imprint of her pillow still fresh on her cheek and a dusty crust of dried saliva running from one corner of her mouth. This unwonted situation did not entirely distract her from the good looks of her fingers and toes (she gave them a glazed and dissatisfied appraisal), but her crazy

71

eyes rolled in a random nervousness as we had seen before, and she perched her large, wobbly self by the front door step. The good thing was that her hair was utterly wild now and it gave her a savage look. If she could muster anything of a growl in the event of an interloper's appearance, they would surely turn to see her and vanish with their tail between their legs in convulsive fear of this ball of knots and sticks. Uncle Heap gave her a growl to suggest how things might go, and she recoiled, looking moon-faced.

Being back on the trail with Uncle Heap felt as unfamiliar as it had done the first time. This was mainly because I had not been given enough time to beg use of his supple bone-beaded hat, so my bare head gave a constant sense of exposure, which I had not experienced before, as well as an entirely broadened perspective on the changing view. I noticed the blue flowers with the radiating stripes (if you looked closely), and the yellow ones with lots of petals (whose leaves Curlywurly had favoured) and thought it funny that we should be making our second trip in this same season of flowers. The wiry-stemmed pink flowers with the cushion leaves were not quite there though, and only showed their tidy buds with a tip of teetering pinkness at the point. But behind all this the backdrop was enormous. The swathes of charred roots rolled away this way and that to meet the various textures of the outside world: prickles, spikes, hopeful grasses, rough rocks, tearing blackness and even, far far away, a hitherto unnoticed huddle of trees still holding up their spindly winter branches from their ditch (or were they dead?). The white sky sped frantically across the blue sky, and the blue sky skidded past in a more covert way. My forehead felt enormous and blank, like an overdue egg emerged from a dark womb, and I clung to Uncle Heap's hand, always, always watching, trying not to be so distracted by the small flying things that sprung from the ground under us, that I might miss a larger thing from another direction.

It was an interminable time. My nerves were so stretched that I felt like days of tense agony passed. Maybe it was days. Maybe time had been ground down to a virtual halt until we finally arrived at the half way dew tree (at which time the speed of things got going again, as I observed it). The tree wasn't dewy any more, but I remembered with vividness the gnarly scar on the seaward side of its trunk. This time I fingered the wound curiously and conjured images of the many lightning strikes I had seen, wondering how it would be to have something like that go through you and then still live. My hands were pretty gnarly themselves from so much chopping and so on, but the dew tree was tough in a way I never expected, or even hoped to be: delicate branches, gracefully yielding to the prevailing winds, intertwining to make a lacy awning over the bare earth; the precision of its leaf-buds, still hard; the way it cupped itself away from the sunlight. All this showed that the tree was refined and meticulous. But this furious gash running the full length of the main trunk was a symbol of the catastrophic realignment of self it had surmounted to meet circumstances reduced beyond imagining. I hoped things would never be that bad for me, but I guess one never knows.

I suppose I must have cast a forlorn look toward Uncle Heap as I touched the sad, strong tree, because he raised his eyes to the sky, then beckoned me with his hand to come away. Once I was back safely in his hand, he made a little 'tssst!' sound and pointed at what I realised must be the descendant of the purple flowered plant that had grown here before. This one had several shorter stems hung with the dripping blooms. They looked stunted, but hairier inside and meaner and purpler and angrier and drippier and more poisonous. I recoiled as the saliva came to my mouth willing me forwards again to... eat them?... lick them?... touch them?... I'm not quite sure, but I allowed Uncle Heap to draw me towards him and all was well.

It's odd how, when you start to look at something, you quickly see lots of them. Sure enough, one little thought in that direction and all the poisonous plants seemed to leap up around my legs as we left the shade of the dew tree and journeyed on to my building place. In this horrible open land I had close encounters with many of the clawing ones and twice met something that wanted to etch through my skin to dissolvingly eat my flesh. It can't be a nice death, to be dissolved, but the thought of it took my mind off the speeding, skidding sky, and this was no bad thing.

If I'm honest (and I am), I have to say that the second half of our epic journey seemed much quicker than the first. It was still epic of course, but nothing dangerous happened, although we thought it might at one point and walked back to back for a long stretch across the charred root area just to make sure nothing surprised us from behind or in front. I noticed myself making involuntarily little coughed 'haha!' noises, which I know meant that I was frightened. My waterfall had started up again and somehow got stuck in my throat. I had to clear it or choke instead, and my attempt at clearing it came out as 'haha!'. But the tufty green of the soft grasses was making a valiant invasion bid into the black burned areas, and it shone so brightly here that the colour felt as though it existed just to inspire me and lift me from these terrible gloopy fears. Life can be very testing, but it usually turns out all right so long as you keep going and don't forget to notice the goodness of the earth under your own feet. I noticed it. I was grateful, and still frightened.

Of course I had hitherto imagined that the Wild

Times were the source of my fear, but I shortly found out that there was something which frightened me altogether more: my heap of Granite. As we came close, it loomed. There is no better word. It loomed, and I pictured the clawing spirit of it climbing to the top of the heap to snarl down on me and yowl its threats with bared, algae covered teeth. I had previously imagined its enormity, but enormity is much bigger close up, you might know already. The weight of all that rock felt so precarious and, in each moment, I lived with the imminent danger of this heap running after me and crushing me to death. After all, it had already mercilessly crushed uncountable small blue flowers. I guess I felt a bit like a flower: small and blue and squashable. I imagined it all vividly: my head caved in and my brain stuff randomly escaping, my mushy face unrecognisable, trailing guts running out through a bloody cavern in my belly, various limbs pointing in ways they were not formerly able to, a general all-over grating, and perhaps even some dismemberment as a result of this avalanche of razor-sharp cutting crystals lumped together into heavy crushing blocks. I allowed myself to be absorbed by these thoughts as I soaked up the vision of my Granite heap, spread as it was over an area covering at least one third of my building platform (and possibly still creeping forwards). I even lost fear of the Wild Times when we were close. I knew instinctively that nothing I had ever seen before would be bold enough in its badness to come anywhere near this knee-trembling presence of rock. Uncle Heap took me closer and closer, and then closer still until I couldn't believe there was any closer to get, but still we went on. He held my hand tighter and tighter and my joints became different in my body: they worked still, but everything was stiff in between and my head could not turn from side to side any more. All I could do was stare at the heap.

We went right up to it and Uncle Heap said a long, protracted 'Yeessss!' and the sparkle came from the sun and ricocheted off the rock crystals and into his eyes. I felt feeble and churny and runny and gushy again. I actually touched it. He made me. He took my hand down there to touch one of the smaller pieces at the edge. It was just as I thought. And when I was there I could smell it. Except it wasn't like smelling something, it was like tasting it. I tasted it and my waterfall stomach rushed away into a poisonous jungle, my tongue went loose and heavy, flapping from my rigid face and, at this taste in my mouth, just the mere taste, I could feel my teeth being grated away, eroded to the nerves, soft and crumbling in my mouth. I blinked.

I remember blinking, but the memory goes a bit misty after that. What I do remember is that when we eventually got back, (goodness knows how many steps, pants and gasps later), Menith had fainted and wasn't on watch at all. I was exhausted by the pitch of the peril we had all survived so I just left her on the doorstep in a loose pile while I wearily went back to the watch blocks to do the job properly with my bucket.

Long weeks of waiting and wondering and recovering followed. The nightmares that had visited me since our first outing had generally become less as time had gone on, but they made a resurgence after the epic journey, furnished with a new suite of images, smells, feelings and colours. The Granite had made a big and frightening impression on me and it revisited me often. I sweated night after night, sleeping in its coldness and tasting its glowing green algae on my softening yellow teeth. As I scraped my dream-gaze over the imposing pile, it scraped me back. It scraped my face and my eyes, and my vision blurred and my eyes ran with water, then with blood, and even the blood ran down my face, cutting channels on its journey across my cheeks before it trailed under my chin, down my neck, and slipped away into my tunic's dark secrets. On some nights my gut-churning waterfall of perpetual rushing change would visit me again, but this time the bed of the river was made from my Granite. It was sharp and glistening and evil and a freezing brown on its upper surfaces, clawing to hurt me through the water, but in every crevice and hidden place it was green and slurping, sucking like a plughole at the contents of my abdomen, drawing the life out of me.

And the barren black burntness of the land around was in my dreams too. In my dreams my feet were often black, the same kind of black as the land. But they were not black from walking, they were black from being burned themselves. The skin was swollen and crunchy and charred, and the bottoms of my leggings were frayed and sooty and uneven. I could feel something oozing through the cracking skin and felt that perhaps my feet might fall off, or perhaps the burn might travel up my legs and over my body and I would become crunchy and charred and splitting open all over, I wasn't sure which. But I still felt a general sogginess about my insides. The worst of it was that in my dreams I could no longer distinguish between the Granite and the Wild Times. My rocky heap would give me fear just like all the horrible things that had threatened me all my life. It would leap after me with a deathly intent just like everything else always had. This was confusing because Uncle Heap had led me to believe that the Granite was there to save me. In my head I knew it was too, but my dreams got me in a muddle sometimes.

Thus muddled, I waited for the big, silent builders.

Chapter Nine: The Wild Times

Ordinarily, before the great Granite arrival, it was the insects and insect-like things that frightened me the most and made my nights rancid with dreams. There were a lot of startled, early morning hours which found me awake, vertical and damp over images centring on the juxtaposition of my human juiciness and the armoured precision of these pointed nasties. But my dreams were inseparable from reality, and both were too often hung with huge, crunchy, glossy flying things. They came so fast that there was no kind of vigilant watch that could keep them away. The best you could do was to hope that they came in a swarm and you could easily hear their approach and get everything shut up in time, and that they weren't the extra extra large size that actually once pierced our wooden shutters and dripped a deadly looking drip onto our floor from its iridescent spike (the burned mark of the puddle was still there last time I looked, a long time ago). They weren't subtle. They weren't sly or coded about what they did, and nor were they calculating. They didn't need to be. They just came to kill and suck out the juices of whatever came in their path, homing in with their thousand faceted eyes. If they didn't kill you outright, you were sure to die of a most grim illness which they harboured and passed along in their digestive juices, or worse still, nearly die and then continue to live on for a while, or whatever. Some of them were enormous, with bodies alone bigger than my head, and all bore appendages that, if they weren't needle sharp and dripping with some fatal goo, were hideously barbed such that you could never escape from them once hooked. The hum of even the smaller ones on the wing so much brought to mind the really big ones that it was natural to feel jumpy. Even ever-placid Great Uncle Lollo jumped (in a blobby way) from time to time at the coming of an insect. There was no net that could keep these beasts away and no cloth that you could rapidly sweep across you that their evil appurtenances could not easily penetrate in order to reach the quivering target of your flesh. The spherical ones had a particular way of spinning in the air which was disconcerting and I imagined I saw their glossy black smiles as they hummed and whirred and darted, malevolent and twirlsome. After each insect encounter I made a mental note to remember some of the forgotten members of my close family who we didn't talk about any more, but I usually forgot this pretty soon.

My insect dreams were difficult to deal with and wore me down from time to time I admit, but when the screaming came this was more wearing and even less escapable than the dreams. The screaming would go on for days at a time sometimes, not at a single pitch but as several voices in one chorus on different pages of the torture requiem, blood curdling here set against mere agony, howling emotional pain, purely physical pain (I always imagined amputation) and a few recovery moans where screamers were catching their breath again. One could never tell where the racket came from (the sky? the ground? everywhere? nowhere?) and it was an obvious thing to conclude that it came from inside yourself, belonged to you and was your own pain. I would sweat pebbles after a few days of this and when it left I had such a ringing through my whole body I felt like my empty bucket after I'd clanked it to scare something off. In the virtual silence that lay in the weeks between screaming sessions, the soft sound of the wind through the grasses ran straight through the perforations left in my brain from the awful cacophony.

Noises that happened less frequently or for shorter periods included shouting, which, again, was difficult to place. Any human kind of sound was alarming, because we so rarely saw other people, not least these frightened I've-just-found-something-that-I'd-rather-not-have shouts. These were spooky and I couldn't help but cast my eyes around in search of the caller, even knowing I would never find them. The long, dying away, as the voice trailed off, bore in it a loneliness which conjured in my mind a scenario involving lonely, puny me, lost and adrift in a bad, bad world that was about to eat me up, one limb at a time. That's what was spooky. A repeating 'No-o-o-o-o!' or 'He-e-e-e-elp!' would occupy me for hours with turbid thoughts and murky feelings and a zigzag battle of will as to whether I should go out and actually search for the shouter or not (I never did).

Night always seemed like a different country. Not that I had any experience of different kinds of countries (apart from what I had read on various torn pages of old books that had become writing paper), but it was all very different indeed, the colours, the mood, the scale of it all, the scale of me. Things, shapes, and other things came close because light wasn't between you and them anymore. Whispered maledictions came from the sky on the darkest nights. Now these definitely came from the sky. I can't say why, but they did. These curses often followed a sticky, poisonous downpour, but not always. I reckon the peeved utterer of such unpleasant words and not nice thoughts was just having an unlucky time and was picking on me because they could, because I was set up to take all this. Fortunately for me, I was also small enough that most of it ran past me without sticking at all.

Of course the darkness didn't always just come at night. Sometimes it was dark for weeks together because the sky got choked up with something or other, and I always hoped and hoped, with a simple heart, that whatever was up there would stay up there and not fall down to bother us. It was an altogether different kind of darkness to the kind we had at night though, usually being purple and often warm too. I've mentioned the acid gloop that fell from darkened skies. Well, that was bad, but sometimes there was ash which fell too, from fiery clouds still aglow with whatever it was. When I saw a black period coming I'd sigh and gather up all the perseverance that I could and pack it all tightly around me. Keeping watch became trickier and trickier with the black times: sheltering, seeing, staying awake, breathing, that sort of thing.

When things seemed particularly prosperous (this did happen), we often became the haunt of a strange, but not exactly dangerous creature that would limp by with its scabby skin, then hang around, sniffing pitifully and never meeting our eyes. It was sly and unkind, had two legs and didn't mess around. I doubted the truthfulness of its watering eyes and sunken cheeks, but nevertheless it ensnared my sympathy and hypnotised me with its wan stare. Its objective seemed to be to get close to you, really really close, so that it could pluck pathetically at your clothing and spread its rotten smell over you as it pawed your limbs and torso. I assumed that the deposition of this horrible odour was lest you forget the creature later on. It came from time to time with another scabby friend, both wearing their rags. This second one was always eating a little smackerel of crust or whatever from its dirty hands and retching and puking. I even saw it eating its own vomit once, which I found less than nice. Of course, I was always sick when these two were around. I didn't like them at all and looked forward to a day when I would never have to smell them again and I could eat whenever I wanted.

A few times I witnessed cases of what Uncle Heap

called 'breakage and destruction'. This was a curious thing to see and I found it rather entertaining, but I was soon old enough to catch the drift of its potential danger to us. Breakage and destruction was spontaneous, unprompted and random, as far as I could glean. There would be preceding rumbling noises and then everything would begin to destroy itself. Trees would shatter or explode; room sized lumps of earth would pop into the air amidst soily scatterings; plants and bushes would be torn up and fly through the brisk winds that sprang up; birds and mammals would be seen fleeing, often on fire or smoking or bleeding. It came pretty close to us one time. I saw it spreading slowly like a violent, regurgitating disease over the scrubland and pictured the implosion of our little house, pictured mother being swallowed into a soily hole and never flinching, pictured Great Uncle Lollo conducting this middle part of a tragic work with climactic percussion and maybe never getting the chance to shape the stately birdsong under the clouds again.

Randomness is worrying, you'll agree. Another thing which made random strikes afflicted a bunch of people at the Wild Times Fair one year: madness. I hadn't seen it before, so was no expert, but Uncle Heap said that it was difficult to tell the difference between mental and physical madness. I don't know anything about it, but after seeing it once I'm very glad madness didn't visit our house ever. The affected people were normal until the convulsions came, then they became all wrong. There was drooling at the mouth, rolling of the eyes and crying out strange things repeatedly like, 'He made me do it!' or, 'The purple ones!' in a tone of desperation. Most dropped to their knees or lay on the ground and some scratched themselves as though they no longer wanted skin, tore their hair out in handfuls or struck the trees and earth with their heads and limbs.

Some attacked their loved ones rather than themselves, one managing to scratchingly extract an eyeball and squash it in his fist with a slurpy pop. But we still managed our fun and games without their participation. Sometimes I wondered if a few of the Wild Times animals I'd seen were suffering from the same random affliction, but it was difficult to tell, obviously.

And talking of animals, as well as all the usual slithering and clawed and toothy threats that you'd expect, from what I deduced there was regular, evil, hairy, inter-species rape. This didn't sound nice to me at all with the limited knowledge I had of what it might mean. It had never happened to me as far as I knew, but I suspected that Menith had been a victim of this sort of thing once or twice. She had a particular disgust for saliva and went pale at certain smells which could have been signs. When I thought about this possibility, my fear-stricken mouth would hang open and allow my tongue to loll as my imagination went in search of some dripping re-enactment of these scenes, a search which left me exhausted and depleted. I was a very young girl and none too strong back then.

Uncle Heap talked of weird things, like the giant tentacles of sea monsters that rose over the deathly drop cliffs in search of tasty morsels of flesh, slammed over the tops and suckered onto anything they could find, tearing up rocks and trees and occasionally happening upon an unwary warm living body to squelchily draw down into their belly depths. He said these monsters had beaks. How could he know that? He certainly was a big mystery, Uncle Heap. But almost anything was believable.

And there was a lot of general stuff that went on too, stuff that characterised our lives in the Wild Times, war for instance (or that's what's Uncle Heap called it, that or 'revolution'). There were muddy, bloody troops that tramped by with weapons far in excess of our own.

They were armoured and spiked to a degree as sophisticated as many of the insects, but they were not nearly so joyous or efficient about their journey. I didn't know who these soldiers were, where they came from or whom they served, but I was reliably informed that they were patrolling for pockets of disagreeable people. When I had my smiling problems I feared that I might be suspected of being one of the pocket people, appearing, as such, to be an obvious non-resident of these parts. What the troops' tactics were I never knew, but I do know that I smelled a big cooked meat smell and saw smoke for two days when they came by last, so I suppose they found someone or other. Anyway, there were always lots of distant rumbles, smoke, that kind of thing, which I could loosely attribute to 'war'.

So many small things troubled us daily that it is difficult to catalogue them: sudden cold that could freeze parts of you off if you weren't prepared; sudden heat that could desiccate slender people like me easily too; there would be ear-splitting silence followed by ear-splitting noise of something metallic; everything could be endless and boundary-less, a monotone pain and a monotone landscape as clouds passed by, scary clouds importing who knows what; the lightning you know about, a lot of that; throbbing, often throbbing, a booming beat of impending devastation, a mounting horror which was just there, and you knew that there was a gut-thirsty murderer around, a big one the size of the hills, transparent, but still hiding himself in the briny fog and licking his fingers in a self-satisfied way.

And rumours abounded in response to all this. The kinds of wealth and ease and serenity that people must enjoy in the world beyond our Wild Times were always the subjects of these whispered hopes at the Wild Times Fair. And the hope rumour was, of course, that wealth and ease and serenity could somehow connect, marry, mingle with or at very least touch our lives in these Wild environs. Jewels of red and green and gold, and metallic gold itself, could all be found somewhere on a lonesome beach being driven out of the muddy corners between the rocks and washed clean and shining just to be picked up by anyone who happened by. That happening person would be happy forever in a palace in a safe place far from here, naturally. But unfortunately the lonesome beaches were lonesome because of their deathly drops and their hungry tidal monsters and their exposure to all kinds of not nice things. This sort of talk was just the sort of thing that kept people going from year to year between the Wild Times Fair gatherings. They would hatch vague plans and share improbable desires with virtual strangers and live for a year at a time knowing that someone else was working on their escape too. Unlikely. I believed that Uncle Heap had taken the practical approach to escape when planning for my safety, shunning jewels of any hue or the silly idea of running away to any Wild Times-less place where we did not know how to live, instead embracing the Wild Times right at its heart, fighting fearfulness with fearfulness: Granite. That was my hope at least, and I hoped it was not silly or embarrassing.

All in all, it was a tiring and bothersome life, one way or another, and even though I knew no different, I imagined how frightening and blank and amazing and confusing times might be without the Wildness. Would I have anything to do? What would there be to think about? If everything was nice, would I still appreciate memories of Curlywurly? And bigger, scarier questions like: Who would I be? Would my family talk to each other? This latter question was so in-the-stars impossible that I knew, once and for all, that I would always belong to the Wild Times and that they were as permanent as the impossible stars. I accepted it and set to wondering how things came about, which unfortunately remains a question I have not fully answered. Certainly mother was never in a position to explain something like that in a parental way and, as ever, I had most of my glimmer of information from Uncle Heap. He never said anything directly either, but I gathered from his whispered ramblings on dark nights that whatever kind of Wild Times we each suffered, it all stemmed from something that had gone wrong a long time ago, generations ago, in a vague and distant era, and no-one specific was to blame exactly. It was difficult to imagine that my people had lived in an easy, not frightening way before that, but I could imagine the part of the story when the bubble of Wild Times swallowed them and then started to swell and fatten over their once happy heads, held aloft by their own sadness. The way Uncle Heap told it, I could not help but feel a niggling sense of having been cheated, as though everyone had somehow been complicit in letting it get really bad rather than just being positive and dealing with it firmly, shooing the nastiness away and letting life be nice, which might have been possible early on. Pity.

Chapter Ten: Dribbling with Great Uncle Lollo

So, life is very inventive. I learned, over much time, that all the inventions that had already gone on were not the whole story: new stuff was always coming up. I can only talk for myself and Uncle Heap, but we lived a nail-biting life of watching and wondering what new marvel of horribleness would next stir us out of the tedium of all the things we already knew about. Our watchfulness and anticipation had been so much greater since the arrival of my Granite of course: now we were also awaiting the next Granite move, the next Granite phase, the manifestation of the architect's next Granite thought. Basically, we were waiting for the builders.

I hadn't talked to Great Uncle Lollo for some time, so I decided one morning during the heightened watchfulness period to saunter his way casually and ask him if he had heard the explosions the previous night. I knew he wouldn't have because he didn't like the night and always kept himself shut away in brain and body.

'Hello Great Uncle Lollo, did you hear the explosions last night?' I whispered brightly.

He was staring out to the west with is chin cupped in his hands, sitting on an upturned wooden box that used to be used for storing things that needed to be hidden (it had a big lock, now disused since there was nothing left to hide, obviously). Next to him on the ground sat his friend Toobit Lonkins in a defeated pose that he adjusted only rarely when his discomfort became unbearable. His crooked legs and grotty, twisted feet stuck straight out in front of him, pointing equally to the west. I doubted very much that his flea-bitten eyes were enjoying the same visual feast as Great Uncle Lollo's. Nevertheless, there they both were, staring west, where there was a strange wobbliness in the air that made the view look like it was under water. I briefly imagined that some new kind of air was mixing itself up with our usual stuff and that this was somehow fascinating the simple part of their minds, but the thought was not interesting enough for me to hold onto.

I sat down on the ground next to them and repeated, 'Hello Great Uncle Lollo, did you hear the explosions last night?'

I saw a small tear of liquid fall from the corner of his mouth. It caught momentarily on his bristly beardiness before it fell to his knee, but otherwise there was nothing that I might call a response.

'There were some big explosions Great Uncle Lollo, out in the east-ish. I was on watch and saw the sky glowing red over that way, with some flashes from time to time. I suppose it was between about ten of the clock and dawn, although I had a nap in the middle for a while you know, so I'm assuming. I wasn't worried, of course, but that sort of thing makes you wonder.' I don't wonder what those things are anymore, because I know, but at that moment I paused to let my curiosity run through me as if it was fresh. 'Does it make you wonder Great Uncle Lollo?'

I thought I heard a quiet 'hm' but wasn't sure. This wasn't like him at all, usually he was so attentive. I changed direction, hoping it was just the boringness of the explosions that was keeping his attention put away.

'Of course my Granite house will be proof against all explosions,' I ventured, 'and anything else too,' I added with a sweeping gesture of my hand. 'Granite, Great Uncle Lollo, it's very tough indeed, and hard as well. If it hits anyone...' I stopped short, 'Oh no, you probably wouldn't want to remember that, but it is very hard and heavy and deathly you'll recall, and my house will be made of pure that, to keep me safe, and it's going to be high and thick and safe and safe and safe and...'

'Nya,' said Great Uncle Lollo rather more flatly than was his custom, and a full blown dribble trickled from the corner of his mouth as he rearranged his hands.

I still felt that his concentration was elsewhere, somewhere in the wobbliness of mixing, unknown gases, but I knew I was onto something talking about my Granite house.

'I've told you the stories about when Uncle Heap and I went out to the building place and all the things we saw. Remember?' No response. 'Remember the tree, and the other tree, and the flat place, all ready and waiting to be built on, and the roaring sea keeping me even safer to the west. At least I think it will keep me safer, and...' I couldn't think of anything else that I had told him, although there must have been much more. 'Remember us sending Toobit Lonkins to the architect and back, time and time again, to get the plans sorted out?' Still no response, except I did notice Toobit raise an eyelid. 'Well, it's all going to happen soon I know, we're just waiting for the builders to turn up now that we have the stone.' Nothing, nothing, nothing. 'Stone, Great Uncle Lollo, Granite, you know, amazing, terrifying.'

'Nya,' he repeated, still flatly, without enthusiasm, but with an air of definiteness and positivity.

I was just beginning to feel that the day was wrong, when he rose slowly from the wooden box for hiding things when there used to be things to hide. He stood up, straight-backed and strong in the thigh, never taking his eyes from the wobbly west.

'Nya,' he said again, quite loudly, just once, and lifted both his arms in the air to begin his conducting.

I was definitely being a bit excluded now as he started, waving his arms, up, up, one then the other. This sense of exclusion was not altogether unheard of around Great Uncle Lollo when he got to his conducting. However, the strange thing was that somehow his rhythm just galloped away this time. He became more urgent right away, then quickly the tempo became verging on frantic as he threw his hands alternately out towards the western horizon and the distorting view that seemed to fascinate him. Even Toobit Lonkins became a bit agitated. Each punching stroke was accompanied by a soft 'nya!' which became progressively louder, and louder and ear-splittingly loud as the tempo increased until I abruptly exhausted my sense of safety, and the world seemed full of nya's, and I was suddenly sure that the Wild Times would be stirred to murder us all. My heart started to leap about and my legs made the decision before my head as I jumped up to try to quieten him. This meant touching him, which was something we usually did not do (apart from my hidden hand-holding with Uncle Heap), but this was beginning to be an emergency. I orientated myself facing in the same direction as him and in front of him so that I could try to jump up to catch his arms but, as I faced west with his arms flailing above me and his nya's bouncing into my ears, I heard myself take that sharp, cold intake of breath through my mouth that means shock. I left my body momentarily, and consequently my body stopped, as if it had been turned into an inert lump, with eyes. My breathing ceased, and the only way into my being was through those eyes, as they were the only bits accepting anything. And it was through those eyes that I saw them. There they were, a suggestion of reality, clear enough to recognise despite the wobbling air syndrome, the two big, silent builders that I had asked for, picking their way over my magnificent Granite heap.

I think Great Uncle Lollo's conducting stopped as soon as he heard my breath go into me so cold and sharp.

There was a big silence that dropped in like a heap of stone must drop in and everything apart from the wind and Great Uncle Lollo's gummy jaws went still.

Sometime later I became aware of a dribble curling thickly out of the corner of my hanging mouth and I came round from my stupor, finding both of my arms (that had been raised to quiet Great Uncle Lollo) still outstretched towards the two big, silent builders. So deep was my awestruck state that, even when I recovered my arms and used one to wipe away the dribble, I did not entirely come back to normality. The appearance of the figures in the distance was momentous and signalled a way toward a less puny future. Maybe it was because I was with Great Uncle Lollo, or maybe something odd happened inside me, but I didn't run off to tell Uncle Heap about their arrival, I just stayed right where I was for a brave and strange moment, staring and staring at those two men, and in those moments I think I claimed them as my own.

Chapter Eleven: Finding Out Things and Wondering Some More

A door in time clanged shut, and another one clanged open. I could never turn back to the life that had got me this far since those two builders had turned up. Now I was obliged to be thrust into an enclosure of life where I would find salvation or ruin, because there would be nothing in between. Did the builders have any idea what kind of heralds they were? Could they hear my quavering heart as I watched them? Did they know they had come for me?

As I looked, one of the first things that I noticed was that, of the two, the biggest one was pretty big. I watched him first because his bigness was so fascinating that it drew my eyes and locked them onto his bulk. I guessed that he must be about six of me, (although much later I revised that to a larger statistic). He was so wide that it appeared to be only a short distance that he needed to stoop to pick up the rock, but I knew it was not. I could see his massive hands wrapping around the pieces he handled and I shivered at the strength in them alone. He had a ruddy, round face and, over the space between us, I saw him wearing a pained expression. His movements were stiffened by the encumbrance of his great muscles as he climbed right onto the peak of the Granite and picked out the smaller rocks, sorting them one by one to a lesser pile that was being created nearby. At first I would not believe my ears, but I thought I might have heard him grunt somewhat as he picked up a rock. Then I definitely heard him grunt, and loudly, when he threw another onto the lesser pile. Then, even more shockingly than this, I soon saw him stop right on the top of the pile, take a huge breath (I estimated his tidal volume to be at least eight thousand millilitres, so this breath could have been even more), raise his head to the sky, beat his chest, then lift his clenched fists upwards. He flexed his muscles, filled out his massive chest once more and made a small roar. This, at first, made me creep behind Great Uncle Lollo just in case, but in time I came to know that it was just his way, and that nothing was out of control at all. His roaring growl would have inspired any growler, and certainly inspired me (after I had got over the creeping feeling, mostly).

As you can imagine, it was a long time before I gathered enough concentration to draw my regard away from this mighty fellow and peer at the other. He was a different sort altogether: lean and, not puny like me, but certainly what many people would call small. He worked hard, that was for sure, but he chose to work from the edge of the great Granite heap rather than to climb it. I could barely see his face because he was stooped all the time, but his very posture told me that the expression on his face was as pained as his colleague's. I did not feel his pain as an angry pain though, more of a dejected and broken down kind of pain, like a man whose pride had withered over generations until he became a rock carrying slave. Unlike his mate, this one moved constantly and fluidly, but always with this air of resignation in his stance. He never looked up, or at anything else apart from the rock in his hands. When the big fellow looked at him and grunted I saw him flinch, shrink and scurry faster to the next rock, cowering more than before.

'Nya, nya,' said Great Uncle Lollo, and sat back down on the wooden box that used to be for hiding things when there were things to hide, Toobit Lonkins slumping in relief next to him in the dirt.

'Yes Great Uncle Lollo, you're not wrong, nya, nya, two of them,' I said back in breathy, rushing words of excitement and nervousness.

'Nya, nya,' he repeated with a self-assured happiness.

And that is how it turned out: my two big, silent builders were not! Well, they were. I had one of each I suppose, but there had definitely been some straying from the order that I had placed with Nitzo Pits-oh the architect. One was huge and noisy in the extreme, the other small and fawningly quiet. I considered that I could probably be content with that, but also wondered if I was shortening my hopes too soon and should try to stop this ugly habit. I still do not know which is best, even today.

Over the next many, many weeks Uncle Heap and I paid very close attention to the goings on with the Granite. Nothing much really changed, not even the wobbly air. The big one and the quiet one were simply always there, clear as clear, two builders, but somehow cloaked in a wobbly dream quality that always left a tiny bit of doubt. I even tried squeezing my vision through the light of the murky hours before dawn and after dusk, but I could never find a moment when they were not there. I noted that one or the other might disappear from view from time to time for a few minutes, presumably to fulfil some animal function that we don't need to think about, or perhaps just to go into a deeper wobbliness of air, but there was always the reassuring presence of at least one worker, humphing a way closer to my lovely house.

Sitting on my watch block one night in a lightning storm, the flashes revealed momentary scenes which both answered and created questions. What I saw in a couple of big light-ups was a momentarily frozen big builder there on top of the Granite still with his fists outstretched to the sky, and a quiet builder mid-scurry at the bottom of the pile, cowering from life as well as danger, just like he did in the daytime. How curious. I thought the only reason to remain awake was to be watchful of the Wild Times attacking, but these two did not seem to be bothered by any of the kinds of things that ruled our lives. Where had they come from, and did they have nowhere to go back to? Was the fearsome Granite really protecting them from lurking evils and, if it was, what was it that kept them warm, especially at night? On some of the most doubtful nights when gruesome happenings were creeping about close by and I could smell things much worse than animal functions, I went so far as to consider if perhaps they were not human, despite appearances.

Uncle Heap was in a rather nervous and subdued state about the whole thing, which inevitably expressed itself in his great agitation and sense of urgency about everything else. It was hard for either of us to maintain our concentration for our own safety when there coexisted the constant fascinating show of the continuing rock-sorting on my far away building site, and this nearly led us into big trouble a couple of times. The agonisingly inching pace of change at the rock pile was a terrible strain to bear, but neither of us could tear ourselves away.

One day, returning from a minor skirmish with a small, clawed creature that normally hunts in a pack, I found Uncle Heap staring, slack-jawed through the haze-wobble, at my builders again.

'What's happening Uncle Heap?' I mumbled.

'What's that stuff?' he mumbled back.

'What's what stuff Uncle Heap?' I only cast a cursory glance to the west.

'What's that stuff?' he repeated.

'What stuff do you mean Uncle Heap, the Granite stuff?'

He didn't mean the 'Granite stuff', I knew that, I was just trying to catch him out of his trance with an exciting word, and 'Granite' is a very arresting as words go, anyone would agree.

'What's that stuff on their clothes?' he elaborated, still transfixed.

I hadn't really looked properly at their trousers and shirts before, but now I came to a more concentrated inspection of my builders, yes, there was a lot of stuff all down the fronts of their trousers and their shirts, dark and smeary.

'What, that dark stuff you mean Uncle Heap?' I ventured.

'What other stuff?' he retorted, irritated, still not lifting his eyes from them to me.

Uncle Heap was, I think, genuinely puzzled, but I had an idea of what it was on their trousers and shirts right away, a speculation that I was able to prove to be correct much later in time.

'I don't know Uncle Heap. You're right though, it's very dark stuff, that's for sure,' I said confidently.

'Well...' Uncle Heap concluded, sighed and sat down looking very old and done in.

Several days later I caught him in exactly the same staring, slack-jawed pose as I swung by on my way back from exchanging a few nya nya'a next door. I noted right away that he was unaware of my arrival and that he seemed as fascinated by the air wobbling like water as Great Uncle Lollo had been on that first day. Wearily (and I don't deny a possible sigh), I made a full turn around search of our environs to verify the probability of our continued existence. All was fine, so I took little time in deciding that it was best to follow his gaze and have a good look westwards before getting involved in any discussion of what's and what else's. There they were again, Big and Silent, covered in a dark smeariness of I-guessed-what. This time the dark smeariness was on their faces as well. Big looked more pained than ever, and when Silent turned away from me with his loping arms hanging limp by his sides I saw the dark smears also blodgeoning on the palms of his hands. No wonder Uncle Heap was curious.

Chapter Twelve: Building Begins

Me, I began to feel rather worried. I felt like a microscopic, blob-like and ineffectual being. I couldn't tell this to Uncle Heap because he just would not understand my sadness on this occasion, and the new building happenings had robbed me of his attentions anyway, which made me feel even more shapeless. I knew that my big thoughts and inflated plans and rocketing hopes and exploding desires had started all this off and now I was not in control. Perhaps I had never been in control. Maybe I had been stupid to venture into something without thinking to notice that I was just much, much too puny to take it on. I felt frightened and things started to slip from their usual state of hyper-reality into another space that I did not recognise at all. And there they were, always, Big and Silent, smeared in their own, dark I-guessed-what, angry or dejected. What dark and smeary stuff had I unearthed with all this digging towards my future? The sane and happy nugget of me that had been packed away safely for so long, away from all the silliness of my world, twitched. It wriggled and squirmed and let me know that it was not comfortable, that a kind of danger we had not seen before was close at hand. I wasn't sure if the meaning of this danger was good, bad, or maybe good-bad, or bad that would lead to good, or good that was about to turn bad, or what. I went to talk again with Great Uncle Lollo.

'Great Uncle Lollo?' I whispered into his afternoon ear. 'How are you?'

'Nya! Nya!' he replied, grinning loosely.

'Oh good.' I did say this, but I didn't feel that it was

good at all because really I wanted to talk to him about my woes and someone who is happy is not easy to talk to about woes. 'I'm very glad about that,' I lied, passionlessly, 'but have you been watching the builders?'

He didn't seem to notice the 'but' I had put in to hint that all might not be well and he enthusiastically replied, 'Nya! Nya!'

'Yes, they're great, Great Uncle Lollo, I know, but I'm worried about the stone and the blood and the sorting and the slowness and the speed and the aggressive anger in Big's gestures and the sadness of ages in Silent's stance and wondering if it is all heading where my teetering fantasies knew it would or is it going to some scary place that is the scariest of all that my fantasies never suspected existed.'

'Mm,' he said after a bit. There was another epic pause and then he continued, 'Mmmmm... err, mm,' looking thoughtfully at his hands before putting his chin in them and going quiet.

'So, what do you think? Should I be worried Great Uncle Lollo?'

I bit my lip and felt rather weak during the next silence that then followed, but I had not fully expired when my dear Great Uncle Lollo finally made his urgent reply.

'Nyaah- aha!' he declared, and sprung up on his old, but still springy legs.

There was a flurry of faltering flight from a nearby patch of dusty looking scrub as a few small birds took to the wing. Great Uncle Lollo's hands followed them, making smooth movements, then tiny, shivering shakes in the air to describe their little beating hearts. His hands drew the thin flock out to the west towards my builders where they departed, upward, over the wobble. At this, his gesture drew a great pause. His fingertips were lightly poised together in a static breath of time. The builders both stopped the rocky things they were up to, and even Silent, my not quite puny embodiment of sadness, turned towards us and looked with his face upturned in our direction. For just a moment I saw his crumbled visage and pitted eyes, before Great Uncle Lollo set them both in motion again with this, his second attempt at the building symphony. I really did admire his conducting, moreso now than ever before perhaps, and some kind of warmth spread through me as I saw the joyful way that he directed them. He was joyful at least. Great Uncle Lollo had taken directorial control, and I felt like Granite had taken to the wing, just like the birds had. He could be enigmatic at times, I admit, but his sense of things was positive, and I was very grateful for his involvement which I had not suspected might come about.

Thus the pained expressions of the Granite humphing duo were eased in my mind. The worries that had been weighing on me were less burdensome, and I was able to watch the rock-sorting finish itself and the actual building begin, sometimes with a sense of calm set into the general slush of fear that was plunging and swashing in my chest. I got used to my new fears and new calm, as one does, and was able to keep a solid Wild Times watch either with Uncle Heap or alone, and still have a whisker of attention touching the building works.

'Look Uncle Heap, they're building a very thick wall,' I whispered excitedly one bright sunny day with a black cloud coming over.

'Well...' he returned. Of course he had seen the thickness of the wall already. Of course! 'Well...' he drawled again ('it must happen,' I imagined his voice in my liquid head).

We didn't talk much, we just watched when we could, and that took up all our attention. We watched the hulk of my big man, to and fro in serial grandiose displays of strength. We watched the scoop of my quiet man's back on its ever dipping journey. We watched the Granite change at an inching pace from a huge mountainous heap, to several, size-related lesser heaps, to the very beginnings of a unified wall of meeting stones. We watched the whole scene stunned by a brightness of sun, and the same place transformed to a cold monotone darkness when skies were heavy. We were bereaved each time the building work disappeared at nightly intervals or behind a heavy cascade of something from the sky. We wore ourselves out thinking about it.

Thoughts I had:

1) How do they ignore the Wild Times like that?

2) Or do the Wild Times ignore them, and if so, why?

3) Will they run out of blood?

4) The other side of the building work that I cannot see may look better, or worse.

5) This side looks not quite as I'd imagined, pretty rough really.

6) Maybe rough is the big answer to everything?

7) I'm feeling something. It may be pride, or it may be fear or it may be anger.

8) Everything is finite, surely.

9) I believe I can see this project through, if nothing else major happens.

10) I will feel differently or work something out later with more information.

And the last proved true.

Chapter Thirteen: Bog Inheritance

As far as I have been able to tell from my own limited experience, people can always become used to things, almost anything in fact: changes in the weather; changes in the availability of things that are needed; changes in the composition of the people around as some die and others are born. Even the change of day to night is something quite extraordinary to bear if you think about it. My life during the Wild Times was a subtle blend of utter monotony and alarmingly sharp jump-ups of things that I needed to instantly invent hitherto unheard of ways to deal with. That on-going situation is, essentially, what I was used to. Having said this, fundamental changes were taking place as building work began though: the heavens realigned their stars so that now the great club constellation rode toward the western sky; green got greyer and black got glossier; jungles grew for the first time in my armpits; everything became finite, especially monotony; my western horizon started to have the beginning of a Granite building on it... and so on. I just couldn't depend on anything, especially not on the monotony side of things. But the biggest readjustment, the mountain-sized need for acceptance, the wall to jump over that drove way up, high into the sky, it was all to do with that twitching nugget of mine that I have already hinted at. That nugget of a sane and perhaps even cheerful me that had been stashed and cached away so long ago, before the Wild Times took hold of me, was bothering me and pricking me from the inside and upsetting my normal blend of what appeared to be balance. The transformation that it was asking of me was still vague, but I could tell from the outset that it wasn't the kind of adjustment or acceptance that simply means sighing and stuffing your hands in your pockets, that this transformation would drown me if I didn't grow big enough to encompass it and somehow keep it afloat. I became a slave to it as it threatened to unhinge me daily. Its uncomfortable twitching was irritating, to say the least. Now that the world was looking as though it may have a rosier future, supposedly, in a safe safe house, it made this wilful assertion of its right to demonstrate itself, and the ensuing struggle seemed like it might last well into my future, paining me forever. And all this suffering for a nugget of me that I had never met! I considered that perhaps this nugget of me was a boring or bad person, that she might be selfish and require things that I thought of as over-opulent and vulgar or, worst of all, that she would squash and smother the me that I knew, the me that had kept me going for so long (she did, after all, seem rather potently persuasive). This thinking simply made it harder to come to terms with the whole situation though, so instead I tried to keep falling back on the sure and golden knowledge that Uncle Heap had seen and recognised and nourished my nugget, so it must be a good thing. He knew, because he saw everything and was always right, and thinking of his take on things kept me in a good place with myself even when I would otherwise have felt shaky and in a state of aloneness. (Of course, I had to ignore my continuing doubts about his endorsement of smiling, but nothing is perfect.)

One day when I was just thinking, 'I wonder if my nugget has jungles in her armpits?' another thought jumped out of the grey-green sky and landed in the front of my brain. It was red and alarming, but rather full of life and attractive at the same time, like flesh. The red thought went something like this: 'If Uncle Heap has recognised my nugget for so long, he must have nugget knowledge, which means he too must have a nugget. I have never seen Uncle Heap's nugget, but it must exist. If Uncle Heap has a nugget, where could it possibly be and, moreover, why has it not shown itself? Am I nugget blind?'

The redness was shimmering as I then considered that if Uncle Heap had not been able to bring his own nugget out of hiding and let it free then there was no reason to believe that he could help me to do that for myself. My wobbling mortal world teetered on the brink of an abyss as I considered that I might have been wrong about Uncle Heap, he might be false, a forged Uncle, he might be faulted, he might be lying, and I would be left with all my silly hopes destroyed and smeared on everyone's faces, hands, trousers and shirts.

The bleak rhythm of mother's curse started to boom-boom, boom-boom in my head: You're Doomed! You're doomed!... Could I be doomed? Bigger, stronger and much less pathetic people than me had been felled by fell felons of the Wild Times, people with hair much less wispy than mine and limbs much thicker and thoughts as sure as Granite is Granite and just as tough. I quivered, shivered, got goosebumpy all over and felt a strong surge of longing to be not alone pass through me like a thick, wet wave. The red and shimmering thought of doubt hovered close in front of my face all the while, fleshy, alive, dead and taunting. I bit my lip and tears welled up, but soon Uncle Heap was there holding my hand, just as I liked him to.

He held my hand for a long time while I sobbed and he knew nothing of what it was all about (unless of course he did know everything after all?). I couldn't even help him keep watch much because all the water around my eyeballs was distorting my vision, but I did my best to keep the slurpiness of the crying as quiet as possible.

Eventually I blew my nose in my hand and flicked the slop onto the ground before wiping myself on my tunic. I could breathe and talk again at last, but I was sure that the redness of my thoughts was now blossoming around my swollen eyes.

'Uncle Heap...' I whispered tentatively.

'Yes?'

'Uncle Heap... I just wondered... you remember we talked about my nugget, safely packed away for better times?' I continued, sniffing.

'Well...' He was up to his old vagaries already.

'Well...' I didn't quite know how to say it.

'Yes?' He narrowed his eyes, with an air of confidentiality this time.

'Well... I have to know something,' I ventured.

'Well...' he repeated, doing little to urge me on.

'Uncle Heap, I have to know where your nugget is, that's the truth. You must have one and I'm worried about it.'

My whisper spilled out of me in one big relief, but as I said it I knew at least some of the answer to my worries already. He was looking at me with a coolness in his expression, very calm, very hard, very solid, very loving: there in his gaze was a glint of a hint of his nugget, maybe.

'Well...' he started up, slowly pulling himself out of a verbal slump and looking away to the still wobbling and possibly semi-aquatic western horizon, 'before you were born all the land here was bog. It was smelly, with oily pools. In the pools were dark shapes of things that used to be alive. They were covered in the soft sludge of the bog.'

'Surely your nugget didn't get lost in there Uncle Heap?' I interrupted, confused and somewhat horrified.

'No. But there were the lost voices.'

He made a dramatic pause to allow me to shape the

sounds in my mind as the lost voices lisped like the wispy haze that hung over the oily pools and curled around the clumpy plants that slid brownly into the gloomy water that sat stiller than stagnancy itself.

He trailed off. 'I didn't like the bog.'

'I wouldn't imagine anyone did Uncle Heap.'

'No. Not unless they had a turn of mind.' He stopped again, I think to let me consider this idea of someone having a turn of mind, before beginning his revelation. 'My brother Hanult was...'

'Yes, yes, you've told me about him Uncle Heap!' Was I beginning to understand something?

'No. You know Hub, the one with the tree thing,' he whisperingly affirmed.

'Ah yes, I just didn't know his name, or the other name, or any name really,' I retreated before he got upset.

'No. We don't talk about Hanult. He had a turn of mind.'

'Oh,' I whispered, trying to sound understanding, intelligent, sympathetic, embracing, curious, serious and a tiny bit servile.

'He started seeing a girl. His loins grew. His mind turned.'

'What happened when his head got turned then Uncle Heap?' I had heard so many tragic stories in my short life, surely this could be nothing new.

'Staring. Mumbling.' (Yes, I had heard this sort of thing dozens of times.) 'Not coherent.' (Of course not) 'Talking to the bog. About his inheritance.' (Really? Like treasure or something?) 'He wanted it.'

'But what was his inheritance Uncle Heap?'

'Well...' (Go on...) 'We'd lost a few to the oily-voiced pools already. (Same old, same old. No treasure.) 'His loins shrank and he smelt badly bog-like.' (Maybe he was rotting by then?) 'Got away one day. Joined his inheritance. That was that.' (That was what?) Uncle Heap looked satisfied and dreamy and, above all, had an air of having finished his story. I let him sit for quite a while just in case there was something else he had to say which would enlighten me before I whispered, 'And your nugget Uncle Heap?'

'Well...' he started up again, 'Family voices, whoever they were. We don't mention them.'

'Yes Uncle Heap, I know who you mean. Well, not that I know who exactly, but you know what I mean.'

A forbidden story started to rattle in my head which I knew I knew, but didn't know how I knew. Lianan (whoever) disappeared with a particularly sharp implement, heading bog-ward and leaving a trail of his own severed fingers and other bits, the bloody dribble leading to an oily pool which looked somewhat murkier than the rest on the day they went to look for him. Aha, so this must have been the bog of old. His end was assumed I suppose. What could have called him there? Those voices must have been particularly persuasive (to a turned mind, that is).

'But what about your nugget Uncle Heap?' I was nearly dead by now.

He looked at me curiously, as though I had my nose on upside down, and he whispered slowly and deliberately, 'Well, my nugget saved me.' He paused the long pause again, read my lack of comprehension, sighed and continued. 'The voices. My inheritance.' He trailed off again, still looking out to the wonderful west. 'Well...'

'Of course Uncle Heap,' I whispered back, not feeling very of-course-y at all.

Maybe those charming voices were enough to make a relation believe that their destiny was just as redemptive, just as tragic, just as beautiful as theirs, and that he was just as frail as all those who had already disappeared into their inheritance. Maybe that was what the turning was, and Uncle Heap wouldn't. He had had some tricky happenings in his time I know, and I can forgive him most things, so the fact that he left his nugget slippery and vague, and me still without hope of grasping it, was something I could accept. His wonky stories and his big hand on mine left me only marginally less wobbly, and I felt a torturous squirm inside me still wiggling tightly and frantically about. For his part, Uncle Heap was being particularly distant. He just kept looking out, far far away, with his hand wrapped around mine as though it was separate from his body today.

'It's not hopeless,' he reassured the breeze.

'No it's not, I know that too,' I reassured the breeze as well.

We both knew what all this was leading up to: I was leaving. I could see it looming over him when I dared to look his way, and he could probably see it over me too, which was what kept his eyes somewhere else. It was a bewitching and heavy shadow to bear but we shared the burden, separately, because it belonged to us both. Our bond was fracturing and sticking at the same time, meaning that some hugeness of destruction, restructuring or effacement was likely to come, along with its rumbling promise of change, creation and the dusting off of long forgotten relics. My smallness hardened in readiness, and the new impartiality of my stoutening heart allowed me to see in Uncle Heap things I hadn't noticed before. For one thing his feet were becoming too heavy for him to bear, such that he seemed to have trouble lifting them at all. He was less and less able to raise them from the ground and his walk became shuffly and rapid to compensate. For another, his squinting had begun to afflict him. His vision seemed to reveal to him everything it used to, but he now had to squeeze the information out in a particularly concentrated way which accentuated the criss-crossed furrows of age across his cheeks and forehead. And for a third thing, his shoulders had sunk in at the front of his chest so that his power seemed in defiance of normal forces, his arm muscles flapped loose in their skin when not in use and his ear lobes hung thick and low in a way that they formerly had not. All in all, his eternal body looked suddenly derelict.

As for his nugget, I wondered in the end if it was derelict too. Maybe it had crumbled and returned to the big mixture of the world long before I was aware of anything, and Uncle Heap himself was outlasting it. Such was my discomfort at its mystery that I fantasised about taking it away in my tunic pocket, hard and golden, and my future unfolding in a perfect, golden way with it in my possession. These dreams usually ended with images of my nugget-searching fingers delved into a boggy sludge and my heart sinking. I tried to avoid the dreaming.

Chapter Fourteen: Preparations, Goodbyes and a Nugget Gift

In my preparations for leaving I gathered everything I thought I would need for my new and independent life in my Granite house, bearing in mind that the building had barely begun. I packed a bag which I could sling over my back with two straps that I had sewed on for the purpose. In it I put my vast selection of seeds that I had been quietly stealing from plants for a long time. These were not all for food. I imagined that in my safe safe house I would have beauty as well as food to nourish me, and so I had shaken the seed pods of the blue flowers (with the radiating stripes if you looked closely), and the yellow flowers with lots of petals (whose leaves Curlywurly had favoured) into a little purse, ready for growing beautifulness in crevices or wherever I could find.

I also packed a pencil and some precious paper for writing on now that I had discovered that they could be uniquely useful in certain situations (which, as it shortly turned out, was very good thinking). Of course I picked out a bundle of particularly interesting pieces of paper with the writing in mind but, further, I went to great pains to raid and ransack our stolen-bits-of-books supply to select a much larger pile of surreptitious reading material so that I could continue my secret and important learning about the normal world. (The thought struck me that it might not have to be surreptitious any more, but that felt shakily unusual.)

Sadly, life had been too busy to mention to Uncle Heap about re-spiking my bluntened club, but I tied it on the side of my bag just as it was, in the hope that whoever had made it, made it good enough to last until my Granite walls did the job of protecting me. Its counterpart metal bucket (for racket-making and other things) was tied underneath so they would not clank together as I made my way on the great voyage.

I took my spare leggings and tunic; a bottle carefully filled with fresh water from our not poisonous well, and a bunch of portable leaves picked from near our watch blocks, both to sustain me lest I should feel hungry or thirsty during the journey or early in my arrival; a needle and some sewing thread to go with a length of fabric that I had 'obtained'; some round things that I was sure could find a purposeful existence in a new world (but never did. I liked them anyway); a brush small enough to brush my teeth in case the weather suggested it; a hank of string that I had spun from a particularly stringy plant and, of course, Uncle Heap's perfect and magically adjusted house building knife with all its mysterious appendages that had been promised to me so long ago and now magically and mysteriously appeared in my bag without being asked.

Despite my preparations having been meticulous, and certainly complete for some time, I still splashed in a swamp of hesitation for several days during which time Uncle Heap became increasingly grumpy and difficult to be around. He glowered in any direction but mine, let the cheek part of his beard grow all grey and stubbly and could be heard making mumbling grunts whenever he was moving around. Maybe he wasn't sure about giving me the knife after all? The stoutened part of me fully planned to deserve the building knife, but most of me held a shivering doubt in my ability to flick out the right appendage for the right job at the right moment and not appear foolish and pathetic. At night I took it out of my bag several times to feel the weight of the thing in my hand and imagine all the amazing things I would be doing with it under my control. It felt very heavy indeed, but I did not flinch even when it was right there and I was touching it. I imagined exquisitely carved panels throughout a massive residence; a large garden embroidered with stone statues who would host the new, colourful Wild Times Fair; walls thick enough to repel a storm of rocks and high enough to be unleapable by the highest leaping creatures; the sky clear and shining above and, of course, me surrounded by happy safety and filled with upright confidence that the world could draw upon without depleting me even slightly.

Each morning showed the slim reality of my paltry bag. The new day tried vainly to creep into the shadows of my wizened family life and it depressingly re-illuminated the vast journey across the land that I had to make to get to my hardly-even-started Granite house. Basically, my grandiose self-concept got trodden into the dirt whenever the sun came up, and I was left unsure that I could even carry the weight of the knife far enough, never mind take it out of my bag and build a marvellous Granite house with it.

Lurching between these days and these nights finally catapulted me out of the hesitation swamp and I began my goodbyes. First was Great Uncle Lollo. I took my bag to show him all the things that I had considered, chosen and handled, as that was the sort of thing that interested him. The crying was my fault because I started it. I knew I wasn't crying because of him, just because of change and all those unknowable things to come that I would have to deal with alone. I don't know why he cried. Maybe it was a bit like wanting to vomit when you see someone vomit, a natural thing. The flesh of his face nearly fell off with his tears and his delicately suggestive hands remained glued heavily to his knees which made me feel like crying more. He could hardly look at the things I pulled out from my bag because he was so upset, but I believe he was just as interested as usual. I made a point of staying with a him a long time to get all the sadness out of us both, and the fear out of me, then I packed my bag again, stood up and waved with my hand.

'Goodbye Great Uncle Lollo,' I sniffed, 'I'll send some birds if I find any.'

Next was Menith. I had to wait to say goodbye to Menith because she had risen late from a particularly thick, lengthy sleep only to disappear behind our ablutions door, lock it and spend two hours making random crashing noises. I thought she might be killing small insects because they liked the constant wetness in there. She eventually emerged looking flushed and swooshed heavily past me, streaming her long, dark and now tamed and stick-free hair on her way to begin her nails. I rarely looked closely at her, but today I did, and I saw her lumpy body, solidly aware of its own gracelessness, and her tapered eyes, once those of a vital animal, sunk still deeper into the fat of her face and having a tired greyness about them that I put down to the endless concentration that so much nail-painting demanded. She landed in her corner and drew a soft cloth and her nail varnish remover from her capacious tunic pocket. Those tired eyes focussed inward, the harsh smell of the open bottle rose from her and she began her day.

I sat down close to her on the floor and whispered, 'I'm leaving today Menith.' My eyes were full of tears from the chemical vapours. 'I'm going to live in my new Granite house that isn't built yet.'

Her gaze flickered once across me and her hands shook slightly as she began wiping yesterday's pink off her left thumbnail. Easing the soggy cloth into the cuticle, she slowly transferred the colour from her thumb to the rag and the nail looked slowly natural, in a morning way. She worked, as usual, with that inconceivable patience she had, but I never knew if it was born of disenchantment, devotion, or merely a misplaced mind.

'I doubt I will be coming back Menith.' I tried to ease myself into her patient world.

She made no reply, but continued her shaking and her wiping for some time. I sat there hoping she would nod or something, then suddenly she dropped her cloth, drove her hand deep into her other pocket and pulled out a bottle of hideous purple nail varnish.

'Here,' she said, and banged it on the floor in front of me.

I was just about to give her my thanks for the exceptional gift when she came over all flustered, grabbed it back and rammed her hand back into her tunic pocket once more.

'No, here,' she corrected herself, slamming garish red nail varnish in front of me this time, then one more, exactly the same. 'Take it.'

I gave her a minute of wiping time to calm down and be certain that she wanted to divest herself of the elegant small bottles then whispered, 'Thanks Menith, I'll remember you and your nails, thanks very much.'

I left her and loyally put the garish red nail varnish in my ready-to-go bag, but to be honest, I had a sick feeling about it. Somehow that nail varnish seemed bent on existing just to remind me that there was something, or someone else I should have been that I wasn't. I hated it, but as an only reminder of my sister I took it anyway in case it became important. I had a momentary lapse into strangeness and my stomach rose to my throat as I considered, in horror, that my nugget might be a nail-painting heroine who appreciated garish red, but I hoped that she was not.

After this draining goodbye, I came to mother for

more draining. I considered the possibility of not saying goodbye to her because she was always so busy with her sitting, but I finally decided that was just an excuse and it was better to make a gesture. So, sitting next to her, closer than I had been for years, or possibly ever, I just sat. The knowledge of her former cleverness (that must still have been buried somewhere) made me think that she already knew what was going on. She let me observe her and didn't move a muscle. I saw her scars: tears and splits in her skin, sores that had never fully healed, thin patches worn away by the flaking of years with cracks full of warty infections, hairless parts in the midst of hairiness and thickened tissue that covered over-used spots. I imagined with some distaste the over-used spots on her seat that supported her weight these days. I looked further and saw her luminous bones shining with a cool sadness through her skin where they were close to the surface: her face, her hands, her shins, her shoulders. And then deeper, I saw her heart, turned dry and crumbling inside her chest. And through her eyes I saw into the space inside her skull, filled with compressed ash, tightly compacted and neat in layers.

I didn't say anything. I don't know if she heard me saying nothing, but I heard her sure enough. Silent words flowed out of her, dusted with that ash and smelling like I imagined the oily pools in my ancestral inheritance bog to smell. I had to leave her quite soon and find somewhere close by to breathe again.

Last of all, I needn't say, I found him on our watch blocks looking rough but keen on his watching. I sat down close to him and rested my little hand on his big veiny hand, just as I think he wanted me to. There was a lot of quietness between us.

'We-e-ell...' he whispered eventually, drawing out his vagueness more than ever.

'I know Uncle Heap. I'm going now.'

'We-ell...' I felt he had nothing else to say, and nor did I really.

The wobbling air out toward my building place was in full wobble and we could see the two builders' unrelenting movement through it. This should have been a comfort to me but, as we sat there one last time on our watch blocks together, hand on hand, my brain was spiralling into all manner of difficulties that might visit me in my new future, first and foremost amongst which was breathing. I kept looking at that wobbling haze and wondering what gaseous mixture might strangle me on my coming journey away from the past and into the future, and if it had been worthwhile packing my bag so carefully after all. I gave Uncle Heap's hand a squeeze so he would feel all right and we kept watch together for an hour or so like that before it was all over.

Without explanation Uncle Heap got up and left me. I was gagged by confusion, my little legs swinging nervously off my watch block and the bag filled with my future life on the ground at my feet. Was this it? Did I have to face it all alone now? Slowly mulling these questions over at a very fast speed of circle-thinking, I slipped my hand into my pocket to see if a crumbling or golden nugget had secretly appeared. It was empty. My silly heart plummeted, then soared a moment later as Uncle Heap reappeared. It was at this moment that I discovered where another small part of his nugget was really stored.

'Well...' he whispered, and held out to me the first of two large piles of the high quality cardboard that had been filched by my forbears to sustain them through the Wild Times in former years. 'I've been keeping it in the rafters. It's the right moment.'

I had never seen such marvellous stuff: shiny, thick, flat, almost unbendable in any direction and decorated by printed words and pictures. This would change my life, change my chances of survival, especially until my safe safe house might be ready enough to fully shelter me. I felt the alarming wash of yet another smile pressing itself through my face and was powerless to suppress it. I didn't even let that bother me too much, I felt so good. He went to fetch the second pile from the rafters, and my spirit soared in the knowledge that I would be taking this measure of endurance with me, this chip of his nugget, this tried and tested family reserve.

When he came back, I pulled out the string that I had spun from the particularly stringy plant and together we tied all the ancestral cardboard into one big bundle. There was no possibility that I could carry the lump of it, so I planned on it being a raft that I could carefully navigate through the territory as I pulled it behind me.

It was time. At the last, Uncle Heap pulled out his broad-brimmed, bone-beaded hat from his back pocket and pushed it onto my head. I peered cautiously through the hole in the brim that the poisonous gloop had left and saw his loving gaze on me. Maybe I would still be breathing when I got to my building place, after all.

He waved with all his ten fingers extended as I left. I could see him squinting severely and knew he was keeping a careful eye on me and my progress. I had a lot to think about, so I couldn't spend much time waving myself: there was breathing the wobbly air to come; there was steering my cardboard safely; there was placing my feet carefully and, of course, keeping a lookout for danger between the swinging beads of my hat. My bucket clanked a bit whatever I did to discourage it, but all in all things were going well and I was grateful that the day was dry so that I could safely slide my ancestral cardboard over the grasses without soggy harm. The wobbly air (or wobbly gas mixture of death, as it might be) seemed to be getting no closer, so instead I began thinking about snakes. Were there snakes in the grasses? I'd seen some fairly shocking snakes in my time and didn't want to meet one now, encumbered as I was. Then I thought of snails. I know it was dry, but I still thought of snails, and that was Uncle Heap's fault. He had been talking about his brothers and reminded me of the story of the brother who turned out to be called Hub, who had the tree thing happen to him. Basically he was out 'collecting' fruits from branches high, high up when he fell out of the tree due to an impossible lack of friction as a result of an unusual quantity of snail slime.

So, I tried to worry constructively, worry away from real worry, as I approached the air wobble. The funny thing was that, the closer I got to the (perhaps?) evil, clammy, throat-clenching, lung-melting haze of contaminants, the further away it got. I hardly noticed the pink tufty flowers on wiry stems that had impressed me so much before, I paid little heed to the scratching and clawing and milky-poisoning plants that had bothered me in former times and I barely nodded at the stunted tree with the lightning strike scar that marked my half way point as I sped past, devoted as I was to my cardboard's safe passage. The black, black burned earth was more difficult and, I admit, my cardboard suffered some marks from the contorted stems of charcoal which twisted out of the ravaged earth, but I forgave myself that.

At last I looked up through my bone beaded fringe. Suddenly I was there, breathing the air of my building place, not inwardly melted by any noxious wobbly mixture in the air and generally exhausted but well. The proximity of the deadly drop cliffs to the west immediately came back to me. The memory of them batted me in the stomach and my stomach responded by bouncing in my insides for a minute, but I stood tall(ish) under my hat and looked around, pretending I was brave. I almost felt brave, I was so good at the pretending. Then, weirdly, close by, next to and on top of my Granite heap I again spotted my two builders, each uniquely surrounded by wobbling air and plodding on through it with their Granite tasks, presumably breathing just as I was (except more, of course). So they were the source of the wobbles, or at least the wobbles were solely attracted to them. The whole notion that I had left home with a building knife and some cardboard to come and be here with these two people who walked around in wobbling air felt less than solid, but maybe it was real, maybe I really was breathing my own breaths, all by myself in my building place. I could not quite let go of the idea that I was somewhere else, somewhere pretend, somewhere in my head or somewhere in a different dream (or nightmare), but it was difficult to tell, being alone (possibly?).

Chapter Fifteen: Big and Silent

Calamity stopped in mid-fall as I looked around my building site; time stood still and the Wild Times waited for me for a change, rather than the other way around. I could hear the pulse of it all, paused nearby and watching me as I stood, shrinking inside my clothes. My cardboard bundle was huge next to me and hung idly from my hand as I wandered my gaze about the vicinity. My back assumed a slight backwards arch due to the weight of my bag hanging from it because I had made the straps a bit too long and my surreptitious reading material was, indeed, a big pile. The bone beads hanging around the rim of my hat were heavier and stiller than ever, while a breeze of hot breath seemed to descend through the hole in the brim. The exertion of the hurried voyage had made me sweat in the sunshine and my head was wet. I imagined one trickle of sweat running down my forehead or through my hair for each dangling bone bead because the symmetry appealed to me. In this posture I listened to that pulse watching me for what felt like a long time. I also listened to my breathing, which sounded a bit thickly wet at the back of my throat, and my main thought was that, surprisingly, everything seemed all right ('so far...' was my other thought).

The beginnings of the great walls for my safe safe house were thick and rough and low and so big that I now saw they would encompass and hide some of the Granite heap when they got taller. There were two and a half of them. I wasn't too close, but I accepted their qualities straight away, as questioning them didn't occur to me. I was still too small to object to anything. After spending time gulping in all this new information I then began weighing the prospect of activity and action against how long I could expect the Wild Times to wait for me before it got ready to pounce once more. I eventually sidled around the side of the knee-high wall, becoming bold enough to get close until I accidentally slipped into a dark hole which I observed ran right under the wall. I made an involuntary squeal as my ankle discovered a new flexibility it had not formerly used and I shot an embarrassed look in the direction of my builders, but fortunately they were not looking. Dusting myself off, I untwisted my ankle and composed my thoughts. 'Aha! Something for important draughts or other things to come and go through,' I considered, with enforced calmness, 'a ventilation hole, haha!' I carried on, less bold about my proximity to the wall, shortly coming upon the place where the gnarly fruit tree grew. Of course, this was the second tree of the day, the first being the lightning strike halfway tree. If it hadn't been for the Granite, these trees would surely be the parts of the landscape destined to endure through the most bleak times, beyond and above anything else. I noted how they both bore the marks of their trials already: weather-beaten and bent and scarred and wizened and fighting to retain the most modest of twigs and tiniest of waxy leaves at the ends of their twisted boughs. I blinked from them to the Granite and marvelled at the two strategies for survival: one to yield, take the blows, shape itself around the onslaught (and wear the evidence for ever more), fruit if possible and make frail beauty hung on depleted resources; and the other to resist, resist, resist, never give ground and remain unchanged, adamant in the superiority of its own stony elegance. Which one would I turn out to be?

My two builders, despite being there just for me, had not yet made any gesture of recognition at all concerning my arrival. I was understandably nervous about meeting such Granite heroes but realised that they were not going to help me make an introduction easy. So, gathering up my ancestral cardboard bundle, I shuffled close to the great Granite heap, goosebumping all the way as well as sweating, and angled myself behind my cardboard protection before I delicately cleared my mucky throat.

'Huh-herrmm,' softly escaped my mouth.

For a long, terrifying moment, nothing happened. From this distance, I could see wisps of the wobbling air silking away from both of the figures, floating across the Granite or upwards to dissolve in the sky and, if I squinted, I could make the wobbles go rainbow coloured. This was interesting, but not interesting enough to distract me when, more terrifying still, both builders stopped their Granite work in their wobbling worlds and turned to look at me. I tried to clear my phlegminess again but my mouth went dry and hung open so I waved with my hand instead, even though it was full of string for the cardboard leash.

'Uff!' said the big one in a grunting way, staring at me aggressively, while the quiet one simply raised his eyebrows.

'You seem to have a lot of blood on yourselves,' I whispered, stating the obvious.

I had not been wrong about what I saw from a distance: both builders had the unmistakable brown smears of blood all the way across their thighs, down the fronts of their shirts and across their faces. Now I saw the blood on their hands clearly too: fresh and red on the palms and the inside of their fingers, crumbly and darkly leaking through each finger gap and hanging around in each dead fingernail's crevices.

The silent one looked at his hands as I spoke, turning them over and over again, then wiped them once more across his chest, sniffing as he did so.

'You can't expect anything different in this bloody work,' roared the big one in response. 'We've certainly got plenty of it.'

I was so shocked by this fellow's volume that I covered my ears as best I could and my eyes involuntarily squeezed shut in pain, but I still managed to fawningly reply, 'Ah... I'm glad to hear that.'

My answer seemed to usher in a still longer silence, and I could see that the silent one was fidgeting and contemplating going back to his Granite tasks. He seemed genuinely as frightened as me to hear his compatriot speak and I had seen him flinch in a not dissimilar way to myself.

'So?' bellowed the big one.

'Well...' I said in my tiny voice, feeling tears pricking inside already, 'I've just come because...'

'Yes,' he shouted, 'you've come because?'

'I've come because I wanted to see the building. It's my house you see,' I squirmed.

'Speak up! You've come because what?' he shouted back again and I watched him lower his huge bulk down the Granite slope to bend his ear and hear me better.

'It's my house you're building,' I whispered simply, with a slight quaver in my voice due to the lump forming in my throat.

'Ah, right. Your house eh.' He considered this evenly. 'But why are you talking so quietly out of that bloody little body of yours?'

At last! A conversation!

'I don't want to upset or attract the Wild Times and get us in trouble, that's all,' I quietly explained from behind my hand.

'Wild. Times.' He contemplated it loudly, as two words to be considered separately, but seemed to reach no conclusion.

'You know, all the bad and deadly things that live in these days that might kill us or worse. I don't want to excite them into noticing us if I can help it,' I boldly elaborated, and I heard Uncle Heap from across the miles growl and make a rattle that preceded a large scrawtching sound, as if on cue to substantiate my words.

'Wild. Times.' He repeated it less loudly then cried out, 'Never heard of them,' and looked around, puzzled, this way and that from his Granite perch as though he might notice something new.

'Ah, well, I'm glad to hear that too,' I got the words past the growing lump in my throat, completely confused.

His appearance was even more impressive than I had imagined. His width was wider, his height higher, but it was his thickness that weighed so heavily on my impression. His every stiff and graceless movement was accompanied by an animalistic grunting and he exuded resentment and anger in his whole demeanour. The painful look that I had previously noticed seemed to have been savagely slashed in, scarred over with the skin which was his face, and his whole head seemed hard, as though it had been baked hard, with a glossy, earth-colour about it. As well as all this, I could now smell him, a warm and damp and old smell, a little rotten but somehow homely too.

He told me his name was Nursten and declared, 'I don't know anything about these bloody Wild Times you mention, but he might, Wort,' flinging one of his great boughs of arms towards the quiet one standing sheepishly at a little distance. 'Wort's his name. He knows about Wild Things. Do you see? In his eyes?' The huge man opened wide his own somewhat wild looking eyes as he asked me with a genuine question in his rumbling voice.

'Ah...' I had no smart answer to this and feared offending one or other of them. 'I'll have a look a bit closer Nursten. Thanks for the information. See you later perhaps,' I still whispered out of old habit.

'Grrrrm,' he grunted in a dissatisfied way and bowed over, setting himself back onto the Granite.

As I approached the quiet one known as Wort he looked panicky in his wobbly bit of world. He blushed, cast his supposedly wild eyes around, hung his arms by his sides helplessly and remained glued to the spot. He had a kind of beauty about him, a balance of features and form, a timidity that would win hearts, given a chance, but closer to I could see just how limply this beauty hung on him, how abraded his skin appeared, how his slimness had sunk around his skull and how he was left with a somewhat death-like appearance, the blood which adorned him not forgotten. Everything about him looked strained, bruised, bloodshot and, above all, powerless, despite his constant physical exertions.

I wasn't afraid of this quiet one, so I plonked my cardboard bundle close to him and sat down on it. Wort's inner panic increased immediately until he was shaking and he began to stutter, 'It, it-it-it, it used to be tuh-terrible,' he said blankly, waving one hand just enough to let fly a drop or two of blood from his fingertips. 'The anguish.'

'I'm so sorry to hear that,' I said, and I could see that he trusted me straight away.

'But no-one else knows how buh-buh-bad, and no-one wuh-wants to know, no-one believes it at-at all.' He threw all his words out in the kind of hurry that secrecy revealed in a pressed moment might provoke, then wiped his forehead with fresh redness. 'What shuh-shuh-shall I do? I am left alone with all the anguish.'

Now this really was perplexing. What should he do? And why should he do what he should do if he did it? I hadn't come prepared for such difficult questions so suddenly.

'I wish you wouldn't shiver like that,' I responded, for better or worse.

'Suh-sorry,' he muttered, hung his head melodramatically and began to cry (but he did stop shaking).

I wondered if he was just trying to make me feel bad, but it didn't bother me if he was. He was my builder and, as such, was supposed to be working for me and I wasn't about to get involved in any shivering discussions.

'Anguish can be terrible to bear alone,' I comforted, 'but maybe you could tell me what all the terribleness was about and then you'd feel better?'

His legs buckled at this and he collapsed onto the ground, snivelling and heaving a little. He dropped his head into his hands, filling his grubby hair with blood too and continuing to mutter, 'I'm suh-sorry. But it happened. Suh-suh-sorry. The anguish is like spuh-spinning knives inside-side me and this buh-buh-bleeding is end-end-endless.'

It was nice to talk to someone who knew how to whisper and fawn in front of time and space after conversing with the brute above on the heap, so I decided that this quiet one could talk to me after all.

'Buh-buh-buh-bigger pain went through me than you cuh-can imagine. It lasted for an eternity and I cuh-could not esca-escape. So weak. So suh-small. My whole wuh-world my torturer.'

He never looked at me, but kept looking up towards Nursten, presumably to be ready to flinch in time, but Nursten showed no interest in the snivelling and continued instead to steadily work and grunt as he went, which grunting gave Wort enough occasion to flinch somewhat anyway.

'Luckily you've got this nice building work to keep you happy,' I whisperingly suggested.

'Oh the buh-blood! The buh-buh-blood! I'm suh-

126

sorry.' He began to rock backwards and forwards in a way that reminded me of mother. I reflected that mother was, at least, clean in her self-pity.

'Well, maybe I could lend you my hat one day then,' I sighed, somewhat exasperated at the depth of his gloom already.

He didn't answer and I tried looking at him with my eyes squinty to bring on the rainbow colours in the wobbles and cheer myself up. This last worked, but I wished straight away that I hadn't offered the hat when Wort started to calm down. He stopped crying and began to stand up at which point I sinkingly felt the beginnings of the disappearance of my lovely hat gifted from Uncle Heap, of it being swallowed into the black hole of Wort's depression, my special bone-beaded head apparel absorbed into all that muddled darkness. I had only just arrived and already my few necessary belongings were about to be raided and depleted. I was wrong about him though. Somehow the idea of the hat had not inspired him to gobble up a generosity. My hat words were something else, like something that didn't fit him. At the sound of them his world stopped momentarily, long enough for him to reorient away from his plague of thoughts, to shake himself out of his painful rememberings and his pitiful fight against them. He simply got up and began working again, sorting the stone, bleeding on it as before. I could hear his breath from where I sat on my bundle as his mouth sagged open and salivated over the rock. For a man who used so much energy to punish himself with memories, he had remarkable stamina and agility with the work. I witnessed the same graceful persistence that I had guessed at from my old home and again was touched by his sad, sad beauty.

He didn't speak again that day.

Chapter Sixteen: The Red, Neo Cardboard Era

The familiar Granite fears were twitching me, despite the cheerful rainbowness of the air, and I moved off to find the best place to leave my bag and bundle and bucket out of danger from the tumble of stone. The Granite heap was extraordinarily Granitic, filled with sharp crystals and slimy crevices, but most of all it was big, and let on nothing about its intentions. The separateness of each stone made me feel queasy about the whole thing shifting and burying me along with my ancestral cardboard, but I laid my trust in my builders and their confidence in their own work as I skirted around it to find one of my walls again. My walls were sure. They were my safe safe house, so I came to them with a proprietary sense of security. Safe safety first. Or the suggestion of it to come at least (at last).

The walls were terrible, but they would work. 'They will work!' I kept saying to myself. I could see the buh-blood, the buh-buh-blood all over them. It wasn't exactly holding them together as far as I could tell, but maybe there was a magical property there that made the wall stronger or more effective against the Wild Times, an odour perhaps. That was a strange thing that I had never thought to think that I might have to consider. I found one of the two existing corners of my two and a half walls and decided that this was to be my bedroom for the time being and there put down my bag with its attached bucket and sufficiently spiked club, which liberated me enough to use both my hands to untie myself from the stringy leash of my cardboard bundle and plonk that down too. Home.

I was pretty exhausted by all the new stuff the day had brought and I sat down with a sigh onto my grass to try to bring it all into some focus under my hat while my body flopped. Unfortunately, the sun was making its way towards the deadly drop cliffs by now and I soon had the dull but practical thought that it would be wise to make camp before night fell. I begrudgingly began to empty the contents of my bag and, by trial and error, slowly found suitable homes for each small item in the bloody crevices of my wall. In the hour or so that I spent doing this, both Silent and Big came close by to lay stone on my wall. Neither acknowledged me at all, so I took great and repeated care over fitting each of my belongings into its given crevice then testing it again and again to be sure it would work in the longer term whilst I was eyeing them sideways and equally not acknowledging them either.

First it was Silent Wort with the tear-streaked face. He carried one bloody rock in each hand, seemingly stretching his thin arms which dripped red at the ends. He placed them in a dejected way on top of the wall, stepped backwards and forwards, away from and towards them repeatedly, sizing up how badly they fitted, waving his dripping arms. Without moving the stones at all, and as part of one complete arc of bodily movement, he began to apparently knead the rocks into some sort of tessellation with the existing stone, salivating on them from his hanging mouth as before. It was to no avail and they remained as ill-fitting as when he had laid them, but this did not bother him and, without ceasing in his fluid gestures of work, he left them there.

Shortly afterwards came Big Nursten. He, of course, carried much bigger but equally bloody rocks, one in each hand, one under each arm and smaller debris weighing down his smeary trousers, which had straps going over his shoulders, presumably for that purpose. He was grunting with each step and sweating wetly. The sweating was no surprise because it must take a lot just to carry around his body never mind the stone as well, but I was intrigued how it cut paths through the red blood on his face, just as the tears did on Wort's. He did not salivate on his rocks as did his fellow, he actively spat, very actively, as he threw them down. Each throw was carried out with splintering force and accompanied by a throaty sound of fury. After all the stones had been thus placed, he commenced the most bone-juddering part of his performance: climbing onto the wall, kicking the stones angrily once or twice then closing his fist and beating one large beat on his chest, (enough to crush my ribs I thought) and making a short roar to the sky before storming back to the heap in his heavy boots.

And so it went as I placed and replaced my seed packets, my clothes, my sewing things, my purposeless round things, my pencil and paper for writing, my reading-and-learning-interesting-things paper, my hank of string, my wonderful building knife, my spiked club and my bucket in my new home, just so, and began wondering how best to arrange my ancestral cardboard for sleeping. I tried not to look at the shocking stonework as I did this, despite being as curious about it as I was about my builders. It was disappointing and confusing but my stinging feelings for it did not matter because I appeared to be invisible anyway, so certainly my grief was beyond consideration, even to me.

When darkness fell I crawled under my cherished cardboard. I knew that dear Uncle Heap would be keeping an extra special watch while I was out alone like this on my first big living adventure. I knew this because Uncle Heap was good at that sort of thing. I was washed by the waves of gratitude that I had felt for him since he had given me my cardboard, and I wallowed in the ancient safety of my ancestors as I handled it. My thoughts rambled around possible scenarios for the 'acquisition' of this particular cardboard: what could the cardboard story here be? Given how thick, strong and shiny it was, the stealing of it must have been a good moment for whoever got it. It may have even travelled great distances to be with me there. It may have been involved in countless Wild Times stories just like mine. It may have saved lives, made lives, even destroyed some wild ones. This was good thinking. I welcomed my cardboard past in a way I had not formerly thought possible, relaxed and felt myself travelling back into the old days and ways, the ones that must have ensured my coming into being. And deep in those old days and ways I felt the safe safety of Uncle Heap's love for me and the crystal hardness of his nugget that must still have had many treasures I had never seen, some of which might also be stored in the rafters. Round and around, I relaxed, didn't relax, then relaxed again, falling into a cardboard sleep to dream, dream... about cardboard. In my dream I was flying on my cardboard through an inky night alight with flashes that I thought were beautiful but were probably dangerous. I didn't know where my body was, but all my sensations were on that flying cardboard. I started to panic about my body. Was it safe? Was I alive? Where was my cardboard taking me? And I awoke jumping between ancestral thoughts like: will I marry the wrong man who will strangely die? Will it be messy? Will I grow mad? Am I mad already? Will I be one of the remembered and talked about members of the family, or one of the forgotten whose demise blights any suggestion of hope?

By then I had simply tumbled long, long, into my whirling head which had been whipping into ever faster spinning by all the newnesses of the day. I found myself clutching what seemed in that moment to be my most precious possession: my nail varnish. It seemed valuable just by virtue of its fabulous colour which had penetrated my sense of obsession and taken hold of me to such an extent that I could even feel its power in the darkness. I held it to me as part of my own body and I wondered if there, against my chest and wrapped up in my little hands, was the answer to being a real female, perhaps a real person. Could I ever be a real female? A real person?

Would answering questions make me less or more confused?

In the morning I still clutched my nail varnish and I was exhausted. Each of those first nights was just the same. I lay there under my cardboard with my reasonably spiked club nearby and with fearful Granite surrounding me, quite out of my depth and trying to get bigger to fill my own life but never really believing in anything but my own puniness in the big world. There was an emptiness that lay beside me like a silent cadaver and I became desperately afraid of it and its lurking. There was space enough for it, and I was in shivers about the possibility of warming it up lest it should live, or rot, or smother me, or all three. I lay quite, quite still, feeling the intensity of aloneness and even missing Menith slightly.

The first days during the light hours were not much easier either. The Wild Times were quiet as I remember, but my brain was in shatters, so a lot could have passed me by without biting, I don't know. The building work continued and I became depressedly resigned and sadly adjusted to its badness. I bolstered my heart up with thoughts of its useful safety and tried to ignore the complete deviance from the wondrous, shining dream that I had so long nurtured secretly with my beloved Uncle Heap. And in my acceptance I felt myself become passive. Was this what I was, passive? I became a furtive encourager, and ornament to the work as I shadowed Nursten and Wort in their daily duties, and I began to believe that this safe safe house, whatever it turned out to be, would happen for me, to me, around me, and would change me without my doing anything or being able to do anything apart from decorate the place by my simple presence. It had a sickening feeling of endlessness. So much for being a resisting rock or being a yielding tree or being a real female or being a real person.

Needless to say, during all this time I heard Uncle Heap busy at work, watching for and deflecting the deadly Wild Times. The many signs of his diligent labours came to me at all hours and brought on a variety of random feelings. For instance, sometimes I felt comforted that he was there looking out for me, sometimes I felt scared that there was stuff around wanting to eat me, sometimes I felt sad not to be out there on the watch blocks doing something useful with him, and other times I felt bored of having nothing to do.

The building knife saved me from all that random variety, that and my stomach, which was beginning to shrink and gurgle. I knew I had to plant some food seeds, and this urgent necessity to act to preserve my life sprung up in the light of my virtual invisibility most of the time with Big and Silent, making it no easier. This sudden knowledge of hunger was what snapped me out of my helplessness: I began my pots.

It caused me no blood, but some sweating I admit, to roll some of the medium sized stones to my corner where I was able to flick out the right knife appendage and carve a beautiful pot for growing things in. Each pot was nicely rounded, rather thin walled, and had a single drainage hole in the bottom. I worked on the first six or so over three days and, strangely, I noticed that my builders were becoming increasingly intrigued by my activity as the days passed. From the corner of my eye I saw Wort actually stop in his fluid path through life. He stopped, shuffled shiftily closer and leaned over to see better what I was up to and how I was up to it. I let him be there for a while then turned to say hello, thinking I may be ceasing to be invisible, but he jumped and scampered off when he realised he had been spotted, even before I had opened my mouth. Nursten on the other hand, came boldly and hung over me (much too damply, smellily close) breathing heavily, 'Grrr... hisss... grrr... hisss... grrr...' for ages, then made me jump by stamping his big-booted feet, kicking the wall and storming off again in his usual rage.

The pots were a great success and very soon I was plucking the odd leaf for lunch, although the little blue or yellow flowers that came from my flower seeds peeked only very shyly from between the hearty eating leaves, showing little enthusiasm for life. Nursten and Wort did not seem to need to eat, and when I noted Wort furtively watching me chewing I could not tell if his curiosity arose from his own hunger or a lack of comprehension as to what hunger might mean. I arranged the pots around the building work and they became my first project. I planned for their future removal to higher parts of the construction as it progressed and placed them to receive optimum light and shelter. With the pots' swelling numbers and the increasing harvest of greenness, so my confidence swelled and my invisible body got coloured in little by little. Maybe this was me: not a rock or a tree or a female or a person, but a planter, a pot-maker, a grower (of leaves, at least).

As my solidness grew, I felt much more like talking to my builders again. I suppose I was getting over the trauma of my arrival and beginning to find my way. Each morning when I woke up I would find them already working and dripping on the rock.

'Good morning Nursten!' I would whisper.

'Why are you talking so quietly still?' he would bellow in response and I would try not to fidget.

'The clouds are coming,' I would whisper a bit louder.

'He needs a wash,' Nursten would grumpily respond, nodding toward the innocent Wort.

'They might be the wrong kind of rain for washing though,' I might suggest.

'Grrr!' Nursten would growl and thus end our greeting, leaving me to pad around to see what Wort was up to.

'Good morning Wort!' I would whisper.

'It's buh-been bad in the past, very buh-bad,' he would counter, mumbling.

'Watch out for the clouds, they might be the wrong sort for washing,' I would suggest.

'Oh, tha-thanks. I don't want any buh-badness again.' And Wort would make his way back into the stone.

And weather did come, black clouds the like of which might drop thick burning ash or gloopy burning acid depending upon your luck. Although they never dropped anything in the end, they spent a long time coming and we had two days of darkness so thick that it hardly allowed me to make out the shape of my Granite heap or my walls. I groped around as best I could and thus learned a bit more about how things were in my home from a different perspective. I could still make out Nursten by the sound of his grunts as he continued to work, and I could just about still make out Wort by his sniffing and shuffling. Thus I was still able to offer, 'Good morning Nursten!' and 'Good morning Wort!' despite the inconvenience. I believe they appreciated my effort and it caused me to wonder if I might be a 'hello-er' as well as a planter and a grower and a pot-maker. On one occasion a smile nearly happened again, when I felt particularly appreciated, as Wort uttered, 'Ah! A-a voice in my duh-darkness!' Somehow I did not resist the idea of it spreading across my face in the same way as I had before. It didn't quite occur in the end, but it came close enough to let me notice that my brain was changing and maybe one day there could be smiles and smiles without reserve or guilt in my world. Shockingly, could I also be a smiler? That thought ended there, it was much too disturbing, as yet.

Despite no longer being Uncle Heap's little girl, or the object of mother's silence, or the one who took an interest in Great Uncle Lollo's conducting, or the recipient of nail varnish bestowals, or the Wild Times growler, or the witness of spider killings, I was feeling like me, finding out whoever that was, and altogether I was managing quite well in life when another good thing happened: I found a new pet snail. She was larger than her predecessor and livelier, with a healthy appetite for the same leaves of the same flowers that I had witnessed my previous companion enjoying. Although I never felt the need to give her a name, the good thing was that I no longer had to hide her, and I no longer needed to feel bad about having feelings for her because there was no-one to tell and nothing to be afraid in front of if I happened to care for her. She wasn't shy and lived in her own special crevice in my corner and would even sometimes roam on my ancestral cardboard. Uncle Heap would not have approved at all, but I was filled with new happiness to have her there. One day I found three precious red berries growing on a low bush nearby. I knew right away what their purpose was. I crushed them carefully and painted my dear snail with their dark juice and she became red, vivid and even more mine than before. Red had become the signature colour of everything important. As she joined the suite of redness in fine style it made me realise that I had been putting off a profound trial for some good while: painting my nails with the garish red nail varnish gifted from Menith as a parting offering. So, with new energy to face the unknown given to me by my new snail friendship, I started boldly out upon the red task. I understood straight away that all the hours Menith put into practising the art of varnishing her nails really did make a difference, because my attempt was blobby and globby and all over my cuticles, with a few dobs on the floor too, and the brush went splayed and gritty and everything was wrong. My brain got painful as I let the varnish dry on my nails because I couldn't move or touch things and it took so long, so so long. The endurance of those forced tense hours made me feel that maybe whatever Menith's obsessive madness was, it was becoming less remote to me in those moments.

At last it was done. I accepted its imperfections (as I had recently learned to accept imperfections) and I span in a red heaven with my snail, sure of myself for an hour or so before it all started to get chipped and I quickly needed to admit that this was not the kind of girl I was.

These were my days, leaping between different experiments, some overt, some subtle, but none overlooked by anyone or anything Wild or family-like, secret from my former life and shrouded in the hard shadow of my Granite. The rock itself still made me nervy and I still feared it deep inside but, on the other hand, I had begun to live with the fear more comfortably and realise that my cardboard was always there to come between us if needs be. Living next to the stone, touching it sometimes, watching it and thinking about it at such close quarters had made me stand up to the idea of it, meet it on some level. I had gone up a notch in bravery and sneakily I knew it. On the third day after painting my snail and myself, my clandestine bravery rose up and I made the most courageous act of my life thus far: I scraped all my red nail varnish off on the frightening

Granite, scoring my nails and cutting my cuticles, bringing on a slight red leakage of sorts. I threw one of my jars of nail varnish as far as I could towards the deadly drop cliffs in a huge gesture of rejection and reclaimed my redness as my own blood.

Chapter Seventeen: Snoring Discovered

'A luh-leaf,' said Wort quietly in my ear under the cardboard, 'for you to puh-put in our mouth this-this morning.'

My insides nearly jumped to the outside. It was the first time either of them had talked to me without my inviting a conversation, not to mention that I was still asleep when he said it. He withdrew his bloody, tear-streaked face from my cardboard peephole and replaced it with his red hand holding a single, dark green leaf tenderly between its fingers. He laid it down right there, inside my cardboard bed. I heard him sniff and move off, so I'm not sure if he caught it or not when I said, 'Urr...' as I prepared my voice for daytime action and thanks and such things as might prove useful.

The leaf, and the gesture of the leaf, caused me much thought. I wiped Wort's blood off it then chewed it contemplatively, hoping insight would leach from it into my system, but nothing meaningful happened. One of the unanswered thoughts was about the wobbling air around my builders: had it touched me when he came so close? I still had not determined what it was or what was its goodness or badness rating so, as my next project, I gathered my bucket and spiked club and set out without delay to find out what was the nature of the wobble.

'Good morning Wort!' I said brightly, if quietly, when I got close enough to my wobbling first builder.

I had found him methodically moving some small chips of Granite from this pile to that pile for a reason I could not discern. He had planted his feet far apart, swayed slowly as he threw each chip individually, and I imagined one stone thrown for every two of his heartbeats. He was sweating very well, and I could see freshly wet tear tracks down his sunken cheeks whose cause he seemed to be muttering about.

'Suh-sorry... buh-badness around... suh-so weak in this lonely-lonely world of... and it doesn't buh-buh-buh-bear thinking... pain... puh-pain... the nightmare of eter-eternity...' And so on.

The pressure must have increased behind his eyes from the talking because they started to leak again, causing me to draw the conclusion that it was time for me to confidently approach him about the subtle subject of the wobbles. But, when I was just about to say, 'My club is mostly blunt, really,' something happened that was not normally allowed to happen to Wild Times residents, something that made me think my blossoming confidence was misplaced: I tripped. My bucket clanked under me and removed some part of the skin on my shin as I passed swiftly over it and my club dangled from its leather strap on one of my outstretched arms that raced towards Wort with me behind them. I had just enough time to see his dinner plate eyes (with my dinner plate eyes) before my hands briefly met a strange but familiar slipperiness across his body, like spilled guts, I felt a soft phut! sound in my ears and then landed on Wort's chest. This was another gaspable shock moment and I ceased to breathe as I drew away from him, because my gasp had been enough to sustain me for a while. Untangling myself to retreat, heart beating, I let out a small involuntary growl and noticed that Wort's wobble had disappeared. Strange, had I popped its slipperiness?

For his part, Wort quickly resumed his Granite chip chucking as if nothing had occurred. My dinner plate eyes retracted into my screwed up face as the rainbow wobbles danced and slithered here and there on the Granite and the ground before me. I looked at my hands in wonder (they had touched someone else, after all). The texture of the wobble had been delicious on them and I stared and stared at the hands that had felt it: smooth and warm, and with the kind of knotty windings that I knew from so many guttings I had participated in when we'd killed things or things had died of their own accord. My hands quivered slightly, from the excitement I suppose, and I noticed a strange drip of colour fall from one. Shaking them, I found that I could toss out splashes of coloured wobble from my fingertips. Strange, but I was fine.

Back in my ridiculous confidence, I walked over to visit Nursten, flicking my rainbow flicks with some pride. I sensed a new something in me, something sharp and thin, like a good blade.

'Good morning Nursten!' I whispered when I came near.

He had no wobble on him either, but looked particularly bright and shiny at the top of the Granite pile as he paused, towering over me to bellow, 'You're still whispering! Fool!'

He grunted and waited for the reply which I did not know, so instead I said, 'Nursten, the wobble's gone funny today, and yours has disappeared.'

'Little fool!' he bellowed again, still waiting for what I didn't have.

I did feel little about then, I admit, so I growled fiercely back at him, baring my teeth in a way that would have made Uncle Heap proud, tossed a bit of wobble at him from my fingers then rattled my club in my bucket. His reaction was to put his two dirty fists on his hips, swell up his chest, roll back his head and laugh a huge fake laugh, as though to fill a vacuum.

'Sweet little girl!' he roared eventually, which sounded no nicer, nor more plausible than little fool to me. 'Ha!' he coughed out his parody and calmed himself.

141

'So what do you think of your little house, sweet little girl?' He bent over, leering out of that ruddy face of his. 'It could have been a bit better with the help of the planning man, but we're doing our best for our sweet little girl, me and Wort.'

'Which planning man?' I asked indignantly, my voice coming out sounding like the squeaking infant of a small furry animal without decent teeth.

'Why, Sir Ar!-chi!-tect! Sir Snore himself,' he contorted his face most unpleasantly.

'What, you mean Nitzo- Pits-oh didn't help? Not even after all those letters that Toobit Lonkins delivered to him that I took so long over?' I squeaked, even higher because of my astonishment.

Nursten seemed to enter a bubble of anger at this, which I can reasonably describe as 'combustible'. Through the roars and growls and screams and shouts that accompanied his long, loud story I gathered from the few comprehensible words that, after many begging croaks from Toobit Lonkins, Nursten himself had gone to the architect's office only to find Mr Ervil Nitzo snoring at his desk, a weedy character with limp hair, half spectacles and an ink-stained nose. Despite Nursten's grand blustering (and I'm sure it was grand), Nitzo-Pits-oh had demanded his right to sleep, on the grounds that his chief boss bigger architect man had told him he could because there was nothing important to do, and he simply waved my huge builder away with an arrogant gesture of his hand, repeated for emphasis.

I stood my ground while Nursten's anger blew past me taking the light hairs on my face with it. I marvelled at how such a weedy pen-pusher could resist the persuasions of such a blusterer, I was awed by Nursten's gentleness of spirit not to have flattened the man's inky nose on the spot, and then, finally, I understood the implications of what was being said.

There was a stampede in my awareness and I became rigid and shatterable on the outside and all hollow and swashy on the inside at the same time: my ragged house building that had gone on so far was undirected, unplanned, unfinished, unconsidered and perhaps even wrong, maybe it would not even stand up, and a lack of building skills may not have even been part of the problem at all. This explained everything: the shortening of my dreams and the shoddiness of my walls. It sounded like I only had my builders at all thanks to dear Toobit's scabby persuasions. I was so upset that I could no longer even hear Nursten's anti-architect tirade and my digestion went back on me, my thought-provoking morning leaf visiting my mouth again in a less than pleasant green flavour.

It was then that the screaming-from-who-knows-where started, but I don't recall exactly what happened after that. I just remember walking, and the sun coming out with a terrible viciousness that wrinkled everything and caused the air to creak like the old roof panel on a long-abandoned shed that flaps lightly in any pioneering breeze. My brain creaked, the lone fruit tree creaked and the earth made ready to split, creaking as it did so, all amidst the din of the awful screaming which, as usual, came from everywhere and no-where. My anger was blistering but passive: talking and listening had exhausted me and I barely had any energy for it. My rigid exterior collapsed and was shipwrecked on my inner swash, while my breakfast kept revisiting me in a way that I did not want to get used to. Wort's continuing words, 'Infinite puh-pain... alone...' reached my ears as I swung close by his sniffing. 'He was snoring!' I managed to point out to him, which only inspired him to continue in the same vein as before. I felt as though in the middle of a white-hot desert atop a tower from which I was about to be thrown into a bottomless, burning pit, that no end could ever be mine, that suffering and falling towards death was all I would do as I spiralled in the infinite twists of the uselessness of me and the lack of prospect in my life.

The next day it got worse. Still consumed by my tower nightmare, I also noticed that Nursten and Wort had been working faster than my brain had processed my observations of them and the first ring of wall, the ground floor as it were, was just about to be holed in, blocked up, sealed and closed forever. A panic rose above my tower and through it I smelled the comforting closeness of Uncle Heap, and all the familiarity of my old home that was just about to be cut off from my new, unfinished world. The wall's gap narrowed and my mouth got stuck so that I couldn't speak. For the first time since I had come to my building place with my ancestral cardboard I looked back towards the east, towards Uncle Heap and our watch blocks, towards our raggy flagpole topped with its plastic bottle glory, towards Great Uncle Lollo's bird symphony and Menith's nail painting and mother's inertia, back towards my memories of spiders I had loved and Wild Times I had clubbed to death and nights when I had slept peacefully. A rush of feeling spoke inside my chest about loss and about separation. Then the clang of permanence rose up my throat, rocket-like and accelerating.

'UNCLE. HEAP!!!' I cried out, screeching, shouting, screaming, screaming, loud loud loud, louder than ever, louder than the white wall of screaming all around me, parched tears rushing down my cheeks. 'UNCLE. HEAP!! UNCLE. HEAP!! UNCLE. HEAP!!'

It came firing out of me and three faces turned to me in response: the blank stare of Great Uncle Lollo as he paused in his conducting, which shortly fashioned itself into the conducting of my jagged voice; the curious but nonchalant up-turned visage of Menith, whose attention I only briefly held before she got back to her life's work; and of course Uncle Heap, who simply stood there and listened.

'UNCLE. HEAP. HE. WAS. SNORING! NITZO. PITS-OH! SNORING. THEY. SAID!' I squeaked frantically. 'NO. PLANS. UNCLE. HEAP! MY. HOOOUUUUUSE!!!' I screech-sobbed.

As I was letting all this anger and astonishment out of me that I hadn't known about before, Nursten and Wort were busy around me, piling up the bloody rocks on top of the thick Granite wall. I stood on my toes and turned my ear into the remaining gap to try to catch Uncle Heap's words.

'NO. TURNING. BACK,' he shouted in a deep voice that I did not recognise. 'MAKE. THE. BEST. OF. IT. NO. OTHER. CHOICE.'

Who would have guessed that Uncle Heap could shout? I knew I would never hear that deep voice again as Nursten placed one big stone just so and blocked my view forever. I waved my hand above the rocky mess and hoped Uncle Heap saw me. I knew I would hold true to him in whatever way I could.

The time that followed on from this was a flop, although thankfully the screaming-from everywhere-and-nowhere stopped after a few days. I did try to keep my feelings a bit stiffer and less floppy by tinkering with my blunt club or stroking my snail, but all the quiet spaces of me opened up again, left empty after my last words with Uncle Heap, and they just sucked up my happiness and left me limp. I flicked wobbles idly from my hands from time to time, screwing up my eyes and following the drifting colours. I looked around me now and then. As a function of my inner dullness, everything looked brighter, but I noted this without caring at all. In this lolling state of despondency that I had slithered into, I no longer cared about myself or my safe safe house or the Wild Times. I listened to and tried not to listen to Uncle Heap's perpetual scuffles with badness. I got so dehydrated from crying that I began to cry dry tears, which hurt and, at this, I knew that I had been wrong about smiling being part of my future, it could never be so. At first my angry voice subsided and went squeaky again, then it went quieter than ever, then my words became a mouthed silence, then I gave up speaking altogether. I clung to my ancestral cardboard for days and days, staring into space, mindless of peril as the sky strode past and so did the weeks and minutes and nights and jagged corners of time.

My dear builders, Nursten and Wort, turned out to be golden fellows, and little by little I came to know that I was still cared for and therefore worth caring for. They were kind enough to move my dozens of plant pots (that I had carved with my precious building knife) up onto the new higher level of the walls so that they would continue to catch the sunlight when it came. Wort faithfully plucked and delivered blood-stained leaves several times a day along with gentle encouragement to eat them.

'Another luh-leaf!' he would say quietly near me. 'It will make the puh-pain lesser.'

And so they did slowly tempt the pain in me to lesser and lesser itself and the need for him to place them in my mouth became the need for him to place them in my hand became the need to let me take them from him.

Perhaps I should not have done, but I asked after my shy flowers and all Wort said was, 'Puh-puh-pathetic,' and 'suh-sorry.' But I put that harsh thought aside as best I could and let his kindness come around me instead.

Even noisy Nursten spoke in a gentle bellow to me when he came to enquire, 'How's our sweet little girl today then?'

And eventually their bobbing in front of my face and waving their hands there to try to bring me back did work and my gaze was drawn outside of me once more. I saw before me two bloody, damaged, unfortunate men with the kindest hearts, all the kinder for whatever they suffered, who gave what they could with little etiquette but much grace.

The leaves they supplied gave me back the will to think new thoughts. Perhaps, if I never made it back from despondency, my builders could share my safe safe house as their home, and be happier and happier there (one thought). Maybe, now that my walls had got so high, Uncle Heap would not notice if I never reappeared (another thought). My body might or might not work well if I stood up (a third thought). I could tell that it was sunshiny at the tops of my walls and considered that it must be lovely up there (the best thought).

I took up another leaf and chewed on all that.

Chapter Eighteen: What I Did with my Pencil

The power given to me by the leaves and the attentions of my builders at last sated my battered heart and spilled over into nourishing my ancient genes which had lain ravenous as I languished. I got up, gently put aside my beautiful cardboard, clenched my fists a few times and gave a small growl. I was ready to see this pooping architect from a different standpoint.

I was semi-aware of Nursten and Wort watching me as I ferreted around in my rocky crevices and pulled out my precious paper and pencil, but I got right to work without saying hello.

Mr Nitzo,

I know you are employed by someone who you think is God, but he is not. I know you are trying to sabotage my safe safe house but it is unsabotageable. I know you think you can sleep and snore and be a bore and be mean and still be the boss and the best in this situation but you cannot and you are not because things happen while bores sleep.

Yours,
Me by the Deadly Drop Cliffs

PS You didn't reckon on the cardboard, did you?

It was a bit of bravado really, because I could see more clearly and rationally than ever what the state of my walls really was, but I just didn't care, it felt great to write it. Above all, I knew that my house would work now just because it should and must, despite the sleepiness and dullness of the architect and however many twists and turns there had to be in the story of making it.

As I neatly folded the paper and scribed Pits-oh's name on the outside I looked up from the shadowy pit inside my walls and found my builders still looking at me. It was then that I realised that I had no way to send the letter, as Toobit Lonkins was all the way over in the other world, living cagelessly with Great Uncle Lollo. Wort saw the blood and force drain from my inspiration and the word 'Toobit' written in my eyes and made an immediate and surprising response: he curled his two middle fingers in and stuck the other two one at each side of the inside of his mouth, raised his eyebrows and blew a gigantic whistle.

'Wow,' I said, astonished, 'where did you get that from Wort?' My voice worked once more all of a sudden.

Wort looked proud and I could see him blush, even beneath the blood stains and, just as we were living through this awkward moment, Toobit Lonkins flapped in and landed atop my Granite heap next to Nursten, followed by a waft of his bad smell. I saw Nursten give a large wink in the direction of our newly arrived friend, and then try to cover it with a small cough, then Wort bared his teeth slightly in Toobit's direction and moved his hand in a suggestion of a furtive wave.

'Toobit!' I cried out, almost forgetting myself and feeling happy for an instant.

My old pal the retired postmaster rolled his globby eyes this way and that, showing off the new extent of his cataract, and croaked a hello. He looked much as ever apart from his wig was skew-whiff, his feathers a bit raggier and his dumpy feet sported claws that were somewhat more randomly curving than before, and possibly a little more painful to look at. He already wore the little chest pouch for letters and there was nothing else to do but to give him my bitter and damning message to forward to the Snorer. Because Nursten had learned to be kind and soft recently, he came down and took the paper from me. It looked a tiny scrap in his mighty hands and his fat fingers fiddled with the buckles on the chest pouch for a few minutes before all was settled, he picked up Toobit, stroked him briefly, and launched him off the very top highermost bit of the highness of my walls.

'Thank you Toobit! Don't delay!' I shouted after him as he dipped then regained himself and started to make for the east. 'That's Toobit Lonkins, the postmaster,' I said proudly to Nursten and Wort. They were obviously (covertly) well acquainted with him already, but I had to say it to feel that lovely pride. 'Can you teach me that gigantic whistle Wort?' I finished, hopeful and expectant and excited again about my future.

And he did teach me. It was the most odd sound to hear coming from this scraggy little man, and probably sounded not much different coming from me once I learned it. I suppose the sound did not carry so far from my dark little pit corner in my safe safe house, but Wort reassured me, 'They're luh-listening! You call-called them!' as he peered out over the wall and whispered back down to me the state of things at my old home.

Blowing my gigantic whistle helped me one way or the other over the next short while, but mostly it just made me feel good, and I made frequent growls to keep my spirits up too. Nursten loved it when I growled. He would swell himself up and bellow back in the mightiest, bone shaking way, often beating his chest with his fists as well which never failed to make me feel a little undecided about his intentions.

In between times I came to a more level way of looking at the characteristics of my safe safe house.

There were my walls: crude, rough, bloody things which would remain standing, by an act of will alone if nothing else. The building itself was a clod of a thing whichever side you saw it from, therefore bearing no relationship to its surroundings which bore all kinds of delicate flowers, charred remains, the swooping cliffs, an inland foreverness, the many paths of the beasts and the arcing journeys of the stars. What my house lacked I could not say. How would I know? But I was sure as sure that things must be missing and I hoped against hope that these were things I could get along without. The extent of the shoddiness stretched my mind, but did not change itself however much I thought about it. No reply came from Ervil Nitzo, so I wrote this second, more considered and less emotional letter to him:

Mr Ervil Nitzo

Keep your inky nose out of my house plans. We don't need you and never will. There are me and Nursten and Wort and Toobit Lonkins, some pots and a tree and my Granite and my building knife and willpower and that is enough. Go back to your snoring and remember in your dreams that small people can make big things happen, especially because they are small. It is always amazing what years of being ignored can do to a person's determination. To ignore is to invite ignorance and to be determined is to be alive.

Yours in determination
The Small Girl With the Knife

It made me feel much better to write to Nitzo Pits-oh, so I did it as often as I wanted. It was, after all, a good excuse to use my whistle, hail Toobit Lonkins and say hello and farewell to him. My letters started to become much of a muchness though, like this one:

Nitzo

I still have no response from you. All I can say is that you have no being. You are not being at all, and you must be radiant with a deep kind of blandness that only snoring can fully express.

Building continues.

Yours
The Smallest Participant

Despite getting many things off my chest, I wondered if I was misdirecting my anger and blame as I again began to have spiralling thoughts about mother that I could not eject from my turning brain, and less and less in the way of disgust focussed on this architect type. I began cowering next to my corpse-like loneliness under my ancestral cardboard at night once more, missing Uncle Heap and being oftentimes visited by dreams. In one dream the nail varnish that I had thrown over the cliff was screeching at me, 'You touch something and it wastes in your hands! You're fated to fail! You're destined to be demeaned!' in a small but commanding red voice. But mostly I had the doom-doom dream, where mother's curse went, 'Thump-thump, thumper-thumper'. I would wake up in a tumult of rejection of the doom, energised, loud and sweating. In these moments I wanted to break my house across mother's face and be done with all the badness that her inertia had blocked into me. I wanted to destroy and never care if anything could be rebuilt, just to destroy. Instead I sweated and screamed back inside, and sometimes screamed back outside, then slowly came back to myself to touch my safe safe walls and welcome the blood of my builders.

They were confusing moments, so I wrote to Ervil Nitzo again to make me feel better.

Dear Mr Nitzo

Stuff the nail varnish.

Yours
Me With Naked Fingernails

Chapter Nineteen: A New View

As I cowered below in the stuffiness and rummaged in my cardboard corner, I did my best to focus on thoughts of my ever-tightening safety but, I admit, in my increasingly murky world I was hard pressed to push away certain other thoughts about the highering walls and how dark it would shortly be. My faithful team would surely be putting in a floor for the next level above my head soon, a ceiling, which would block out everything, and this did not make me feel very homely at all. It became so humidly hot down there for a short time that I extricated my brush for brushing my teeth from its crevice, lest the weather should bring on any rot in my mouth. I didn't know if it would ever turn cooler again (although later it did). In general, I was worried.

Sure enough, the walls grew extremely tall. Occasionally I felt brave enough to practice my two fingered whistle, and sometimes I felt sure enough of myself that I could plant both feet far apart on the floor, brace myself thus and muster enough courage to look up at the frightening perspective of the walls which had become so enormous so quickly. My eyes moved over it quickly as well, and the perspective itself was quick in an arrowing awayness of up towards the sky.

Nursten and Wort inhabited a lovely world on top, I could tell. They would wave and sometimes chat. I could hear that Nursten continued his relieving bellows and I frequently saw some part or other of Wort, an arm perhaps, swaying out over the edge thus letting me know that he was still working in his silent rhythm. There was a dry, hot light up there, it was outside, and I saw the breeze lifting their hair and rippling their clothes from time to time. The sky rushed about them and the air they inhabited looked so fresh that, in my imagination, I likened the experience of it to a really good wash or the discovery of a new and interesting thought that would make your brain shine with surreptitious curiosity.

'A luh-leaf from the top for you to-to eat,' dear Wort would whisperingly declare several times a day after scrambling down sweatily to me in my dark oven with the blusterous coolness of his rushing still running off him, his loyalty to my diet undimmed.

'It must be bright up there to make leaves Wort,' I might put forward timidly.

'Oh yuh-yuh-yes, luh-lots of light at the tuh-tuh-top,' he would confirm.

'I suppose plants need air to grow too,' I might suggest. 'Is there lots of air?'

'Oh yuh-yes, luh-lots of air at-at the tuh-top,' he would equally confirm.

Some days when he came to see me he would arrive without any tears staining his bloody face. At first I noticed this with concern and regarded it as a suspect change but, at the same time that I began to become accustomed to the uncomfortable thought of this changeableness, I also began to notice that his face would definitely brighten and his wiry body lighten in its swing as he approached me with his nourishing gift. He worked no less and was no less quiet than before but seemed to be what you might call 'happier', so I revised my doubts as I crouched thoughtfully by my cardboard.

'Ha! Ha! Ha!' Nursten would pace his big breaths between each sound so as to have maximum puff to punch out the syllables. He knew he had my attention and beat his inflated chest once or twice, roaring out his usual belligerence before leaning over the edge of the wall and shouting down, 'Funny little girl!' through his cupped hands. 'It's great up here!'

He shouted it with the same crushing delivery as his bellows, and this both frightened and excited me. I had little to say in response, so I would shout back in my squeaky voice, 'A new view Nursten!' as if he needed to be told.

As time passed slowly on, the increasing bright lightness of Wort's comportment and the addition of what might be called humour to Nursten's repertoire of anger contrasted ever more with the darkening dankness and climatological isolation of my cardboard corner. I had told myself that this space was only for the time being, but I had no better idea or other source of hope that had thus far presented itself. The weight of my saturated situation was heavy and the effort needed to remain balanced increased as speedily as the height of my walls. Nursten and Wort brought or sent their rays of optimism to me, but deep down I felt I was losing touch with them as my Granite crevices turned greener and slimier with algae, and fungi started to push themselves through the sopping floor covered with dead leaves (that used to be alive) and muddy soil (that used to be dusty and warm). After such a recent and painful severance of contact with Uncle Heap, this sliding away of my builders was hard. But I was hard, and I continued to shuffle around, wondering about life, my life, trying to keep the last few, as yet unrotted flowering plants alive that grew in the sopping floor. I also spent a lot of time going over and over memories of some of the times when I had lived, when perhaps I might not have done if Uncle Heap and I had not been such a good Wild Times team. These were lovely thoughts to have and they cumulatively filled me with a powerful knowing about my survivability, whatever badness called itself mine. I would go over a scenario in full gory colour, beating out the blood of an evil creature under a black sky, smelling the foulness of its innards and remembering the slickness of its slippery organs as they spilled. Or it might be a crunchy sort of creature that I remembered more as the crackly sounds of being crushed. Whatever, I liked the bloody creature memories best and I would go over them again and again and fill myself up with the steady normality of being alive, always alive, and let it solidify in me for comfort.

When my builders put the first floor in above my head I learned that, however solid that solidity in me seemed, the normality of it could still vibrate. As my gloom shivered and was swallowed into blackness, my normal aliveness that I had worked to solidify vibrated to the rhythm of 'doom-doom, doom-doom'. I pictured mother sitting at her window on her Wild Times chair and felt the queasy thump of her words, but fortunately my solidity never cracked or gave way. The water started to crawl up the lumpy walls with the algae in pursuit but my heart never split, and the cold smell of loneliness fell heavily around me but my lungs never shattered, nor did my stomach implode, nor did my liver crumble, nor my brain, nor my shiny kidneys that I felt cleansing me each day. Safer and safer, the safety felt good and better and better still, but the agility was draining out of my aliveness and I became a solid mass of resistance to breakage, hanging onto the edge of doom-doom as the sky gradually disappeared.

You can imagine my quaking relief when I realised that the floor they were building did not go all the way across between my walls. No, down at the nether end, far away from cardboard corner, my new ceiling ended in a rough line and light still slithered down between the walls from the distant sky beyond them. Once I had accepted these parameters I loudly told myself in my head that I must be blessed to have such a hidden and protected corner where I could shore up my well-being and belong in the safety of both my Granite present and my ancestral cardboard past. Much less loudly, I told myself that Wort's light brightness and Nursten's humour made the wetter parts of me squirm and I knew I was vegetating, becoming ever closer in nature to the creeping algae in my damp world. Then Wort changed this.

My courteous leafy deliveries still came in Wort's dripping hands several times a day, and he preserved their intactness in one hand while nimbly climbing down a diagonal row of jutting stones that had been built into the wall at the lighter end of my abode with the somewhat obscured notion of stairs in the minds of the craftsmen. He was now often preceded by a tumbling shower of hot dryness that his activity had driven to a minor avalanche, and he sometimes trickled a little wobbling air after him whose colours I would squint to see before he entered the gloom.

'A luh-leaf from the tuh-tuh-top for you to-to eat.' He would hold it out to me and reach into a gentle reverie to describe the fare. 'Yuh-you and the sun and the-the plant and the water fuh-fuh-from the sky and the gift of-of the wind made it together and huh-here it is for you to-to eat.' And he would sway a bit on the spot in his usual elegant way.

'Does it take a lot of sun to make it do you think Wort?' I would ask timidly as I chewed.

'Oh yuh-yes! Buh-but there is luh-lots of light at the top. Hot too ruh-right now.' And he would cast his eyes toward the corner of grey that made a slight suggestion of the light above.

'And is the water from the sky so different to the wetness of down here?' I would probe.

'It's fuh-fuh-fresh and light and always cha-changing, from cooling puh-puff of vapour to cuh-cuh-crystal splash,' he would tantalise me as he swayed.

We took a lot of time over these familiar

158

conversations with many pauses, and we spoke in the most soft way about such dreamy things.

'But what about the wind Wort, is the wind nice up there?'

'Oh yuh-yes.'

He always said, 'Oh yuh-yes,' until one day when he began nodding repeatedly and slowly then said, 'Cuh-come and fuh-fuh-feel it for yoursel-self' instead.

This was the beginning of everything that hadn't begun already. I insisted on pulling my bone-beaded hat out of its mouldy crevice and plonking it on my wary head as well as putting on my extra tunic so that I would have more padding when I fell. Then Wort took my hand and led me to the jutting stones that went up. He had never held my hand before, so this was a very sharply felt sensation. His hand wasn't as wet as I had imagined it would be, and was significantly rougher. I could feel the friction as his coarse skin gripped me like a poisonous weed seed clings to your clothes and I knew he would never drop me. Nursten peeped the ends of his great boots over the edge of the stone, high up, then peeked his bloody face over the boots. He watched, bellowing and guffing with an excitement and encouragement which totally out-paced the inching of Wort and me as we clung to the wall and quivered higher. I was inside and outside myself and upside down and everything felt so beyond any fear I had ever felt before that straight away I could not tell if it was safer for me to go up, then up more, or to come down the perilous jutting stones. My bone-beads pressed into my face and bumped the rough wall as I clung on, trying to make as much contact with the rock as possible. The Granite that I had feared to even think about not long before was now my intimate hope, comfort and companion. My legs were shaky, but Wort's rough hand and Nursten's bold support steadied me and I relinquished my fate to these two. I had no control left.

My mind had stepped completely away.

I screamed and clenched my eyes shut and thought I would die as Nursten picked me up off the top step and lifted me onto the wall of my safe safe house. I felt the deepness of his slow laugh run through me, Ha! Ha! Ha! and smelled, close up, the rancid sweetness of his homely odour. Just like any other new and difficult things, the smell, the being held, the unconnectedness of me to the earth, the breeziness of elevation: it all lasted for ages and I can recount it in every detail (but I will not). My brain shrunk to the size of something I could squash in my hand easily and then it dropped gloopily into my stomach and swam around in a pool of countless time before, at last, Nursten kindly put me down. I squeezed and squeezed my eyes shut, pushing myself into the rock and lodging my feet and hands in between stones, searching for a sense of gravity. Could I fall up into the sky I wondered? It felt like the normal forces of up- and down-ness might abandon me at any moment.

'So what do you think of your house from up here sweet little girl?' Nursten boomed in my ear.

He had sat down next to me and I also felt the gentle presence of Wort at my other side, close by, so I gingerly opened one eye. The impact was breathtaking, so much so that I could not even scream and the only sound that came out of me was a small squelch. My bone beads did not shield me from the deadly drop cliffs which plunged below me, announcing with an alarming verticality the water spread out below. I could look right out to the infinity of ocean. The blueness of it was as monotonous as forgetfulness on a vacant day with no Wildness in it. The colour stretched for ever and until an unknowable end. Not only did the falling away from the land to the water make me feel giddy, but I suffered with the blueness and could hardly tear myself away from its alluring suggestion of depth and breadth and width and liquid light and clogging death and strangely formed creatures and sinkability and floatability. I could hardly fail to notice the brightness of it too. The sunlight ricocheted off its kinked surface every whichways and sparked into my head because my eye had forgotten how to close itself properly after so much dark and dank time. But I kept on looking and believing that the sun was a good thing and that I would not fall from the wall into permanent forgetfulness so long as I remained sitting down, and nor was I on an endlessly high dream tower from which I could fall into infinite pre-death fear. I made myself as small as possible with my knees against my chest and the rough Granite aggressing my feet and bottom and elbows. I did not dare to look sideways to see my builders to each side of me in case I moved by accident and something new happened that I hadn't thought of yet. I was not fully aware of what forces might be involved in this unwonted situation and I could still feel the prints of Nursten's hands on me where he had picked me up. I opened my other eye tentatively and blinked and blinked to make the light tolerable but, after some great time, its intensity lessened as the bright edge of it was blown away on a flimsy breeze that drifted up from the ragged cliff edge. I sweated.

'Time for you to see the rest little girl,' Nursten bellowed in my right ear.

I barely had time to gasp before he had picked me up again close to his bulky, hard body. I didn't want to think about what might be happening so I scrunched my face shut and curled up and imagined that I was my snail and that Nursten was my shell. It was a bloody shell, obviously, but smelled warm and was tight and snug around the crumple of my skinny body that lay curled inside it. Its open hole pointed at the sky whichever way I tried to imagine it, but luckily I had my special protective hat to shield me from the worst of the world until he plonked me nakedly down somewhere else.

I peeled open my sweaty vision once more when I was sure I felt the reassuring presence of Big to one side of me and Silent to the other. Immediately I wondered how the deadly drop cliffs had followed me, as a little rainbow wobble tricked off the edge down to who knows where, then realised that they hadn't, it was simply the sharp descent from the top of the wall which gave an impression of limitless down to fall through, that same kind of infinite down-ness as I had suffered in my tower dreams.

I was also instantly staggered to understand where that little breeze had blown the worst of the brightness of the light: east. And east, of course, meant all the vast lands between my safe safe house and my old home, the scorched earth and the tufty grass and the halfway lightning tree and the memory of my recent journeys lay there. And beyond lay my old gate, and the scraggier than ever flagpole, laced with leaves and scraps, and my old home. Everything that I used to not notice when I lived there was noticeably there in this harsh glare.

Drawn farther and farther into the mysterious distance (that was not mysterious anymore), I saw the lightly blown light there too, bouncing from the fervent yellows of the duplicitous flowering bushes and glinting off their thorns, searching out barren hills that were pale due to the luckless mineral they had be formed from, soaking into the rolling burntness of lower flatlands that offered no gifts, prising pockets of trees out from ditches and hollows and sucking their green up to the sky. Most surprisingly though, after spending all my life wondering what lay in the east, I could now see other homes in the distant landscape. Squared up pieces of land with buildings nearby signified the presence of people, clearly visible and no question about it. This gave me pause for thought: perhaps they were people like me, or Uncle

Heap, or Menith, or Great Uncle Lollo, or even possibly mother (although I hoped that it was unlikely that someone else in the world was so inertly sad as mother). Or maybe they were new and exotic kinds of people such as would not even come to the Wild Times Fair and might lead completely different lives with different tools and possibilities that I could not imagine. All I could see were half a dozen tiny block buildings in shades of grey and red, scattered over a huge distance and surrounded by partitioned bits of land that distinguished themselves from the countryside by being mostly a uniform green. These 'fields' (as they might be) had corners but were not regular in shape and one contained a cluster of large, dark-coloured animals which I presumed were gathering to attack the unlucky homestead. At that house, smoke rose from somewhere close by, a strategy that Uncle Heap and I had infrequently and ineffectively used to scare things off.

My gaze lolled around the perimeters of this distant smoking house, where the uniform green met the blooming duplicitous flowers of the smelly yellow kind that licked their prickles around each clearing made for living and then cut a big swathe out of the dullness of the land as they plunged westwards towards my Granite house, even surrounding that. Their nectareous fragrance was potent even at altitude. It shot straight up my nose, knifing into my brain and making the sea and the early summer sky still sharper and bluer. The flowers even smelled yellow.

The more I looked, the more my mind hesitated and began to wind through some memories of Uncle Heap and me again, battling the Wild Times together, which all made me notice that there hadn't been much battling recently for me, although I had heard a yelp from Menith and various bangings and screeches made by Uncle Heap which let me know that it was business as usual at my old house. This Granite really worked.

I was becoming hot and giddy, perhaps made worse by the duplicitous smell and the vertiginous height, but mostly because of the heat from the sun which was becoming intense. I had dressed for dank darkness and met instead with a heatwave bursting through clean-washed air, fresh from a drizzle of days (so Nursten bellowed). That clean air gradually filled with small insects whose variety and danger level I did not recognise. Because of this, I was glad of all my clothing because they were too small to penetrate my coarse layers with stingers or mouthparts or spines or spikes or hooks. Nevertheless, I began to feel agitated, stuck as I was and unable to move for fear of the plummeting of down-ness or up-ness or whatever might happen if I got wrong-footed.

'They are as sweet as you if not sweeter little girl,' Nursten thumped into my right ear and held out his hand until one of the insects landed on it. 'See? Sweet.'

He smiled and balanced his insect laden hand under my eyes. Sure enough the creature was gentle looking and opaque, carrying dusty, over-sized wings of an iridescent blue, fringed with silver spots. No spikes or poisons to be seen. I had a sudden feeling for it like I had for my snails and wondered if, as they swarmed, they might be heading down into cardboard corner to, at very least, die in the coolness. They would be most welcome and maybe I could use their wings for decoration afterwards.

Whilst dropping back into my head to contemplate what decorations might be furnished by Nursten's insects, an exclamation made me bare my attention to the stab of the sun once more. I definitely thought I heard a muffled 'BE. CAREFUL!' in a deep, alarmed tone. The sound bounced around under the sky making it hard to identify the place where it had come from. Then I spotted my dear Uncle Heap!

'UNCLE. HEEEEEEEEEAP!!' I bellowed out in true Nursten style, clinging to the rocks that I was sitting on and wobbling my bone beads dangerously. 'UNCLE. HEEEEAP! THE. ARCHITECT. WAS. SNORING! SNORING!'

'YOU. SAID. BEFORE,' Uncle Heap shouted back in that unfamiliar voice which had now been demuffled.

'I. WROTE. LETTERS. UNCLE. HEAP. TOOBIT. TOOK. THEM. NOTHING. STILL. NOTHING.' My desperation pushed out in tears that ran as hot as the air down my already steaming cheeks. 'NOTHING. UNCLE. HEAP!'

'WELL.' He even made shouting sound like procrastination. 'NO. OTHER. CHOICE. MAKE. THE. BEST. OF. IT.'

'THANK. YOU. FOR. TEACHING. ME. TO. WRITE. DIDN'T. WORK. THOUGH.' My voice was going a bit scrawtchy with the crying but I still managed to bellow sufficiently.

'BE. CAREFUL. REMEMBER. COUSIN. HANUK,' warned Uncle Heap.

My mind scanned through the battery of stories of stricken ancestors but I could not locate cousin Hanuk's fall from a great height. I thought he might be another relative with a lot of loose-bowelled off-spring, but I couldn't be sure. I suddenly felt exhausted and just stared and wept my face in the direction of Uncle Heap. He was maybe exhausted by the shouting too, because he just stood there, looking at me on and on with his big hands hung by his sides, our watch blocks to the right and left of him, even more silent than my own bloody companions. It didn't matter that we had no words to say for a long time because we had that big, thick bond joining us all the while. It was such a relief to feel this bond again that it became at first painful, like the rush of saliva when you first taste a flavoursome leaf, but the pain ebbed and the nameless joy grew and pooled inside me.

Much later, Nursten put me back in my snail shell, also without words, and I felt serene as I was transported gently back to the dark dankness of cardboard corner, my eyes shut.

Chapter Twenty: Settling the Ownership of Smiles

So that was my first time aloft, and the next few went much the same: my quivering nerves, Nursten's trusty arms and so on. I shouted with Uncle Heap several times and the noise became more familiar but remained exhausting. Things changed though, and I was soon teetering up the rocky steps alone and crawling about to see what I could see. I got over the novelty of Uncle Heap being there again, and began to see the others as well. Seeing Great Uncle Lollo from such a distance was like seeing him in his true context, with his orchestra laid out before him and his fatigued fan club close at hand (Toobit Lonkins). I observed him thoughtfully, as ever, and tried to hear his music as he conducted. When he was going through a particularly slow movement I shouted out his name and caused him to stop, confused. I called again and he adopted the same stance as Uncle Heap, with his hands hanging heavily by his sides, staring blindly from the end of his tether. I called and called, not knowing if the calling was a good thing that was helping him to understand, or a bad thing that was merely interrupting his creative flow. Repeating his name over and over, he eventually began to conduct me and lead me into all manner of rhythms and tempos and wandering pitches. I was powerless before his decisive direction and he made of me then, and on many occasions afterwards, a bird. Yes, I felt like a singing bird, singing out of my heart and out of the landscape and out of the air. There was no limit to the beauty and power in Great Uncle Lollo's art.

Mother was another story, as usual. I saw her, of course. Her immobile silhouette was distinguishable in most lights, never changing and never changing, because she was never going to change whilst she never changed. She had not slumped or shifted or slipped at all since I last saw her, nor, obviously, had she decided to live. Looking at her made my throat feel raw all the way down to my bowels but I did it sometimes anyway out of some strange compulsion which I believed was given to me by my Granite. If she had ever, ever, even once looked back at me I could never have looked again but, as it was, I was free to be curious and weigh myself up next to her in a pleasant way. Her offer of doom was tamed a short breath by each minute I observed her, the curse deflated and her sole ownership of that doom slowly marked, gasp by gasp.

Less often I would catch Menith at her beautifying chores. I know I had pretty much rejected her garish gift but I did not feel small or silly next to her (not often) and eventually plucked up the courage to call her name from time to time. Clearly she heard me. She responded almost always by looking in my direction for a few seconds before carrying on stroking her nails with colour. I was never sure if she was being disdainful, if she had somehow discovered the fate of her gift to me and was deliberately shunning me, or if there was something she genuinely did not comprehend about my distance. It was despite this (other) unanswered question that I found the inner courage to call to her, just to remind her that I still existed (or for some different reason that I have deliberately forgotten). She was only visible to me when the sun was shining because it was her habit at these times to flirt on the doorstep with her varnishes, tossing her hair and inspecting the twenty-fold magnificence of her digits. The Wild Times made a surprise, squawking visit on one occasion just about then, but her lumpy form still did not shift all that fast. Her wetly lacquered nails trailed behind, dragging her, and I wondered how the odds must be stacking against her and her sunshine-licked nails in a potentially fatal world.

All this was filling me up: breathing, thinking, observing, marking the distance between me and various conditions of life. I was frightened a lot, needless to say, but there was exhilaration in abundance and I passed the time full of the wonder of many things, and of me, me who could climb walls and see all this as though it were mine to see, clinging less and less fearfully to the fearful Granite as each day passed. Wort eyed me warily sometimes and avoided me if I was thinking. Nursten, whose brash and dangerous spirit could not be quelled, injured me badly once by making as though to push me off the wall after delivering a surprise scowl in my face under my hat. I hadn't seen him coming because of the brim unfortunately. My damaged confidence took a slug's lifetime to restore, but Nursten knew his part and carried me once or twice as penance and constantly stood by me as a physical barrier to the abyss at the same time as bellowing the good news of my assured safety endlessly.

After the first bleak season of my new view had passed, as the weather conditions warmed and dried, I noticed that I could smell something very nice up there. I eliminated the possibility of a duplicitous niceness when I followed a dripping rainbow wobble to the edge one day and identified that it was my fruiting tree flowering (which meant getting ready to fruit), just above the level of the tops of my walls. I watched it carefully and saw bunches of tiny green berries form behind the falling creamy flowers as the wall gradually elevated in front of it. I watched them ripen to an almost black redness over weeks and weeks, just as I would in the many years that followed. In future seasons I would only be able to smell, see or imagine them with an unsated lust, but this first year saw the height of the wall rise through the branches of the tree as it ripened its glassy fruit and I was able to lie on my stomach and reach out to pick these beauties and put them straight into my mouth.

The fruit picking added another dimension of thrill to my new climbing abilities but as the walls got higher, the climbing became more difficult and long and I began to notice blood on my own hands from handling the rock. I imagined my face, not just smeared with blood like those of my builders, but daubed in a mixture of dark blood and dark fruit juice, whilst my innards were equally dyed black-red. These were good colours for me, not the colours of memories any more, and they gave me strength as I struggled daily with my nerves as well as my pathetic body. Each time I reached the top of my walls I felt I had summited the impossible, and I wore my victory paint with pride.

This pride grew up from its crawling infancy and, on one day of stifling dark cloud cover, I found myself as tall as I was and standing on top of my brave walls with my dark-streaked, rigid face pointed hatlessly at the unbounded sky. I was gulping the glorious air as it rushed towards me, staving off the total take-over of face rigidity and getting accustomed to the new vertical exposure when something even more wonderful happened. I don't know if it was so much a sound or a feeling, but there was a definite 'woink!' of some sort and I got bigger on the spot. I was still puny, but with each few gulps of air my body would take in enough elation to cause my bones to moan, groan, stretch and, with another impulsive 'woink!', I would expand and occupy a bigger, more solid space. When I had 'woinked' about six or eight times it all began to slow. Of course, if you stood me next to Nursten, I was still a scrap of flesh, but I was definitely stupendously bigger than before. Not only that, but my teeth felt full and hard and bedded in my mouth in a new powerful way, and my hair abandoned its wispiness in favour of a glossy, thickness, which looked like it might repel water and be so heavy that the wind could not lift it. My nails were longer and thicker and had become entirely new tools, which I celebrated by painting them with the red nail varnish then chewing the nasty, lying stuff off. I flexed my fingers, my arms, just so that I could watch them. I wiggled my toes to be certain that those far away things really were mine. It was all so spectacular that the smiling thing happened across my face again. I let it come and stay for as long as it wanted to without any doubtful hesitation. There were smiles in my future I knew for sure again, and that was a good thing, just like Uncle Heap had said.

'UNCLE. HEAP! I'M. BIG!' I bellowed with new lung capacity.

He had been watching me and stood silent for a while at this news. I could see that the stains had spread on his tatty overalls since the last time I had seen him.

'YOU. LOOK. SMALL. FROM. HERE' he shouted back using his discouraging voice.

'I. GREW. BIG. FROM. BREATHING. HIGH. AIR' I clarified.

'YOUR. MOTHER'S. THIRD. COUSIN. TWICE. REMOVED. LOST. HIS. MIND. FOREVER. AFTER. CLIMBING. TO. A. MOUNTAIN. HEIGHT. NEVER. SLEPT. AGAIN. UNTIL. HE. SLEPT. IN. HIS. GRAVE. WHICH. HE. GOT. TO. BY. LYING. DOWN. IN. A. ROCKFALL. INSTEAD. OF. SHELTERING. THE. HIGH. AIR. DRAGGED. HIM. THROUGH. MISERY. UNTIL. THAT. DAY' Uncle Heap added helpfully. 'BE. VIGILANT. FOR. THE. WILD. TIMES. IN. THE. SKY' he warned, 'DON'T. FORGET. YOU. ARE. YOUR. MOTHER'S. DAUGHTER.'

This last remark was disappointing. Thoughts of mother, of doom, of eternal puniness and inertia rushed through the draughty corridors of my head almost before my smile had faded and in this state of mental deflation my attention was luckily distracted by Great Uncle Lollo, who, stretched right to the end of his tether, was busy trying to pull up a fence post. Menith had seen him and gristled her fatty body over the grass to prevent him. Unfortunately, Great Uncle Lollo had a gift for increasing his weight at will and Menith could not so much as lift his arm from the post. A struggle ensued which turned Menith's hair all tousled. She looked about her increasingly frantically as if expecting imminent attack from all sides and, as she slowed and tired, I felt sure I could see her sweating a blubbery sweat before she jellied back to the house in defeat. Great Uncle Lollo had neither the strength nor the tether to lift any fence post in reality, but he was happy playing with the idea and it cheered me up to see him happy.

'I. LIKE. THE. AIR. UNCLE. HEAP' I affirmed to myself as I turned to Uncle Heap again. He had ambled off to the not poisonous well, and now returned, his right arm longer than his left, with a bucket of not poisonous water on the end of it.

He paused thoughtfully then advised, 'BE. WARY. OF. WHAT. YOU. LIKE. REMEMBER. MY. BROTHER. HE. LAY. DOWN. IN. HAPPINESS. AFTER. INDULGING. IN. SMELLING. FLOWERS. FELL. ASLEEP. AND. WAS. EATEN. BY. THE. WILD. TIMES. ALL. THEY. COULD. FIND. AFTERWARDS. THEY. SCRAPED. INTO. A. BASKET. REMEMBER. HIS. WIFE. WHO. WAS. SHAKEN. OFF. THE. LEDGE. BY. A. WILD. TIMES. SHUDDER. WHEN. SHE. WENT. FOR. EGGS.'

It seemed that Uncle Heap had lost faith in smiling. I did not smile as I thought it, but I knew that all my future smiles belonged to me.

Chapter Twenty-One: Words Lead to Chocolate

Following the normal two months of unbearable heat, after which bleakness dropped in heavily, and right away began to last forever one more time, Wort and Nursten began to fuss over me less. I was terribly proud that they had noticed how my liquid nerves had hardened and how my climbing abilities had consolidated and now knew that fussing over me was no longer a good thing but a bad thing. The weather was a challenge, I admit. It rained, normal, wet rain an awful lot and this made just-for-the-time-being cardboard corner more slimy than ever and had a not dissimilar effect upon the crucial grip of the rough Granite steps that were my stairway to loftiness. Algal clods formed here and there, fed almost daily by the green rain, and wishful plants sprouted from the crevices to live only briefly before they rapidly rotted to a brown goo. Days of drizzle only signified that heavy rain was coming very shortly, and the continuing workload became heavier and heavier for my builders as they lugged around their sodden bodies under the cumbersome grey skies. Grey became the colour of the moment (as it would again later, when something happened that only grey could express). The sky was the supreme artist in interpreting the many facets of greyness, and it shed a sullen mood over the Granite and the burnt lands, and even the greener parts. The duplicitous yellow flowers turned a grey shade of yellow and the pink tufty ones expired with the small blue ones. All in all, life was bathed in colours drably shocking enough to have been inherited from the wrecked days of mother's past, or from a battlefield littered with the long-decayed bodies of loved people or somesuch.

I put the increased level of wet precipitation of my new environs down to their supreme altitude. But rain or dry, green or grating, always the sweet duplicitous yellow reached up my nostrils and into my brain, tweaking a resistance in me for beautiful things that might turn out to be tricky. I remain suspicious of tricky things to this day, things that may turn out to be beautiful things, perhaps, perhaps not. But this duplicitous yellow flowered plant spread itself around and seemed to be the first to spring up from the burnt lands. Sprigs of grey-yellow flowers tufted out between the clawing black fingers of death that reached through the scorched blackness that I could see was scorched deep, to scar forever. How could something that was purely good jump up from such a tomblike beginning? Clearly, it could not.

I didn't let the greyness bother me. I had shrugged off at least some part of my mother-poisoned past, which made everything less bothersome. Thus, the lofty climbing was not really a bother any more either, not really. It was not that my enthusiasm had dimmed, just that the novelty of exhilaration had stopped vibrating so fast. I spent more and more of each day wandering around in the high places of my world, gladly letting the normal wind and the normal rain (which wouldn't hurt me but would just be blowy and wet) assault me as they would. They became the new silence, the new page on which to write the day. I never had too much to write and it always seemed much the same, something like: 'Ah! High-ness!', or 'The joy of open space!', or 'Air!' or suchlike things, over and over. Below, in my dim personal seclusion, equally dim thoughts sometimes came to me of course: wondering about Hanuk's fate; feeling still and forever puny despite having grown and thickened considerably; turning over the possibility of nail varnish retribution by Menith... and so on. These were all more reasons to go aloft.

The giant lands that lay now within my sight rippled like the pelt of a once sleek greyish animal, fur like a river, a creature in powerful motion that had somehow been frozen and given brutal mange to scab its dazzling coat with dilapidation. I could feel the smoothness of the green parts of the countryside in my moist throat and I let them roll there coolly as I looked. Amongst the green were smatterings of trees, serene even on days of weather, their whole magnitude so much greater than mine. They bent this way and that, aged, wise and possibly even more resilient than Uncle Heap. I had only seen a couple of trees up close ever, so it became a recurring fantasy of mine, imagining walking beneath them, their green shade soaking my skin and my earthy-smelling clothes. In my mind I could feel my arms wrapped around the trunks of great, gentle trees, alive with secret channels of liquid nourishment coursing up from their plunging roots so that I could put my ear to them and hear the beat of the push of it. My fruit tree was me-sized by comparison with how I imagined the far off copses. These massive plants in the distance took on grand proportions that magnified with my admiration of them. The stories of them told themselves and the trees were always the champions whether axes were buried within them or poison gloop fell from the sky or fire raged past or evil creatures defecated and urinated below them or light ended or the air turned bad. Twisted by scars and stunted from lack, old or young, they were whole, whatever was left of them.

In all the hours of all the days that I spent in just looking and absorbing all this, it was hard not to taste in my mouth, above my damp throat of moist tree-feelings, the bitterness of the blemished and burned parts that the Wild Times had favoured in its rampages too. These blackened and scabby areas grated my green-softened throat where the trees had soothed, so I tried not to think about them even when I saw them. It was only bad (the throat grating) on the rare absolutely dry days, when the charring of the earth stretched right into my lungs. On the worst dehydrated days breathing became harder as the sun rose, and I could think of little else but the blackening of my innards, my breathing apparatus clogged and my pulsing blood attempting weakly to clear a way again.

And all these observations had full freedom. In Nursten and Wort's post-fussing era they offered something much less expected instead: persistent invitations to consort with them. I babbled on constantly and heartily about what I thought and saw. My brain flowed out of my mouth for months of wonderful flooding, cleaning, nourishing hours. I hope they enjoyed it too, a bit, somehow. Every day I would wake, emerge from my ancestral cardboard, do necessary things, then poke my head around under the space that led up to the sky to see what the day promised. Enthusiastic beckoning arms would sweep over the edge of the walls, dripping blood and the familiar wobbly air, which showed its full rainbow colours through my sleep-dazed eyes.

'Drop the cardboard and come up here with me sweet little girl,' Nursten would invite me, and roar as an encouragement because he knew I liked it.

'I'll be up in a minute!' my tinny voice would call back towards the dizzying world above, without a thought for my own safety or the sometimes algal clods and brown goo to be negotiated in between.

Nursten's good natured savagery still worried me at times, naturally, and at times it worried me that I liked it, but it was all so gruff and unbridled and uncomplicated and unafraid that I could not help but wish that I could be that, and not the tinny-voiced, puny girl that I was. I suppose that's why I wanted to run away from Nursten at the same time as let his great arms fold around me while I pretended to be a snail again.

'This rock is suh-so heav-heavy. The anguish is tuh-too much for me all-all alone, I'm suh-sorry. If only I were suh-suh-someone tuh-tough like you,' Wort would whisper-weep through the plummetting air.

This flattery made me blush, and I had no words to answer with. 'I'll be up in a minute!' I staggered out in an embarrassed repetition then, all of a rush and a further blush, hoped that my response did not oblige me to do anything I could not.

Wort was not heroic like his co-humpher but I felt sure of myself around him and his whimperings and stutterings and was comfortable in the knowledge that I was always certain to be the less feeble of the two of us. I felt so much caring for him and he for me too, I believe. I suppose he understood how it was to have a pathetic body for a start. Maybe he wanted to help me to be happy, to cast me up, up and away on a breeze of better life, or maybe he wanted me to climb down into his hole of stagnant sadness, I couldn't tell at first because of the soft spot I had for him.

So, blackness, highness, trees, wetness: they were all shared with my dear builders. I spent many hours of each day squinting out the details of diverse and faraway things to let them know my feelings about them. A particular fascination of my own was the cluster of peopled dwellings to the east, but I'm not sure that these were the most popular topic with Nursten and Wort.

'I think there are two of them,' I would declare, straining up the hillside of our panorama. 'And they have both come out of the door and now are going around the back of the house.'

'Life is exciting up there on the hill,' Nursten would

comment dryly.

'I think they are nice people because their home looks tidy from here, so I hope those black beasts there don't attack them,' I would continue.

'Black beasts, eh.' Nursten was sceptical. 'Those belong to the people.'

'Well, you could say that the Wild Times belong to us all Nursten,' I would counter huffily. 'Look, one is going back inside and the other is going to that little shed of theirs.' It seemed interesting to me, and I stared, open-mouthed, for a long time. 'The one who just went into the shed is taking a long time. Maybe they've lost something, or maybe something prowling is preventing them coming back.'

All this while, Wort would be listening avidly, obviously, and both he and Nursten would be working, shifting always the precious Granite, steadily advancing my verticality.

'Ah good, they're coming back. They are carrying something. Maybe it's a tool, maybe some wood, maybe a weapon, maybe a tool and some wood to make a weapon with. I wouldn't be surprised you know, the way the black beasts look at them all the time.'

'Black beast nonsense,' bellowed Nursten and gave an immense wave of his arms as though to point out how benign the world was.

I wasn't really listening. 'I wonder if they get a lot of wind up there...'

I would banter boringly dreamily like this until poor Wort would stop me by saying, 'Puh-please duh-don't talk abou-about them any more. The puh-puh-pain is cuh-coming back.'

I would change the subject at these moments and talk instead about some of Uncle Heap and my Wild Times successes, battles, the splotches of grizzly, splashing deaths of unkind creatures and so on. I probably brought up the odd suicide too I admit, and may have wondered out loud about Hanuk's fall from a great height, I'm not altogether sure. Anyway, whatever I talked about, Wort always eventually put his hands to his ears, rocked his head from side to side and cried out again, 'The puh-puh-pain,' with snuffles and gasps for effect.

The only thing that both Nursten and Wort seemed genuinely interested in was my ancestral cardboard stories. Their eyes would widen and they liked especially to hear where it had come from (my invented story), and about it hiding in the rafters for my whole life before it became mine (true, as you know), about how useful it was and in which ways, but no information had ever marvelled them so much as when I gave them the news that there was writing on the cardboard.

'Well, what does it say sweet little girl?' Nursten asked me in a state of shivering excitement that even made him cease heaving the stone.

Sadly I could not answer because the words on the cardboard had never meant anything to me before. To them it was a momentous clue in the wonderful mystery of the great and glorious cardboard. To me they were random letters from someone else's life and times.

'I'll have to check it and tell you tomorrow exactly what the letters are, just so I get it right,' was how I put it.

The next morning their frantic anticipation had full possession of them and all four possible arms were beckoning, waving and gesticulating madly as soon as I appeared at the foot of the steps.

'Ok! Ok!' I grumbled.

'But what does it say on the cardboard little girl?' bellowed Nursten.

'Yes, wuh-what are the wuh-words?' whisper-shouted Wort.

'I'm coming!'

179

I climbed the grippy bits of Granite so fast (doing my utmost to avoid the algal clods and the slippery goo) that I was pant-panting when I reached the top. The effort that I had made to memorise the cardboard words was concerted, but my panting seemed to be forcing the memory out of me. Reaching the top I flopped double to get my blood into the right places again. I could still remember one set of words at least and I pushed them out towards my feet as I hung over with my hands on my bending knees.

'It says "Newton's Chocolate Selection" over and over with some numbers and things on several bits of the cardboard.'

I got it all out super-rapidly all in one breath then set to gasping again but, as the verve of my lung ventilation calmed, I noticed that the two figures who had come to stand so uncomfortably close were both still and silent. I peered up from my hunch and saw two shocked faces. The crumblier parts of the blood-crust on their faces were flaking off somewhat as the surprise was written there, leaving pale bands across their foreheads and around the corners of their mouths.

' "Newton's Chocolate Selection"?' I ventured again.

Their eyes widened to unimaginable wideness, especially Wort, and their eyebrows arched almost up to their hair lines while two mouths fell open leaving dark o-holes in two faces.

'What?' I said innocently enough.

As I stood up, Wort was embarrassed at first and drew away from me looking sheepish, then Nursten's face also fell to self-consciousness and he bellowed, 'Chocolate, that's what sweet little girl! Chocolate! What do you say about chocolate?!'

This was a tricky question because I had no idea what chocolate might be, but my brain suddenly warped back to the previous evening's cardboard studying and I recalled what it said on the other boxes, because they featured the same word.

'What I say is that the other boxes say "Deluxe Chocolate Chip Biscuits" and "Longford's Chocolate Fingers", that's what I say,' I blurted triumphantly.

I felt rather proud and superior to have come back with a clever response in such a confounding position, but I had not anticipated the weakening effect my words would have on my builders. Wort dropped down to sit roughly on the stone, drooling and staring at me in wonder and stupidity, and Nursten virtually fell into a faint and had to be revived with a few growls from me.

I had not yet found out what it meant, but after this incident I used the word 'chocolate' cheekily and with very good effect to make either Big or Silent swoon and go peculiar. I liked this a lot and tried different tones of voice to see which had more effect. Strangely, the more gently I spoke, the more cutting the word became, and the more I liked it.

Chapter Twenty-Two: I Become Truly Complicit for a Moment

So it went. The three of us found ways to know each other, to tolerate and enjoy each other in our giddy world. Wort could hardly be said to be the same miserable wisp that I had first met and he talked to me often, if still in a meek voice. Our quiet chats on top of the Granite walls made him grin with pleasure from time to time. This was pleasant, naturally, but unfortunate for me because it meant that he leaned close to me and displayed a nauseating set of rotten teeth which had previously been a secret withheld. His proximity was such that I could smell the foulness of his breath that ran through the black gaps in those teeth. I hoped that the bad odour was the stench of his inner store of sadness and that he was finally breathing it out for good, meaning that the time would come when I didn't have to suffer the smell any longer.

Nursten too had changed. His mindless anger was thrown into my rock still, but he channelled his energies in acts of boisterous playfulness more and more often. Wort and I were both victims of his ambush roars and friendly shoves and pushes. Wort was slower to adapt than me. He flinched and flickered at Nursten's approaches, where I growled and teased back. Although he still called me 'sweet little girl', Nursten seemed to have accepted my puniness. For my part, I took time alone to concentrate on gulping the bone-expanding air which got richer and richer the higher we got. Thus, my puniness became at least a tiny bit more formidable against the billowing muscles of Nursten's immense body, proportioned as it was on the same scale as the clouds in the sky that we forever became closer to.

During my now accustomed rambling talk, I stopped once unexpectedly when I was blankly talking about the past while staring at mother, motionless in the window. All of a sudden I saw that the window was empty of her. I only just had time to gasp, hold it in and then deflate myself again when there she was in the window, as before, as always. Had my eyes deceived me? I didn't really have time to wonder where she might be and why. I was never quite sure about mother, she was a mystery.

Mystery breath-holding moments were mercifully rare, my thoughts were stable and I blathered out out out of me all the words I had, until everything seemed scraped clean inside and I was left with a not-worrying-at-all smile suggesting itself on my face and little else to say which was, in general, a relief to Wort I believe. My life stably rambled on after that, a bit like my banter had, but then something unforeseen happened.

It was a day on the cusp between unbearable heat and relentless bleakness when I was talking a few selected words with Wort about Granite as we sat up in the sky facing west.

'Sparkles sometimes,' I said, hoping for one but the sun had gone.

'Huh-heavy,' he said back, dropping his hands into his lap with the very weight of the word.

'Holds back the sea,' I said with gladness, looking that way (it was a lumpy and an unfriendly grey-blue that day).

'Safe safe huh-house,' he also pointed out.

'Thank you for all your building Wort.'

A well of gratitude surged inside me, despite the substandard finish, and I think it reached out to Wort because he did something special: he took my hand in his for another time. And this was no simple hand-holding thing of mere affection, nor was he leading me anywhere. This was the grasp of instruction, the touch of a tutor which held the momentum of demonstration. In this gentle at first way, smeared in my builder's blood that I had ingested so often on my home-grown leaves, I was first shown how to build by dear Wort, the teaching delivered in his characteristically tender and quiet way. I was the hands within his hands and he cupped them around the chosen rock and placed it with me. His gnarly palms on the back of my hands were barely more comfortable than the Granite I held. Thus, each of my hands was martyred to become the middle of a rough sandwich. I don't know if it was what Wort would have called puh-pain, but it hurt me, although my puh-pain was so sweetened by Wort's attentions that I could only notice it as something beautiful. He persisted, and I persisted inside him, in this deliberate contact with the frightening rock, a contact which flew through my hands, arms, neck, to my brain as all kinds of bright sureness and amazement. I felt that he would have broken all his own bones to raise me to the heights of his modest pride and happiness. As for me, my hands and my thoughts could yield just enough to take up the stone, to tessellate with its coarse qualities, to run our energies together.

I bled of course. But he also showed me how to spit at the right times to make the seal good, and we worked out together how my smallness could lift and move what size of rocks and the kinds of places that they might fit. The first few days were fairly hopeless but Wort's tactile tuition was constant and level. Nursten lumped his great body past us, carrying stone over to the north wall several times a day. He would not stop to talk or help or intervene or participate, but would give an approving bellow of encouragement when his arms were full or a short roar then slap me on the back when he returned to collect more. If his slap was too playful I would just hiss, 'Cho-co-late!' back at him, or sometimes even, 'Chocolate! Chocolate! Chocolate!' and he became instantly subdued.

Thus the first days began when I joined my builders in their noble struggle to monumentalise the ugliness of my safe safe house. I became complicit in its shoddiness but went over my memories of the worst of the Wild Times, spiced it with a few of Uncle Heap's stories, and knew that this building was definitely a good thing to do. I was slow and nervous, and watched the wobbling air flow off my fingertips into the swallowing crevices as I inched the west wall upwards. I contemplated that my wall was not nearly as frightening as the deadly drop cliffs it stood next to, but at least it was made of the same stuff. I worked with great concentration, until Nursten could surprise me horribly whenever he wanted to.

I got lost in those months, fell, reeling through a loop of oblivion, existing only between my eyes and my hands, grasping the grating crystals with the whole of my consciousness. I reserved myself exclusively for that time of oblivion, just as time reserved itself for the same, and I knew in my whole being that nothing else would ever happen.

Chapter Twenty-Three: Time Passes, Things Change

So, time passed, other things happened, of course. I worked, dripped, sweated and spat a great deal of my hours, watched the ascending wall that was made by my own hands. Otherwise I consorted with Big and Silent, smiling after the talking was done, or wandered off alone along the tops to simply soak in the happenings around me until just after I got cold and just before I blew away as a frigid shape in the high air. Since I had ceased my tedious obsession with the other homes and people, I simply soaked in impressions of my environs and let them land where they would in my head. Maybe they meant something there.

My family also became a lot more like impressions. By this I mean that I felt less upset by the upsets that I felt, and calmer about attachments I had formed that still ruled me. Mother's doom lost yet more of its edge, as did my anger towards her. Menith meant close to nothing, she was just 'there'. Great Uncle Lollo was a simple pleasure manifested. Uncle Heap could be himself and I didn't mind at all. The memories of my spider and of Curlywurly rested somewhere just to the right of my heart. The Wild Times were inevitable and surmountable.

Any time that I was in high places and the light was dim (dusk, dawn, heavy clouds, during the bleakness), I saw the sky breathing. Luminous discs and streaks swept grandly across the dimness like an inhalation and an exhalation on a sky-wide if not a universe-wise scale. They were beautiful in a sad way, like loving someone who is dying, and I let them soak into me as I counted

186

them and tried to imagine what tidal volume the air would have in the breath of the sky. I felt human and whole and wondered about the future, whether these magnificent light splodges signalled some sad beauty on the horizon of my life, perhaps some death or some new life inside me or outside me.

I also began to see a particular figure very often. It was a woman because her clothes were so tight that I could tell she had breasts. Her trousers were as though painted onto her legs and she always wore a pinched jacket, black and drawn in at the waist, just exactly like we did not wear, nor anyone I had ever met. Maybe she was mad, I thought. Day after day she walked across the hillsides, fearing nothing, just in order to see the progress on my shoddily built Granite house (I thought). Closer and closer she came each day, until I could see every hair up her nose. And I could see up her nose, despite her being so low down, because she was always looking up, right up, unashamedly at the up- and down-ness, but especially the up-ness of my walls. I didn't like her creeping closer like this, it was rude, so I took to leaping up suddenly when she was close by, standing right on the edge and placing my hands on my hips in an I've-seen-you-and-don't-want-you-here kind of way. She didn't exactly flinch, but might fiddle with the fastening on her shoe, suddenly notice a noteworthy patch of dirt and commence kicking it in an exploratory way, or (almost always) start to sing in a tuneless and strained tone that somehow resonated with the duplicitous yellow odours that were ever present.

All this seemed cheeky and tricky to me, so I began to treat her as though she were a Wild Times visitor (although I knew she was not). Each time she came along I hid silently until the last moment when I could not only jump up suddenly to surprise her, but growl as well, hurl small stones, rattle my metal-spiked wonder club in my metal bucket and the like. I never did anything that might actually hurt her, but she was immune to whatever I tried, unmoved. She equally remained unreached by the plague of Wild Times fear that held everyone I'd ever met in its grip (apart from Nursten and Wort, who lived in their own Granite dream world). Even Great Uncle Lollo showed fear of his surroundings and would skip indoors as though his trousers were on fire if an insect that buzzed at a disagreeable pitch happened by. Especially because I knew Great Uncle Lollo to be a happy and unphasable type, I could only deduce that this dangerously fearless female visitor was, indeed, very strange.

To render my ambushes more effective I began to make them only sporadically, on other times just lying on my stomach observing her instead, counting the silver buttons on her pinched jacket, imagining being inside those constricting clothes (was it nice? Could she breathe?), reading the contours and lines on her face. With this latter observation I came to a clear conclusion about her: she was a woman who was going to die. I could see it there in the shape, hang, colour and topography of her face, she was definitely going to die. Maybe her people would bury her in her suction clothes and she would be forever remembered for them or maybe she would grow so thin before she died that the clothes would no longer stick. Thoughts from idle moments.

Things changed though. My dear Wort became challenging as time passed. Firstly just because he was no longer the fawning, whimpering thing I had first felt affection for and therefore I no longer knew him exactly, but secondly because the bits of his personality that started to come out more and more were not altogether likeable some of the time, and often startling in the context of how I had hitherto seen him (not to mention his teeth again, of course). He cried less and less and then not at all, and then all his anguish began to squeeze out through a new escape hole that was as equally insufficiently sized as his tear ducts.

'The puh-puh-parasites sucked up my puh-power and left me only ang-anguish!' he shouted and shouted, louder and deafening loud, threshing his limbs and tearing at his hair. 'Anguish! And that thuh-thug there is a muh-mirror for their brutal-brutal-tality.' He stood up as tall as he could and made a whole body gesture of accusation and blame toward Nursten who was listening without foreseeing this turn of things and drew his chin back into his neck in surprise. 'I-I will nuh-nuh-not be a rag for their muh-muh-muh-mess anymore!' he raged. 'And wuh-what are you luh-looking at?' he poured his stinking anger into my startled face, and now it was my turn to flinch.

I could not answer at first because my voice had gone, but I soon managed to recover enough to sniffle, 'I was just looking at you and hoping you were feeling happier today,' which seemed reasonable and part of the truth.

'Hap-hap-py! What hap-piness did those an-animals luh-leave me with?' he bared his foul teeth and slavered as he again set about tearing at his meagre hair, this time pulling at his dirty clothes as well and eventually prostrating himself on the Granite.

'Please be nice Wort, you are upsetting me,' I blubbed, the tears beginning their tumble down my girlish cheeks.

'Upset-setting you! Puh-poor thing!' He sprang up and came back at me fast, splattering his saliva in my face as he spoke and then ran a hand of rough and desperate fingers through my hair, mocking, as though about to put a knife in my stomach. But I know that he remembered my innocence, because he swallowed his fury shortly afterwards and spoke no more that day. I could still hear the ranks of raging words warring in his mouth as he breathed heavily near me though. Whether it was from the exertion of his emotions or of the work I do not know, but he certainly steamed as he took up his stones again.

Wort bounced between his former poignant sadness and this spitting ball of blame. I didn't like it, but Nursten found it much more difficult to deal with. One day when Wort was in full flow screaming, 'No muh-muh-more! Nuh-no muh-more!' Nursten simply broke down. This was unexpected. Wort did not notice and continued ranting against whatever it was, but I witnessed the pitiful sight of Nursten, this powerful beast of a man, this constant force, this wall blocking the spread of uncertainty, folding and dropping to his knees, a wretched distortion of his sturdy self. Then he began to sob. He covered his ears with his hands, just as Wort had before demonstrated, and began sucking in air as though it was running out, rocking back and forth as he did so. I could only think of one thing when he started rocking of course, and this caused me to retreat in horror, shaking a bit myself and wondering what new nightmare might be on its way. But thankfully he didn't always rock, and on the many occasions when Wort's voluminous blame and blame and pointless blame temporarily destroyed Nursten I was usually able to offer some comfort. As his huge, bent frame shuddered, I might spit on a small piece of Granite and offer it into his sorry hands, or I might say, 'Good morning Nursten!' brightly to remind him of his pre-feeble life in better times. It wasn't surprising if I thought about it and measured his size once more, but Nursten cried such a torrent of tears that it wet everything around him and he ended up kneeling in a salty puddle, dipping his stained knees and his clumping boots. I marvelled at this and it seemed somehow in keeping with his former heroism, whilst at the same time his bloodied clothes that used to make up part of his prodigious manfulness appeared limply pathetic.

All this was a great show for the passing woman who was going to die. She would turn up most days in her pinched jacket and point her nasal hair upwards. She ogled and stared and seemed to believe herself invisible while she did it. Any attempt on my part at startling her off was not even noticed at such times when Wort and Nursten were busy with their shouting and sobbing matches, so I saved my own performances for other days.

And all of the rest of the time we just got on with the building. All three of us, covered in blood, sweating, salivating over my safe safe house, stone after stone, lugging them up and placing them as we could, dizzying around at the vertiginous tops in our now accustomed sense of camaraderie and advancing into our futures in the steady rhythm of physical work. An aeon of different skies presented themselves around our heads: towering grey things, touched by pink wispiness, swirling infinite blackness cut by lightning, ruthless open-ness. The sea beat out its fury and its pleasures below us at the foot of the deadly drop cliffs, sometimes blue, sometimes green, sometimes white, sometimes dark with the shadows of the sky, persistent in its ceaseless war against the Granite. The land ululated through colour changes (apart from the new and the old scorched bits, where black merely came in seasonal shades). My fruit tree flowered, then leafed, then leafed and fruited together before it dropped everything on the ground and went spindly for the bleak period. The duplicitous yellow smell never changed at all though. They always flowered whatever the time of day or year.

Around this time I finally admitted that I had never been fully sure why Wort and Nursten were there. It seemed impolite to ask now, as though I had never cared. They were simply my builders. There was no question in

191

my mind at first, but now the questions had invented themselves. So I secretly puzzled over it all and tried to glean hints that might lead to answers. There were no hints, so I never found any real answers. They had clearly migrated from the world beyond the Wild Times, but why? I found it ridiculous that Ervil Nitzo had sent them as they certainly did not represent him, his haughty self-importance or his possible refinement, but how could they have known that I needed them? Why did they make their best effort for me? Why did I not have builders whose best effort was better? I wondered if I had been correct in my former wondering that their easy familiarity with scabby Toobit Lonkins signified something important. Perhaps he had made some supplication to them, or perhaps he had seen that they belonged deep in the Wild Times, so helped them to get here. Still, they worked all the time and this was good. I never witnessed them not at work and was never aware of their absence. I never saw them come or go, so I knew that they must have a sneaky side, a secret life, a shifty way of going about their business and, in this respect, I bowed completely to them and fell before their mysterious ways. I did everything I could to make the stonework just as Wort had showed me and also to be a loyal person to them both, chatting until I found what interested them as a means to express my gratitude. Even so, there was always a lingering sense of confusion as to how to deal with them.

Days became increasingly exhausting around this time because of all this trying I was doing. My builders and my building had become my entire goal. I was depleted of body fluid and words by the end of each day, and my heart was depleted too sometimes. I no longer had it in me to wander off along the tops and swirl in my thoughts and look around me at my life. As I clung to the Granite wall and descended my steps into my private dimness each night, a sense of fearful loss gripped me that I no longer had my builders to shape my purpose for hours to come, a creeping loneliness to be without anyone but myself, but also a sense of relief that the hard work was over.

As I looked around my little space, the corner of such a big dampness and a dark safety, I counted and assessed my belongings. My tunics were both shabby and worn, my home-spun string waited for its purpose and my small purse of seeds was not yet depleted. I had collected a few bits and pieces since arrival (nice stones and a black feather and an amber blob that I did not understand), but there were two of my old objects that shone out to me more brightly than anything else: Uncle Heap's magical house building knife, which I had avoided thinking about for quite a while, and the remaining red as red nail varnish from Menith. I thought a lot about them both, but did not have the nerve to handle either of them. The knife had not been used for so long, and it inspired crazy thoughts of branching out on my own and building in a different style. The nail varnish inspired hate and I wanted to crush it. My concentrated wish was for it to stop looking so red near to me. (I didn't start building in a different style, and nor did I crush the nail varnish, not yet.)

I only allowed myself these night moments to be in my free mind. Not only did I spend the last weary minutes of the day staring at my possessions and their possibilities or contemplating the remembered sky of earlier and so on, but these closing thoughts usually spawned sleep dreams. Clinging to and wrapped in my ancestral cardboard, ancestralness necessarily leaked into the rambling night stories as well, blending a potent mixture of family fate, multi-beamed beauty, glistening teeth that slavered, clouds that rose and turned and clouds that fell and hurt, liquid hope running away, legs running away from unspeakable danger, my own legs naked inside my tunic, stinking pools full of dead faces, the drip of juicy fruits for finger licking, and other such stuff. It was quite various. And the cool breath of the stars slid down to cardboard corner while I slept, and the warm breath of the sun reached my cheek to awaken me in the mornings, tired from the night's exhaustions as much as the previous day's. It had all been so simple and easy when I only had the Wild Times to deal with. Things with Uncle Heap had been manageable and understood.

And speaking of Uncle Heap, we rarely spoke during this time. I heard him often at the throats of his Wild Times visitors and twice I heard him cry out to me, 'GROWL. GIRL. GROWL!' during the daytime. I tried my croak, but my fully fledged growl had escaped me. The best I could do was to shout back, 'GROWL. UNCLE. HEAP. GROWL!' as bigly as I could and hope it saved him some bother somehow. He also persisted in telling me a failed suicide story of a distant cousin who had tried to hang himself.

'HUNG. HIMSELF. BY. ONE. FOOT. COULDN'T. DIE. LIKE. THAT. BY. THE. FOOT.' He carefully enunciated repeatedly.

I did not like this story and was not sure why Uncle Heap was telling it to me in such an instructional way. I wondered if it was a sign that he had lost faith in my building project or that he knew of some greater danger on the way that would wipe us all out in some grizzly fashion.

'NO. UNLCE. HEAP. HAVE. TO. HANG. BY. THE. NECK. TO. DIE.' I would make it clear I understood to make the recounting of the tale shorter if possible. 'I. UNDERSTAND.'

'GOOD.' he would close, and go back about his business at home apparently satisfied.

Chapter Twenty-Four: I am No Longer Complicit in Shoddiness

Only one thing stopped our building work around then, and that was the biggest normal storm I had ever experienced. It was on the horizon and also high in the sky as dawn came on. Things had never promised to be so black. All of the sky was already dark as dark, then this storm swallowed up the last hope of light into its vastness and sucked it away to the west. I worked all morning in the weak light with one eye over my shoulder watching it approach. As it neared I could see the glooming and the churning centres of it. Its breathing suck was audible, and the beautiful luminous discs and streaks that I had seen often before were darting in and out of the towering malevolence. When it hit my safe safe house I was wet to my skin instantly, and I feared being slurped into its gasping atmosphere. I became part of the cascade of algal clods and brown goo and black water that crashed down my rough steps as I slurried away to relative safety (or so I hoped). Even from beneath my cardboard I could see the lightning cut the blackness and I waited after each flash in that weighty space until the following thunderclap sounded. The storm mangled the air and I imagined it biting savagely at the clouds, scouring the sea with clawing hail, cuffing the trees to horizontal submission, slapping a deluge of black water at the landscape which would then curl up into small wavelets. The first claps of hammering thunder came close to bringing my safe safe house down around me but I sheltered with hope for my life under my dear cardboard. Without poison gloop and suchlike, this could only be a natural storm and I therefore deemed it to be not strictly part of my world. It seemed an odd accident that it had reached me when clearly it was bound for someone else. Survival was only a matter of endurance, which was no stranger to me, but I could not know or even imagine how Nursten and Wort were doing in this situation. They were not here in my shelter, so maybe they had departed their mysterious ways again. Maybe they had lived through this before, or maybe the storm did not appear to them, just like the Wild Times did not. Maybe they would emerge at the end of it washed clean of blood, happy.

In these tempestuous days I clung to my dim cardboard and the slimy Granite with my fingertips, which I knew would be much grippier than they appeared if a crisis emerged. I went through the various scenarios of flooding, the undermining of my walls, the splitting of the world by a colossal lightning strike and so on, and detailed my certain escape with my extra-grip fingers and my conglomerate wits. Meanwhile, the bursts of electric light assailed the terrified algae, the detonation of the thunderous repeat made slow waves in the viscous air, the rock itself quivered under the attack, and the quivering magnified through my jelly body until my head wagged and my teeth clanked. I comforted myself with the knowledge that, whatever damage the hurly-burly made outside, I still had my string, my needle and thread, some fabric, my building knife and those wits of mine to put things right, even though I was unsure if my old home or my new one or any home nearby might be still there when I climbed my high walls again (unscathed). The more I dwelt upon the picture of destruction awaiting me when the hostile heavens had burned out, the more it became a striking image of a tall pillar of vertical rock, rising from the foaming sea, whose walls grew into the walls of my safe safe house, and I stood at the top of the top, looking out from the highest thing I could imagine. This was not the same tower nightmare. There was no falling. It would be wonderful. The sea would stretch to infinity all around, as all the other land had been swept away. I wondered what use I could make of my string in such a situation, and got muddled without Uncle Heap to clear up my brain for me.

I am sure that the constant battering of the storm caused potential dangers to come closer as time passed but, after some sleepless days, I wore myself out with thoughts of wreckage and devastation and fell into a prophetic slumber. It was as though the storm had knocked me out with a violent bash to the head and, by the time I came back, there was a halted hush around me that I did not understand. All I knew was that it was time to unleash the power of Uncle Heap's knife's many appendages into the world of building (or reconstruction, as I assumed). And so I crawled, bruised, to my algae-stripped steps to investigate, the knife hot in my tunic pocket.

'Thought you'd have a nice sleep eh, sweet little girl,' Nursten greeted me with an air of utter normality as I peeped over, although he looked a bit haggard.

'I've just woken up, Nursten. How are you?' I replied blearily.

Nursten bent close to me and whispered, 'He's still screaming. It does me in.' And he bashed his fist weakly against the wall of his chest to knock out a small cough.

'Ah,' I whispered back, flicking my gaze toward Wort who was swaying in his usual work rhythm.

'Cho-co-late!' I whispered sweetly, just to try and take his mind off things. His eyes widened and he staggered off, dreamily.

Nursten's utter normality manifested everywhere, so I said nothing about the storm in case it wasn't and I'd just been dreaming. I made my familiar, bright 'Good morning Wort!' to Wort, then hurriedly took up my building position on the north corner of the west wall and began re-orientating myself to the building work amidst the blameless sky that presented itself around us.

Previous to the recent turbulent days, I had dared to suspect that I had become better than my builders at building. Whilst I worked in the same crude way that Wort had shown me, I believed I could make a somewhat nicer wall than either of them. I didn't mind this, or think much of it, but now I had become a creeping building rebel with secret knife plans bungling about between my head and my tunic pocket. This could be my moment of downfall or of exaltation. I hunched my back shiftily towards my builders and pulled out the magic tool for a preliminary assessment of its applications. The numerous sibling attachments glinted and whirred as I tried one then the other, and it was no time at all before I saw possibilities budding before me. Even before the sun slipped away that night, I had constructed a short, low section of wall that was of a stunning different quality to any other part of my dwelling. Whilst I bled no less to achieve it, I found that I could finish the stone in such a way as to tame the wild self-possession of the crystals and marry each rock with its neighbours so exactly as to imagine that the blood and spit really would hold it together indefinitely. Above all, what I cherished and felt jitteringly excited about was the look of it: trim and efficient, elegant and proud, impenetrable and enviable. This was the new me. I was more aware than ever that the rest of the building was a shambles, but I used this observation to convince myself that making the walls elegant was even more worthwhile from now on.

Of course I said nothing to Nursten or Wort. I harboured my pleasure and became, as I thought, gracefully detached whilst maintaining a chirpy familiarity. It was so blunderingly obvious that my work had a far superior polish to it than theirs that I did not want to point it out, but just to let it sit and speak for itself.

The next 'of course' was that they soon noticed it. It was Nursten who first stumbled across me and it, in gentle harmony together, with a knife-like interface working its whirring wonder. He had probably come to poke me or something, because he was having a good day, but was abruptly paused instead, looking down on me, mumbling and dripping. I gathered that his mumbling might have been something like, 'I swear by my auntie's twenty-seventh rib that I've never seen anything like that before,' after which words he gave up trying to talk and merely beckoned Wort vigorously to come and see for himself. I never knew he could mumble before, or that he had an auntie.

'The-the rock is her suh-suh-servant,' declared Wort immediately and bowed reverentially, baring his horrible teeth in a sickly grimace.

And this was exactly how it felt to me. Wort had said it like it was and spoke the truth, after which time they both regarded me with solemn respect. A kind of admiration lay on them like a spell.

From then on they were my audience and sat like two children with their chins cupped in their hands, staring at me during every building minute of the day when they were not serving me in some other fashion. I could barely get conversation out of them at these times because they were so spellbound by the flashing appendages, my clever judgement and the overall tessellation of the rock. As soon as I put Uncle Heap's knife away they were released to be the same Big and Silent they had been previously, and swung between their adopted states: roaring and whimpering or sobbing and screaming. It was hard work keeping up with their moods.

199

They heaved stone to the tops for me, but never did any building again. Despite this, the walls shot upwards with greater velocity than ever before. My builders turned out to be better heavers than they were builders. The smooth stone that I set looked like part of a finished house, while I rationalised that the rough walls below it could be seen to be a rough and lanky plinth to display the fine thing atop. I was able to take my marvellous, invigorating gulps higher and higher in odd moments, and my body made its usual 'woink!' sound as it thickened out. I think the air was very rich and I felt very rich too.

Strange things happened as well. In a small empty part of a building day, I once saw Nursten and Wort in close company having a quiet discussion after which Nursten clapped Wort on his back, Wort wavered then grimaced with his teeth and they both went back to their rock. Where this fitted into their roving moods and distant relationship I could not tell. I suspected that they had finally noticed the Wild Times and were wondering how to keep it secret from me that they now knew I had been right all along.

Overall, I felt optimistic. That the building work was proceeding so successfully was something I dwelt upon in most of the hours I was not building. The fact that its new found sophistication was due to my efforts and skills was a source of such solid pride that other (less pleasing) thoughts bounced of it and far away. I enjoyed my builders' admiration very much, and added (rightly or wrongly) to my list of achievements the lessening of Wort's attacks. He spent so much time transfixed by the lovely knife that he usually forgot his anger and, when his violent mood did surface, it did so for a shorter time from which he recovered faster, even if his eruption was no less extreme.

Nursten was brusque and radiant with energy most

of the time, and he seemed to shrug off the shock of Wort's outbursts better these days. He roared as he delivered the Granite to me for my day's building, and when he had dropped it he would beat his chest as an encouragement. I loved him so much for his energy and his thoughtfulness toward me. I did also catch him secretly weeping twice though, when Wort was nowhere to be seen. When I clapped eyes on his squatting figure it was plain as the sky that he was not all right because he never, but never sat down. So, even from a distance I could tell from his hunched back curled around his giant knees that something was wrong again. When I came close to him he looked crumpled and did his best to assert his usual charm for my benefit by feebly thudding both his fists against his concave chest and letting out an unconvincing phlegmy croak.

'See? Fine,' he gurgled.

He got up and turned away to go back below and continue with his rock heaving without saying or inviting another word. The next time I saw him upset I left him alone so that he would not have to hurry his tears. That would be a very sad thing, to not have enough time for your own sadness.

Chapter Twenty-Five: Gratitude and Leavings

The air rushed by very fast indeed almost every day up there and was bothersome because it would blow Uncle Heap and my voices away when we were trying to shout with one another. I don't know how much he heard of me, but from my perch our conversations went something like this:

'THE. KNIFE. IS. GREAT. UNCLE. HEAP.' I longed to tell him how much difference it had made.

'SH   .   .   T. . TH   . R   .' his reply would rush by my ears, too fast to decipher.

'WALLS. VERY. SAFE. THANKS. TO. KNIFE. UNCLE. HEAP.' I tried again.

'GO   .   . DIE.   . AKE.   . PR   .' came the next delivery to render me none the wiser.

'MUST. BUILD. UNCLE. HEAP. SPEAK. LATER.' I lied on both counts.

'   T. BE.   . L   .'

He looked frustrated and unwilling to give up trying to communicate at these times, but I gestured defeat with my arms and he always shuffled off eventually to fiddle with the latest decor additions to his flagpole or somesuch. He left me thoughtful about my fruit tree, which was the only wrinkly old thing in my whereabouts, so I sometimes went and peered over the edge of my wall just after these conversations to comfort myself about the sturdiness of old age and marvel at its twisted trunk that did not exactly grow any more, but rather crept into the air and held its territory out of mere habit, in a gnarly way.

After many blown-out chats with Uncle Heap I

judged that it was a safe time for me to shout some of the contempt I had felt for such a long time toward Menith. I brought the remaining bottle of her gifted red nail varnish to the top of the walls the next day to hold in my hand and sensually focus my scorn upon, and wasted no time in getting going when she appeared. I started up with an almighty two-fingered whistle. I was so eager, I knew that today I was a whistle warrior who could blow someone's ears out with two fingers and a little puff. I didn't let it bother me when she didn't seem to hear at all, and moved swiftly on to my next aural attack.

'MENITH!' I shouted out just as she settled into her nail-painting universe on the doorstep.

She caught the music of her own name and looked up at me, annoyed at the distraction, but said nothing and dipped again to her occupation. She would never have lived had it not been for Uncle Heap's ever faithful watch for the Wild Times, and there he was, still at it, while she painted sluggishly. I was so angry with her for her selfishness, and I shouted that out. And I was so angry with her for making me feel inadequate with my unpainted nails, and I shouted that out as well. I was disgusted with her lardy fatness, and that just began the beginning of a string of abuses that had been nomadic in my head for too long, poking everywhere they went with their pointedness.

'LOOK! LOOK!' I screamed, and with the widest arc my little arm could make I flung the last red bottle toward the deadly drop cliffs. It curved in a gentleness that was the antithesis of my gesture. I like to believe that it went right over the cliffs and, who knows, maybe even into the sea? I dared to envisage it, sinking into the blueness and all its fiery red being absorbed and quelled as I rose up above into the other blueness, the shining sky, smeared as I was with the other red. I shook with excitement over the emotion of it.

203

Meanwhile Menith herself was painting her nails in her doorstep universe. I never said that she exactly celebrated the painting of her nails, but there was an intensity in the importance she offered to this distraction that proposed to elevate nail painting to some imperative and defining act nonetheless. She was so occupied by this importance that I felt sure she would never be idle, not even on the most tedious foggy days of death. Always she would have her little glass bottles and brushes and rags and remover lotion tucked into a fold of her intimate life so that she could delve in there, busy herself and see nothing else. She was not happy, of course. I could not help myself, but I imagined her eating. It is sickening to imagine someone unhappy eating. The slurps and slops and sounds of being in doubt as to whether to be alive or not; the leaden plate populated by morsels of misery. She finished her coat of varnish and went inside, probably to eat and swell her sad lardiness yet more. She never acknowledged me at all as she left my sight, but what also left me as she went indoors were my ugly feelings for her, so I was very grateful.

Gratitude and leavings got mixed up with the story of my builders and me the next day too, strangely. Gratitude was ever present between us, even if it had to lurk occasionally, but the leaving thing was new.

I had got up particularly early and, as I lurched up my Granite steps, it was largely by feel, because the first light from the sun had not much appeared. By this point in building history it took a good while to reach the tops of the walls, maybe four floors were completed, and not skinny ones either, so by the time I reached the summit there was a glow of a suggestion of the east when I looked around for the new day. The first thing that caught my eye was those lovely, luminous discs and streaks, lights of the breathing sky. They flamed up in the swampy green and orange of dawn, cold and warm together, giving doubt and hope for the day. They held me in trance and I did not resist, knowing that the sun was coming and they were leaving soon. But their leaving in the first of the sun was eclipsed by another leaving that I suddenly noticed. I had not even thought to think about Nursten and Wort because they were so always there that there was nothing to think. The two figures, one tall and massive, the other skinny and swaying, were walking away from my safe safe house toward the east, heading for the halfway tree and who knows where beyond. I gasped the same sharp, cold intake of breath through my mouth that means shock that I had heard myself make at other shocking moments, and thereafter did not breath for a long time. My breath let itself back out of my chest without my asking and I mouthed, 'Good morning Nursten!' and 'Good morning Wort!' with little appetite.

Nursten heard me despite the lack of sound and turned his face up, smiled once and waved his big paw.

'Chocolate?' I silently suggested.

I'd never really seen his teeth before and wondered if the smile was to himself, for my work, or simply at the joy of departure. He took his attention back down to himself and began chatting with Wort in that close way that I'd seen once before. It all looked so innocent and normal, but my heart was popping. Then Nursten took both his great, bloody hands and shoved Wort so as to make him stumble. My breath came into me again and this time I felt my face contort like contours in a mountainous land, my eyes lakes filling, and all the weakness of me stumbled with Wort. But Wort was more than I imagined, yet again. He recovered himself, made an exaggeratedly fake stumble back toward his building partner, shoved him in return, then picked himself up in a springy run and skipped away, laughing out loud through his grotty teeth. I could almost smell

205

his rank breath from where I sat. Nursten lumbered after him, roaring, and Wort feigned fear, dodged this way and that. They were reborn children, released from the tyranny of the heavy work they had lugged for me all these years, both of them, chasing their laughter, their friendship and their freedom across the fields.

Behind them rode a weightless trail of wobbling air. I scrunched my eyes and shook a dash of colours from my own fingertips, wondering what the three of us were together. But no more wobble would come after that first shake or two, no more rainbow colours and, above all, no more Big and no more Silent. I wasn't to know it for sure immediately, but this was the last time I would see them. After I had suffered and enjoyed and got used to the fact that Silent had become noisy and Big had become crumpled and pathetic from time to time, that kindness could come in many forms, that niceness is never exclusive, and wouldn't be nice if it was, and that people remain the same even when they change, they left. They truly were gone.

The tidal volume of air passing through my lungs diminished considerably as I went through possible reasons why they had left. I sat down on the whooshing top of my smoothly finished and excellent wall and slumped with my feet dangling into the vacuous space that now fell between me and my builders. I was safe, but I wished that the dawn had never come. I felt that the stars that were fleeing the sky in the new day were deserting the heavens forever, sensed that the day's altitudinous winds were not rich for nourishing me, but there to scour and erode. Maybe Ervil Nitzo had sent orders through Toobit Lonkins to leave such an impudent and ungrateful girl as me alone where she could heave her own rock and solve her own constructional problems (reminding them that he was an architect of note and standing). Seeing that she has the audacity to participate in the building herself, let her do it, as alone as anyone ever before her. Let her invent building from nothing if that is how she chooses it. Let her.

But how could dear Nursten and dear Wort fall under the spell of such nonsenses? Maybe their brush with the Wild Times was simply finished and they had other things to attend to. I had no other thought, and busied myself flicking my knife's many arms in and out and watching them shine in the rising sun. After an enormous, windy silence when the rain threatened again, the figures of my two builders were no longer visible, and a thick, broad, high curtain of time and light, as big as the biggest sky, dropped between me and them. That day I truly felt the safety of my safe safe house: Granite fearfulness and vertical unscaleability. How distant everything was from me, how impossible.

Chapter Twenty-Six: Alone with a Knife

When a whole day had passed and I emerged on top of my walls in another new morning to still find no Nursten and no Wort I knew that things were different. It had been threatening to become another precarious moment, and then it did.

There was a normal wind and a normal light rain, so I sat down in them and let my precarious hours scald through me, hoping that their passing would be fast. I could feel the muscles around my veins spasm and each branch in my stressed arteries kick with the brutish pulse of my new hardship. My breathing came in gasps between a stillness which could have lasted longer, and longer, and forever, but my damp lungs were inside me but outside of my control, a force unto themselves, and they made subversive preparations for each mutinous gasp without my consent. My neck broke, flopping my head, too full of thoughts, down to my chest. Fluid pooled and swelled in my feet and legs and hands and arms that weighed as much as all the stone I had ever seen, and no limb could be moved.

Sitting down was the right thing to do, because only two days later the scalding precariousness started to abate and I started to move again, although my movements were slight and crunchy at first. I soon sat steaming in a fresher and lighter despondency, fingering my beautifully crafted stones around me and detesting each facet of each crystal in minute detail, wanting to reject it all, willing it to melt and ruin and leave me cleansed and impoverished and relieved of the burden of hope or plans or future. At last, those strong new feelings told me that my energy was back. I was grumpy at having to conform to this new despondency of course, but it would not shift. Not only that, but the layers of dried blood and building dust that I had collected on me (as a result of what I had formerly thought to be my noble activity) seemed to be petrifying and shrinking around me, demanding my conformity to a new, smaller shape. I decided to try eating something as a counterrevolutionary act against the despotism of despondency and petrified squeezing, and promptly set off looking for some leaves, learning again to walk.

Eating is usually a good thing, but on this occasion it was not as successful as you might have imagined. I popped in one or two leaves and chewed with a sense of unfamiliarity to get them to sink down to my innards. There they sat, a stale green pool in my belly. Fog-bound images came to me of all the family histories Uncle Heap had told about the stagnant pools, back in the days of the bogs, that would never let a thing out once it had sunk into the murky sludge, and where things and people disappeared mysteriously. So my greens felt: locked in my stomach, locked in history, and me locked in there with them.

I lacked any decisiveness to pull myself out. The bog waters began to rise in my stomach and all those historical thoughts were swimming, floating, sinking, bubbling up again for another foul belch. Basically I could not help but think of mother again. It was not as doom-doom-y as before but there was definitely a reverberating 'you're doomed' tracking hectically inside my head. I began to obsess about her, her every possible thought or move, just as I had done with my distant neighbours recently. The only difference was that I could hardly imagine her having a thought, and she never moved; not even in my imagination could I get her to move. She appeared to me in my dreams. Several times she wafted in like a black ghost come to cremate the insides of my dim and shady head. In the dream she was looking towards me, not seeing me any more than she had ever done, but it was rather disconcerting all the same. The understory of my dream foretold that if I failed to acknowledge her she might stake a new territorial claim and come to inhabit the space inside my eyelids. I never saw exactly what the consequences of her habitation might be like, but the mood of the suggestion was enough to make clear that it was not a desirable option. I could be thankful that at least I did not have to sleep all the time.

In spite of being worn down by all this, I mustered all the tenacity that had ever been instilled in me by Uncle Heap and started fiddling with my building knife once more. I flicked it, in out, this bit that bit, all so shiny and not tarnished by my mood in the slightest, suggesting the odd bit of Granite to it but not really making the absolute connection.

'THEY. LEFT. UNCLE. HEAP.' I declared bluntly one day when I saw him, but he only looked confused. 'MY. BUILDERS. HAVE. GONE. I. AM. HERE. WITH. JUST. YOUR. KNIFE. AND. THE. GRANITE. UNCLE. HEAP.' I elaborated.

He made a hugely procrastinacious pause then shouted, 'WELL.' in a way that connected the old and the new Uncle Heap for a split second in my heart.

'THEY. LEFT. ME. UNCLE. HEAP. BUT. I. HAVE. THE. KNIFE. AND. LOTS. OF. STONE.' I reiterated.

'WELL.' he stalled again, 'AT. LEAST. YOU. ARE. NOT. ALONE.'

I hadn't thought of it that way before. 'YES. THANK. YOU. UNCLE. HEAP.' And we left it at that and I got on with the building.

Now that I had to carry my own rock up from the dark and gloomy depths below, things were not as fast, but I gained confidence rather quickly in working alone, as happens whenever some imperative comes along. I also improved the quality of my Granite nimbleness until there was a seamless flow of pure art that rose from the tops of my walls. I bled and spat and married the stones in perfection and cursed the Wild Times with venom and felt bigger against them each day. I took the odd gulp to thicken the blood I lost and the blood I retained, and my hair swooshed around my crispy cheeks as the air screamed around my safe safe house. The passing of time lifted the days out of blackness and into a world which merely resembled the murky depths of a bog pool instead. That period was not too bad when I look back, all considered.

The building work had taken its toll on my limited garments over the years. Both my tunics had looked crumbly for a long time already, due to such blood and Granite punishment. So, I willingly took a break from stone lugging and setting for a brief time, and dragged my stolen length of cloth and sewing things to the tops of my walls for some tunic making. I made three. Two were to serve me in the same way as those that had come before, but the third I made in a spirit of commitment to the success of my hopes and I vowed to save it until such time as my safe safe house was safe and all bloody Granite work was at an end. I pictured myself wearing it, but didn't try it on, not yet.

I also had a lot of contact with Great Uncle Lollo during this recovery phase. We never conversed, but I often made noises and shouted words for him to conduct and he conducted me into making more noises and words with his graceful hands. I wondered how his heart and his breathing dealt with the continuous, rhythmic hesitation that seized his whole body when he was in full conducting flow. He worked more and more and seemed to live an intense existence with his music, which rivalled the intensity of Menith with her nail varnish. (Although this is an unfair comparison because Great Uncle Lollo's art was an awesome gift.) He was very active with the birds, who flocked to him and his musical enterprise. Together they reached towards a poetry of sound, somehow explaining the unexplainable in a wordless eloquence that, obviously, I cannot describe in words. His ever faithful friend Toobit Lonkins hopped over to be at his side often and was duly acknowledged with what I gathered were a series of happy nya, nya's. I felt Toobit was staring out from his louse-chewed plumage at all the fit young birds that Great Uncle Lollo gathered around him and trying to absorb a revitalising force from them much like I gathered from my wall-top deep breathing sessions. I saw him coughing once or twice and imagined his scabby eyes pressing to leave his skull under the punishment of those rough splutters. I hoped I would not have much need of him in the future.

So, variously entertaining myself and being entertained, I tinkered on. I felt rather alone some of the time despite Uncle Heap's helpful words and Great Uncle Lollo's musical explanations of all the difficult things. When I went down into the shady bowels of my safe safe house I felt myself in a vacuous space. I was afraid to utter a sound there lest I accidentally voiced some turbid thought that an echo might repeat back to me, sending me into an ever spiralling descent to further turbidity. At the bottom of that murky pool (that I had been elevated into out of blackness) I had a clammy feeling when I forgot what I was looking for, and the clamminess brought on visions of the suddenness of Hanuk's fall and the timeless beginning of mother's inertia (amongst other unchangeable things).

I did not forget Nursten and Wort, but my memory of them changed from season to season. During the first bleakness I thought of how feeble I had been and how they had helped me in that respect. I felt grateful and a little sad and snivelly, especially when it was very cold. Then, during the brief transition period to the season of unbearable heat, I could not help but let my thoughts constantly fall on images of their hands. I suppose this was the season when I had first really looked at their hands without shyness about my curiosity. Their hands were so much bigger than mine, even Wort's, and seeing them soaked in the colour of rage, of sadness, and perhaps even of desperation, was very different to what I had imagined when I had first seen my builders dressed in blood from a distance. I tried to pull my attention away from such images by looking out across the vast lands and the infinite ocean around me and by building my clever, perfect walls that I was sure were for safe safety, mine, but this was only useful up to a certain point. I could not help but be often distracted from my intense looking and at these times dwell on my own hands before my face, smeared as they were in exactly the same colour. I asked myself why we should bleed so and turned the question around without ever finding even the beginning of a path leading to a possible answer. I thought I found another possible question which might be the answer, but it was too large to fit into my world, something like: Why am I here? I quickly understood that consideration of such things with a brain was invented for those mystery people who lived outside the Wild Times, so I began to shout some sound approximation of the meaning of what these questions might be all about to Great Uncle Lollo so that he might conduct them. He worked his usual magic and with so many sweeps of his untutored arms he took up my strained tone, smoothed it, stroked it into a sleepy, forgetful place and pretty soon I no longer fretted that I could not answer questions about bloody desperation or existence or other suchlike things.

Chapter Twenty-Seven: I Learn About Normality

Thus things went on: the air came and went rather quickly, Uncle Heap growled loudly, my perfect walls swelled in their upright pride, an ocean of bad moods was displayed in blue to the west, a swarm of the soft-winged insects engulfed my old house once, and so on. The figure of the fearless woman in the suction clothes passed close by just as usual. She was obviously taking note of my circumstances and had, no doubt, noticed that my builders were no longer to be seen. I had grown rather tired of trying to mutate my ambushes to render them effective, so I resigned myself to the fact that she would be hanging around my walls showing off her nasal hair. I was doing just that (being resigned) one day as she was nosily close by, when something altogether surprising happened: she spoke to me. Not only that, but she spoke to me as if I was there, a person to be spoken to, someone likely to answer, approachable and, above all, normal.

'Hello there!' she called up to me.

She had an exceedingly high pitched voice which I found rather startling and my first instinct was to wonder if the condition was due to the pinching nature of her waisted jacket and her paint-on trousers. I looked around me as though she might have been beckoning something else, but there was no hiding my presence, so I simply stared back at her hoping this would do the trick.

'Ah hello! You're building then,' I think she said as she squeaked on.

I heard now that not only was her pitch altitudinous but her accent was most odd and seemed to distort each word in an attempt to disguise it as something else and make it more enigmatic. I thought this was rather silly so I just continued to stare, but she did not give up. Maybe, for her, someone staring at her amounted to much the same as an invitation to conversation.

'I've seen you here a good lot when I've been going by on my way,' was the next bit, or something like.

I was getting fed up and wanted her to go on her way directly, so I growled softly and said, 'What?' in a rather aggressive and rolling way. It was the wrong thing to say, because in her language this meant that I was interested.

'Oh!' she exclaimed, 'I go by this way a fair bit because I just live over the hill,' she waved her arm in that over-the-hill direction, 'and it's a good old walk here, nice views and that.'

In this way, she confirmed in one sentence that I had formerly been correct: she was mad. Nice views? A good old walk? Honestly, where did she think she was? I was now staring at her for a different reason: just sheer incredulity at her very oddness. I also confirmed from these new close quarters that her face did, indeed, seem deformed by the prospect of death, which equally could have been put down to her constricting garments. All around her eyes was a deep black (which could only come from severe illness I concluded), and her lips were an exaggerated colour of pink as though all her blood flowed there at a great pace. She did talk a lot, so I reasoned that maybe she needed a lot of blood around her mouth.

'My name is Clare by the way.' Her imperturbability was already beginning to perturb me when she declared this, her most peculiar name, and thus exaggerated her own oddness another tenfold in my head. 'What's yours?'

I flinched and replied, 'Clare?' cautiously.

'Yes, my name's Clare, what's yours love?'

This wasn't going to be easy. I did know what my name was, but that knowledge was remembered from a very long time ago and I had only the vaguest memory of such a cruelly identifying word ever being spoken out loud, and it certainly wasn't by me. Somehow, to be called by name was much the same as being blamed for everything, including Hanuk's fall and mother's inertia. I felt unsure if my mouth could form the sounds required to utter this disturbing word, and I asked myself why it would want to for this Clare woman with breasts and a squeaky voice anyway.

'M-muh-muh-muh,' I tried.

'Beg your pardon love?

'M-muh-moo-m-m.' I cursed Wort for his affliction.

'Sorry love, can't make it out. Starts with an M, right?'

'Clare?' I ventured with little hope.

'Yes, I'm Clare. Your name is...' She was not in a hurry.

'My name is, is, is Muh-muh-moo-muh-moot,' I managed, feeling rather exhausted by this small and brief effort.

'Maud? Is that right?'

'No!' I moodily expressed my effrontery all I could in one syllable, feeling another growl pushing up behind it. 'My nuh-name is Muh!-moo!-moo!-moot!'

'Sorry love,' she shrilled a patient shrill, 'think you have to spell it for me, a letter at a time. Can you do that?'

I was getting irritated, and I could not be sure if it was because of her or because of me.

'M,' I began, 'then O,' I continued, 'then another O,' I shouted slowly as if speaking with Uncle Heap far, far away, 'ending with a T,' I finished up, finished.

'M-O-O-T.' She spelled it through fast to herself,

like that, and shook her head at the same time. 'Moot. Moot? A very unusual name love, where's that from then?' She seemed to be trying to kill me with questions and insistence.

'You're the one with the funny nuh-name!' I boldly stuttered. This time the growl did emerge slightly afterwards and through it I could feel that my throat was becoming hoarse and dry and not wanting to talk anymore and closing and clamping in protest at all the answers I had given.

'Oo, common enough hereabouts, Clare is,' she gave what I thought was a nervous laugh. 'Lots of folk called Clare, here, up country, further up country, lots. Folk often get it wrong, call me Helen, some reason, don't know.'

She talked in a kind of code that meant I had to listen severely in order to comprehend. Whilst also battling with the suppression of my growl, this was most energy consuming but, through some mystery, I managed it. What I understood made my brain go all stiff with thought: understanding her words did not seem to amount to understanding her at all. She talked as though the far Wild Times-less world and its many inhabitants were in her sphere, and she said it all so casually. This could only mean that some sort of safe, Wildness-free living was within a short walking distance. But then again, where were the Wild Times in her life as she came close to me, walking? She seemed unaffected, which begged the question, did the Wild Times belong to a place or, frighteningly, did they belong to us, wherever we were? Maybe the dark and murky cloud of turbulent Wild Times hung over only those few who deserved it, or needed it maybe, or inherited it even. If she brushed with such a large populace then she must represent a kind of safe majority that I, in my puny life, did not. I was alert as I stared at her.

For her part, Clare's attention was deflected momentarily by a large yawn which she captured in the cup of her hand then used to smooth out her jacket before she continued, 'Tall one you're building there.'

Was she interested or was the laziness I heard in her voice disdain? Despite my plummeting downward view of her, my feeling was that she looked down on me from another kind of height. Perhaps the view of her nasal hair enhanced this sense of belittlement.

'Yes,' I nodded, 'it ascends very high, my Granite house. It's very safe you know,' I asserted, searching for my pride and trying to ignore the shoddy mostpart of my house that spread out between me and her.

'Anyway, nice to meet you Moot. Got to go. Things to do. You know how it is.'

'Yes, things to do, yes, of course, always things to do,' I wondered if she was building too and maybe that's why she was so keen to look at my safe safe house.

The ordeal was over and that's how she ended it. But, for a long time she called round on me tiringly often which I hated and loved, one or the other, and sometimes both at the same time. Whilst I still needed every hour of the day for building, thinking, bleeding, shouting and looking, along she would come with questions and topics that demanded so much of me that they wore out my day. She wanted to know the oddest things.

'What's your star sign then Moot?' she asked one day.

I said that I liked the bucket best, but my answer did not satisfy her. What she really wanted to know, she said, was which stars I was born under. 'All of them were there I expect,' I honestly replied, which fared no better than my previous response and she moved quickly on to declare that she saw me as 'rather watery' which I did not take as a compliment.

'Is that club with spikes for some special kind of

building job?' was another one.

I told her what my excellent spiked club was for and illustrated my answer with a normal bloody tale of keeping the Wild Times back. She was quiet and still the whole time I spoke, almost as though she had stopped breathing. There was a long pause afterwards and I didn't know what to think until she calmed the turbulent hush by stating that her neighbour had hedgehogs, which sounded similar.

'Where are your family then?' and other domestic questions were favourites of hers as well. At first I told her everything that came to my mind but I realised that it took too much time so instead I did my best to make general answers like, 'Dead mostly,' or 'Pets don't usually last long,' or 'Just the usual', trying to be casual from within my confusion and distraction and hoping not to inspire follow-up questions or I'd never get building work done again.

One of the early things she enlightened me about was chocolate. I still have not sampled chocolate myself but I know what it is and just how dangerous it can be in the wrong hands.

'Oo, it's lovely,' she squealed, 'I'd kill for my favourite dark chocky.'

That's what she called it after a bit: 'chocky'. It sounded friendly, but I could tell that she was one of the people with the wrong hands.

'Holidays, birthdays... my chockies make them worth waiting for.'

'Yes, chockies...' I would affirm and feel squirmy and a bit concerned.

It took me a long time to grasp that I could ask questions back, but even after this realisation I was not quick enough to think of any questions to ask her. I came up with a cunning plan to potentially unsettle her: ask her own questions in return. In practice this did not work from my point of view because she always found the questions very simple and, worse still, gave answers that I could not comprehend. What I could deduce from all these bouncing questions was that I had been wrong: she was not looking down on me from the great below but instead it was me who was looking down on me, which was even more complicated to get to grips with spatially.

There were occasionally normal things which she mentioned like her sister's children and how old they were, the cold days getting colder as it got wetter in the bleak times, her husband's death in an accident that tore his leg off, sleeping and dreaming, that kind of thing, but these were heavily outweighed by the things I could not imagine, like towns filled with people, many of whom were wheeled around rather than walked, people who came to get food and other necessary things that they could not get at home for some reason. Not to mention, she talked of festivities, of bunting and lights, music, dancing and laughter, whose necessity I failed to grasp.

'Anyway.'

This meant 'stop talking and listen' in her language, so I stopped and accepted that I was nothing to do with anything at all apart from listening.

'Anyway,' she repeated when I stopped, 'if you like romance-thriller things there's this show on telly on Fridays which co-stars Johnny.'

Romance? Thriller? Show? Telly? Co-stars? Johnny? I had no idea.

'I get my knitting out and do a bit while I'm watching. It couldn't be better.' And she went on to describe something that sounded like a contrived kind of knot-making exercise which I discerned could be perhaps useful.

'Almost as good as chocolate,' she concluded, and then she went all distracted until the rain started.

I think she liked books because, when we talked about building (her idea), she showed so much interest in all the how's and why's and other details about my physical plan of work that she could not express the size of her impression in any way other than to suggest that I write a book about it. I had, of course, seen a book before, and found the connection she had made a most unlikely conclusion to draw. However, her surprising and flattering comment probably made more of an impression on me than any single sentence ever had done before, and thus I have written the story of my house-building at her suggestion (but without her knowledge, obviously). Her meandering words about chapters and digressions and authors caused me a second (secret) decision: to go off my topic a bit in my book writing endeavour and write my chapter about Granite, as well as arrange my book into helpful chapters. I don't know what she would have thought because she seemed to think I was a builder and I don't think I ever discouraged her in that idea. So, the Granite chapter was my second big rebellion from Clare, even greater than the first. I feel that she probably saw a building book as being more strictly informative, and perhaps even instructive, but I know that the story is the most important when it comes to getting a project right, so I went about writing my book in my own way with all the critical narrative information to hopefully inspire the ability to build in any person who may come to read it. I have, after all, built a house and she had not, to the best of my knowledge.

Through Clare I felt I was becoming modern, civilised, someone: concepts that were nowhere near the realms of even imagination or dissatisfaction in my life before leaving my former home and becoming a builder. She swiftly became my angel of normality, my teller of veracity, my guide toward integration of all concepts in one place, my source. I was amazed at myself and got swept away alternately by waves of optimism and tempests of doubt. It was hugely exhausting trying to be someone, whilst at the same time I had so much bloody building work to do and lived alone and had to carry my own stone and pick my own leaves.

Apart from the literary ones, there were other secrets I kept from Clare. She never asked about any of them in a very exact way, so I didn't tell her, exactly. Here is a list of all the secrets together that I can remember, although I'm sure there were many more:

1. Writing my book
2. Chapters
3. The Granite digression
4. My love for Curlywurly, the fruits from my tree and Uncle Heap
5. The story about Nitzo Pits-oh letting me down
6. Mother's wordlessness
7. Great Uncle Lollo's tether
8. My other name
9. My building knife's full suite of appendages
10. Where the nail varnish had gone
11. My twitching nugget
12. Mother's curse
13. The flying postman's real state of health

Basically, after I got over my dangerous tell-all phase, I eventually learned to act as though everything was low-key and meaningless in my life and always had been so. In this way I hoped to deflect any probing which might lead to the discovery of something which might not be quite right in Clare's eyes. These not-quite-right-in-Clare's-eyes things could be absolutely anything as far as I could tell, so the less I said the better. Instead I hung on her every word. At some point I just started saying 'yes' and nodding a lot, but this became more sophisticated as I did my best to mimic her voice and her way of thinking to train the conversation along.

'Ok, later love,' she would squeak her goodbye and give her nervous laugh again.

'Yes, later love,' I would reply and wave my bloody hand at her departing face, hoping she would not die before I had learned everything I needed to.

Chapter Twenty-Eight: The Absorption of Doom

However gruelling Clare's visits were, in between times my spirits started to climb because of them and perhaps even levitate occasionally. Without my builders to witness my efforts and hardships, things had seemed to be pointlessly aimed at me and only me and my own furtherment, but now that Clare showed an interest in the stars I was born under and my Granitic progress, I had context, meaning and direction again, floating as I was. The sky was also very kind to me for a long number of days and weeks together. I got all the rush of beautiful, nourishing air and the thrill of my head being up in the light clouds, spinning, without anything horrible to put up with. It drizzled a few times, but the darkness and gloop that surrounded the neighbouring hills to the east and ate up the little homes over there never came around my safe safe house at all. The don't-care-won't-care kind of fatigue I learned from Clare was a shield to the droopy side of existence that might have otherwise got me down.

Something in that conspiracy between Clare and the sky gave me my long lost building sparkle back. I no longer tinkered, but was struck by a spangling frenetic energy that ran through me like a sharp stick runs through a soft belly. Strenuous gossiping with Clare followed by all those compulsive hours of arduous rock frenzy left me too tired to think. I crawled into cardboard corner each night with just enough spangle left to wonder what Clare might be dreaming about before I dropped off to sleep to try and answer the question. My thin arms ran with thick blood and became hard and tetchy, even when I was exhausted and sleepy.

224

I had to work. I couldn't stop myself. My walls grew at a vertiginous rate, each stone perfectly hewn by my clever building knife. The faces of the rocks that I placed were so finely made that even the sliming algae could not get hold and the very water from the sky formed a solid sheet over it like a varnish. Thus the blocks remained pristine in their crystalline uprightness and my heart swelled and my saliva flowed and all my terrible feelings that cruelly ruled me were squeezed through the tiny hole that was this contrived and controlled task and it all came out very concentrated, pure, intense.

I asked no questions of myself and worked ever on to a higher perfection. The intensity pushed away a niggarting knowledge, but sometimes it poked through my tiredness to remind me that I had no idea what I was doing. Without Ervil Nitzo's professional proposals my plans were just a silly girl's invention. In fact, I had little in the way of a plan to be honest. It was simple: I continued upwards. Upwards is upwards I would always think, and upwards is better and higher than downwards or horizontalwards. At least Nitzo Pits-oh was not there to see it and laugh at me, I reassured myself.

I was glad of the continuity of the upness and sameness of the building work, despite its lack of direction, because nothing else in my life ever seemed to stay the same for long. Phases, it was always phases of this or phases of that, running into one another or stop-shifting with surprises.

In my next phase that all this high and smooth talk is leading to, I became like a Granite building myself: unbreakable and unmoveable. I say this because the doom still persecuted me, but now I was rock against it. Now I could consider the 'doom-doom, you're doomed' of mother's curse from a rock-like position where it could not necessarily harm me. I saw the doom itself more clearly than ever, like a spear probing one ear and hoping to find the second, its tip a cold sharpness that burst and spilled pockets of rotting thoughts that would infect anything clean.   Discontent with ears, it probed elsewhere, torturing any softness or orifice which opened to the world.   The drips from its point voiced themselves loudly in a steady 'doom-doom, doom-doom, doom-doom, doom-doom, doom-doom, doom-doom' like a pulse. But the only blood I bled was for my Granite.

Mother haunted my dreams again but my Granitic qualities were fit against even this. I willed myself to stone at night and when she appeared, inanimate, I held off her ugliness with an igneous resistance. When she opened her mouth, a thousand foul smelling insects swarmed out in search of some morsel to satisfy her blunt need to poison, to commit to putrefaction. They took flight from her dry tongue and she never blinked. Behind them came a hundred slavering dogs with black, fat teats on their undersides weeping puss as they too jumped from her desertous mouth. The teat-puss filled mother's lap and ran from her knees to the floor and started to cover the floor. I awoke before the flood and the drowning but my dream told me that they were coming. Mother had such a need to destroy.

It was great. All the energy she sought to sap from me, and even the withering curse itself fed me, and I grew harder and stronger and tougher and safer. And as my crystal facets twinkled I felt my counter-curse rising up in me. It was big, dynamic, loud, and more pointed than her stick.

'YOU'RE DOOMED MOTHER!' I yelled.

There was no other place to make my violent delivery than the edge of the precipice on my eastern wall. From here I could gasp the up-draughts, see the inert figure sitting in the window of my old home and nearly plunge to my death, all at the same time. I went right to the very edge of the edge and let myself sway there, as tall and as tetchy hard as I was, and I screamed.

'YOU'RE DOOMED, DOOMED, DOOMED, DOOMED, DOOMED, DOOMED MOTHER!' My voice went all rage-y and it panicked to get out of me and the words started to not come out right because there was too much scream to make coherence possible. 'YOU! YOU! YOU! IT'S YOUR DOOM! YOU'RE DOOMED MOTHER! YES, DOOMED!'

It was a simple enough message but I simply could not seem to get it across sufficiently and it kept torrenting out of me without getting any clearer. The deluge of hysteria and words came from my mouth, just as the insects and the teaty dogs had come from mother's mouth in the dreams when she visited me. And far from being a hundred or a thousand in number, my words and my hysteria would not stop.

'DOOM, DOOM, DOOM, YOU, YOU, YOU MOTHER! YOUR DOOM!'

And she sat as immobile as I had ever seen her, there at the window. I tore at my thickened hair and spat into the open void between me and the far down world. I roared and beat my fists on my bony chest. My hands bled more freely than they ever did when I was building, and the drops and drips of it flew through the air in slow motion when I frenzied my arms around me as though I needed to clean the sky back to its bones. It was wonderful. I was stormed by a glee whose deliciousness escalated with its wickedness. I was uncontrollable and felt like free, clean Granite, beautifully finished and perfectly safe, avalanching into existence.

I was not too aware of anything apart from this lovely rage in me, but I can tell you that afterwards I was very tired. I was so tired that I struggled to get back down to cardboard corner and I lay there in a febrile state for two days before feeling any semblance of recovery. It didn't stop there though. It was like a compulsion, and I was even drawn away from my careful building work for a period of time most days to counter-curse from the east wall. It was never as intense as that first time, but still I could not get to the bottom of it. In my wilting, post-rage condition I saw Uncle Heap standing mute and confused. He never tried to speak to me at these times. I saw Great Uncle Lollo stop in his conducting, unable to find any means to contact my mood. He would wait until it was over then return to his birds. I saw Menith staring at me for minutes together with her swiftly drying brush held in the air. She eventually noticed the bristly stiffness, and I saw her mouthed infuriation before she stomped gracelessly indoors. I was obsessive and could not help myself but scream, 'YOU'RE DOOMED! DOOMED MOTHER! YOUR DOOM! DOOM, DOOM, DOOM!' I was angry and I cried and my hair suffered. I still bled a lot and my saliva came the same.

All this, and building, and occasional visits from Clare, and I was living at such a pitch that I was getting hard enough to crack, to shatter like Granite could not. I was aging rapidly, crumbling with overuse and I could not help but feel exhilarated by this release that punished me so.

Clare heard me once. I know she did, but she never mentioned it, so I know that my screaming was one of those not-quite-right-in-Clare's-eyes things. I still could not help but do it.

After so long of this, I awoke tired as usual one morning and clambered to the tops of my walls for more compulsive behaviour (building or screaming I was not sure at the time, as I had not been compelled more one way than the other yet). I surveyed the environs swiftly to take in the nature of the day and peruse the dangers that others seemed to be facing that I was not. Taking in a deep breath on the east wall I glanced over to mother's window and, lo and behold, she was not there. Now this was something that stopped me. Obviously I had been wishing her doom for some time, but I was well aware that the vat of doom I still had left to wish upon her was very deep and broad indeed and surely such a relatively paltry amount of doom as I had already visited on her could not have had any marked effect.

She was gone, more gone and more absent than ever before. I waited, my raging paused and tense, flickering blood into space from my jittery fingers. There was a big nothingness. I wondered if her camouflage had become so good that now I could see right through her. I longed for Uncle Heap to appear so that I could talk to him, step into the safety of his heart and out of all this rage and now this confusion, if he would let me. He did not appear.

I went back to tinkering on my walls. My tension was high, so I moved some bits of rock to dissipate it, finished and placed some stones to tame it. I went through the recent past in my mind. When had I last seen her definitely? My head went as soft as my anxiety went hard.

Later in the day when I went to sit down behind the half-made wall, I was in a state of exhaustion from the tension. While I was sitting there something happened very quickly (considering what it was), because by the time I stood up again it was nearly over and I don't think I was sitting there for so long. There was a kind of crispy coldness that day which allows you to see very well at a distance, even with the bleary vision of an exhausted builder. The sharpness of all this vision around me was tiring me even further, so I admit that I probably did shut my eyelids down for a moment at least in the hope of respite from all this energy pouring out of me that I could scarcely support. Time slips of course when you are tired, but it just wasn't that slippery on that occasion I'm fairly sure.

When I opened my eyes, still looking for a solution to the missing doomed parent, there was Uncle Heap, just putting the last Granite rocks on top of a big pile ten paces from the house. The pile was about six feet long and one person wide. I realised what must have happened now and ground my teeth for a half a minute considering the meaning of it in general and some of the side-points. I wondered if the dreams I had had foretold that she would die of the black vomit, or maybe drowning. Maybe she drowned in the nostalgic waste that circled her, prowling and stalking her as she sat in her immobility. Maybe the eternalised pain had been magnified after so much solitude, purified by contemplation. Maybe she had burned in her own bitterness. I could not say. What was clear was that her dry heart of running sand would beat no more and the doom had been absorbed and would no longer be my questionable, questioning visitor. I knew definitely, once and for all, that I had been right in the beginning: it was her and not me who was doomed. That was a relief.

'Mother, it seems you were doomed,' I muttered under my breath. 'Ha!'

My howling rage mutated into a muttering triumph which spilled from me effortlessly as I got on with ever-upping my Granite safety towards the loftiest spaces imaginable. I worked intensely again, chatted with Clare, shouted with Uncle Heap, was conducted by Great Uncle Lollo and all of my usual life was restored in one moment. The day to dayness of things was often peppered by the run-off from the absorption of doom event, of course. A nasty spell had been broken, and the aforementioned steady stream of muttering flowed from me in tones that I can only describe as something close to abuse of a dead person (if you can abuse a dead person). It was a quiet and productive time. I felt so much better and nothing and nobody commented or tried to stop me or change me or threaten me in anything I did or was and mother's window remained as empty as any hopeless hope I had ever entertained.

Chapter Twenty-Nine: The Big Dipper

Time never slowed down, however much I muttered. It raced as fast onwards as my walls raced upwards and with just as much energy. It dragged with it trailing clouds, lonely pollen from the brave flowers, mucky smells from the duplicitous yellow scrub, memories of Wild Times encounters, slicing cold and the quickening pulse of my world. It sucked the blood from my hands and spread it with my sticky saliva over all the surfaces of the needy Granite, a thin layer that could only be translated as my real and not hopeless hope, my investment against further despondency. It scattered my childish years and drew the semblance of age on my hard-worked hands as it hurried past and forgot to ever come back to erase the scars. It wafted notions of the future past me in such haste that I could not read them as they went by and I puzzled at the script with feeble eyes.

Over the course of Clare's visits, she showed me ever more clearly that, as well as being a fountain of knowledge, she was also someone who was prone to moods and who suffered failures but for whom everything was always the same anyway. She lived in a flatness of continuity where no thing seemed to distinguish itself from the other things. Her deathly face showed some animation when I paid my respects to her worldliness by expressing great interest in her perception of life, but exuded her moroseness through the same terminal visage. This was all most interesting. Although things had not always been lovely for me I could almost see that I had something she did not. My words and my actions did not fall into a similar vacuum because it was imperative that they mean something because I needed to survive. My inner Granite qualities held me secure when I was shocked to finally understand this difference, and I wondered cautiously and at great length which side it was best to be on, hers or mine.

My interest in Clare's interesting information never abated though. She became ever more fascinating to me in her pinched jacket (she had several of more or less the same style actually). She told me about chutney (a sweet food that is strangely sour); potholes in roads (I had never seen a road but I had an idea of the broad, flatness they must show when not holed, and how disturbing a hole must be when you were accustomed to that usual, unbroken expanse); stereos (machines that make music without being conducted, but need to be monitored, which involves less movement); poetry (words that mean more than words because they are so carefully chosen, and try to go about proving that the loved one is immortalised by the one who loves them) and many other things. She even enlightened me about mother's former hell and damnation, which were quoted from a particularly threatening part of a very fat book.

'You know, the plough, the big dipper,' she squealed with dramatic effect, plunging her hand up and down, 'dips to us up there in the north sky, showing us our way and all that.'

'Yeah, up there,' I said and pointed my nose toward the north, definitely the north.

'Well, you should see it anyway, you're so close to it up there. I don't see it really. Can't, y'see,' and she gave her nervous laugh.

She talked about people too, lots of people.

'Should've seen the look on her face!'

'What was it like?' I boldly questioned.

'Oh, oh...' She seemed at a loss for ideas now. Perhaps I should not have asked. 'Oh... terrible. Like...

233

like her mother had just died.'

I pictured my own face muttering with a glee that was laced with wickedness. What that had to do with being caught eating chutney out of the pot I guessed was something to do with the strange sweet-sour contrast of the food itself.

'Just can't control himself, you know what I mean?' was another one, this time about her neighbour.

'Probably just can't,' I ventured.

'No, no, I guess not,' she mumbled pensively as though I had introduced some new angle on things.

Men were a whole topic unto themselves and one where she could not say anything direct enough for me to understand at all. I thought men were normal things until she made such an obscurity out of them. But, as I said, my discernment about normal normality was not high.

'Had a thing with the guy from number forty-seven, but turns out he was a bit of a bastard. Bit of fun though for a while, nothing extra,' she squeaked her usual squeak of ever flatness. 'Any romance in your life Moot?'

'Oh, nothing extra,' I swooshed, perhaps a bit too hastily but it seemed to work because there was a silence rather than another question.

'Hm, all right then. See you later love,' and she shuffled in a getting-ready-to-go way.

'Yeah, later love,' I returned and we both waved loosely with our right hand to one other.

The relief I had felt by mother absorbing her own doom powered me for years. I muttered and muttered, as required, 'You were doomed! Ha, ha!' and suchlike and my building went very vertically well. I could hardly get better at it now because there was no measure of better for it to be. My walls were perfect. This brought me huge satisfaction and I lived in a relatively peaceful mind and heart for the first time, wondering if I would discover

Clare's kind of flatness in myself next and did it equate to happiness.

Those wonderings went obsolete. My peaceful mind and heart were not to last, of course. A couple of things occurred.

I was just quietly singing, 'Doom, doom, doom-doom-doomed mother!' and skipping with furtive skips along my walls toward the pile of unhewn stone I had left on the southeast corner, wearing my second-to-last last tunic. As the muttering melody spilling from my peaceful heart reached the umpteenth refrain I spotted something flapping in a swift agitation of colours in the distance by the houses, the ones up on the hill that I had formerly obsessed about, that I most loved when I saw cloaked in poisonous gloop from the sky thus enhancing my own sense of safety and achievement. The flapping, coloured sight amidst the homes stalled my little song because I had an immediate suspicion as to what it was. I squinted and peered far, far away trying to disprove myself, wishing it could be anything else. I yearned with an impulsive and immediate desire to see some other explanation as I strained to see through my narrowed eyes, but it was not so. What had caught my eye was unmistakably what Clare had described as bunting (colourful flags of a triangular shape tied in a line to string and suggesting celebration and decoration and frivolity and so on).

Needless to say, I hated Clare for this. She wasn't exactly to blame, but I hated her and blamed her anyway because she was not there and it was easy. In my hate I could not help but picture her as she gave one of her nervous laughs, and in my mind her going-to-die face melted and I saw only her teeth hung in the rank air which was her breath. I was so spellbound by this image that I didn't even mutter for the whole of the rest of the day and the following night. My mutter had been evaporated in mid-refrain and its absence left my mood flaccidly sliding down to a darker depth that I thought I had left behind in the times when Ervil Nitzo let me down or when I first wondered how I felt about nail varnish.

Then, the next day, after the sun had gone past its middle and the wind had dropped to a pleasant rush, something else happened. The bunting was still there, oh yes it was, taunting me and calling me a fool, but now it was worse. From the same direction as I saw these accursed flags, the wind blew to my grumpy ears strains of what I could only conclude was music. I had been attentive when Clare had been talking about the conductorless music from stereos and I had gleaned enough knowledge to guess for almost certain that what I was hearing was undeniably this. I did try to deny it of course, but trying never works and I gave that up. It was music and this could mean only one thing: someone was having a party (a happy get together of lively people to celebrate something). This, in turn, could only mean another thing: the Wild Times were subsiding.

My brain crawled all over this conclusion searching for optimism. I tired myself out in my rummaging optimism forays and was weaker on each subsequent expedition. I wandered breathlessly around my flagging head and searched with my eyes around the not-so-familiar-any-more landscape, searching, searching for evidence of the Wild Times, any sign that anything at all still meant something. Nothing. I found none. The Wild Times were subsiding. Eventually my flaccid state popped, leaked and left the wrinkled remains of me, lost on top of my walls.

If I was honest with myself I could say that I had neither heard nor seen the Wild Times for at least all of my peaceful phase. I had not even heard the clatters and growls of dear Uncle Heap protecting my family and my old home. It must be true. Suddenly it was all for nothing. My safe safe house was safe from nothing at all. The project of my life was extraneous. My hollow heart was opened into a yawning cavern. Sunken hopes were poured out leaving a thirsting pit. Futility reigned in a life that was beside the point.

And I don't just mean the work, the building, it was more. It was me, what I had come to think of myself and what others had come to think of me. I could no longer be obscurely proud of the poor workmanship that the first few floors of my safe safe house exhibited. They did not keep me roughly safe from all danger, because there was no danger. I felt, and must have looked, a fool with a shoddy house. Worse still, it was me who built the house and it could only be seen to be mine and to represent all that I was.

Bunting, eh. Music, eh. It was all so indulgent, extravagant, greedy, fanatical, extreme. My spinning head flew off towards wild thoughts that maybe indulgence would be the new danger now that the Wild Times were subsided, that indulgence could get out of control, take multiple guises and disguises, threaten us all, punish our bodies and torture our heads (me and the other inhabitants of the planet that is, whoever they were). I thought about chocolate and wondered if my walls could keep me safe from it or not. Suddenly I was not feeling Granite-like at all.

Without wanting to state the obvious, it was not a great time for the next thing to happen. There couldn't have been a good time, of course, but my sense of purpose and determination having morphed from Granite sturdiness to spongy sog left me prey to the worst. In all my jumbled and shaky thoughts, I sadly discovered the most obvious thing that I had never thought before. As if the discovery of the unthought thought was not enough, the puzzling knowledge that I had so long missed the blatantly obvious threw me into a new spin of self-doubt. Maybe it was the shake-up of the bunting and music that had somehow jarred it loose in my head, maybe the Granite had seduced my brain into a state of solid unthinkingness, or maybe the time was just wrong in the scheme of things, I don't know, but it came to me in a low moment: I deduced the devastating fact that what Nitzo Pits-oh would have intended (had he taken an active professional role in my safe safe house) was to put in a door.

No door. There was no door in my house. I had no door. For coming and going there was nothing door-like at all. I had simply walked in and built my safety around me, gushing with silly, girlish Granite pride. Now I had no door, but no reason to stay behind my walls either. I was trapped behind my walls, on display as the silly girl I was who knew nothing about anything. My doorlessness must have been evident to anyone who even glanced from a distance and by this sign they would know what I was: the very person I had thought I was building a way away from. It crossed my mind that the sideways looks that Clare had given me early on, and I had taken for friendly interest, were in fact pity after all.

After years of building my walls and my confidence and my peace and my happiness, it was a hard fall I took. My life now appeared to be illuminated by a new light, a bold new message that spelled out just what a huge embarrassing stutter I was. My life seemed only to have halted in moments long enough to find the next stupidity to aim for, ever. I had merely tripped from one folly to the next, each foolishness becoming larger, more ambitious and more permanent than its predecessor, more visible to the wider and wider world who were surely increasingly discerning about such things the wider they got.

I did my best to look out from the tops in the morning but could not keep myself there, up high, it made me sick. I slipped, slithered and fell, down, down, to the shady depths of my prison to wait it out. Descending from the tops into the bowels of my safe safe house resembled a clamber into a grave, my grave, and lingering there all day, until the failing of the light, was an agony, a suspended hope that endings would comfort me. The dusk came on so slowly that I sometimes became certain that the day had stopped in that limbo space. The hindered time and illumination stalled my very blood and my hands no longer leaked. I sat in a slow madness for hours of each day looking and looking over my not leaking hands and only every so often surfaced from that uncountable spell enough to know that if time, my time, got much slower there could be nothing after it, nothing would follow.

I tried to keep myself thinking, about anything. In trying to warm up my will to rage against Nitzo Pits-oh I got lost in a detailed remembering of all the insulting things I had said in my many letters that Toobit had delivered. I remembered indulging in many convoluted ways of calling him a bore, suggesting that his blandness shone from him as light does from the sun, even hinting that a failure on his part could lead to some bloody outcome. I wondered how much I had dwelt upon the matter of his inky nose. I couldn't be sure. Maybe the notable architect would have helped me if I had not written all of them, maybe he would have relented, maybe I could have been more patient, maybe I would have had a door now. It was all my fault, and any other way of thinking that had tried to wheedle its way into my favour was a lie. On the other hand, Ervil Nitzo was a conceited and ugly and incompetent and rude architect who commanded little respect from me, even if he might have thought of a door, which maybe he wouldn't have, I don't know. I went back to my hands.

So, no door, no door and still no door. The

ventilation ditch crossing right under the wall was there, right where I slippingly realigned my ankle when I first came to live there, so at least air could pass from inside to outside. I thought about this ditch for days and examined, blow by blow, all the ways in which I hated it and found it inadequate before I actually managed to move my body over to look at it again. The hole had always bothered me in the bleak season because it allowed an extra freeze to enter, but it was great in the moment of unbearable heat which came once a year. Right at the time I was looking at it, the season was deep in bleakness. I hated my ventilation ditch.

The impossibility of all my thoughts bounced against the certainty of the most unlikely other thoughts. I was sure I could fly from my walls to a distant city and become famous as the flying girl, be revered in their religion, pampered and adored, never want for anything again. I knew I could dig my way out and walk to a warm place where walls were not important and people lived under a light canvas woven from spider silk. I could descend the walls, downwards from the tops like a crawling creature, and run with the wind, rescue Great Uncle Lollo from obscurity and bring him with me, trailing his birds, to a life of refinement. I could slither through my ventilation hole, heroically damaging myself on the way and make contact with whomever I wanted.

I bet my shiniest knife appendage that Pits-oh still thought he was smart and had forgotten all about a snivelling girl client like me. I hated him now. No door, eh. I could do it, overcome anything (if only I could move at all). I moved in a static rage against him, against mother and the doom doom doom years she had inflicted and against the foul and untrustworthy Wild Times who had deserted me, left, gone, dissolved and abandoned their important task of maintaining meaning, leaving behind a space filled only by nonsensical bunting and stupid music.

All my passionate thoughts washed around me like water in a wind, and I lay limp and fretful whilst they rinsed me in a blue drowning and a green nourishing: they were of me and of another realm, each one crisp, like a bleak season sky at night. And a cumulative learning gradually transferred from them to me. I learned what the leading light of the big dipper was, the one that showed me my way, just as Clare had said. I reasoned that on the way to greater things there are usually dips. I had had my dips already, but this was truly my big dipper. It ploughed crude tracks in the front of my brain, just above my wet eyes, furrowing my middle years and drawing in my old age, rendering all the impossible possible (supposedly) and all the possible as remote as redness is from greenness. The northern sky pressed on my heart and I was mute as it held me.

Chapter Thirty: An Important Piece of White Paper

Acting, as I was, like a drifting log in my own sloshy body, I opened my knife in a dimly-lit tinkering moment one evening to find a shocking thing: one of my appendages was rusty. I took that sharp, cold intake of breath through my mouth that expressed the sharpness of my rusty shock, snapped out of my drifting, and examined all the other appendages. They were all rusty and I wondered what this could possibly mean. A restless night followed in cardboard corner, but when I looked out from the tops of my walls the following morning I found the meaning of the sign right away. There, outside my old house, and not too far from the ragflag pole, sat Uncle Heap in the other Wild Times Fair chair we possessed, the one not occupied by the ghost of mother's quietsadness. He was still as still. I had never seen him sit in the chair before, in fact he rarely even sat down on our watch blocks with me unless it was to hold my hand or for one of our intense secret talks. He looked asleep and was wearing his tatty, stained overalls which I thought were probably not warm enough for the bleak season, not for dozing at least. Pinned to his chest was a piece of white paper which flapped lazily.

There was a profound silence that day, which smelled of the bleak season's earth, and I felt uncomfortable and pensive as I slithered below for the afternoon. The stillness followed me and my jarring head settled to a blankness and serenity. Later, the night air that wafted through the ventilation hole to me seemed thick, and in the morning everything had a light dusting of grey ash, including Uncle Heap who still sat in our

242

other Wild Times Fair chair with the paper flapping lazily on his chest. The morning after that, more grey ash had landed and everything, including Uncle Heap, began to take on a monotone monotony. The morning following that again showed the greyness thick and soft and untouched and homogenising the landscape and Uncle Heap with it, apart from his lazily flapping piece of paper, still brilliantly white and valiantly pinned to his chest. The silent night-storm thickened the air the next night and in the morning the land looked smothered by grey grief and Uncle Heap, underneath some of it, could be seen to be looking less well than he had at other times. As the next grey-black night passed in much the same way, the following day I found that almost nothing was discernible around me, the flapping paper being one shining white exception.

'Rusty,' I thought.

Of course I was deliberating in these days. Of course I was. I rationalised that the Wild Times had subsided and that the impossible had become possible, so I vowed to pull out my bone-beaded hat the next morning from the storage crevice where it had taken retirement and slither with it through my ventilation hole, heroically damage myself on the way and make contact with my old life which I now reluctantly admitted remained a part of my present. I needed that piece of paper.

Sleeping did not go so well that night as I lay in anticipation of the wide open journey (so long, so alone), but the good news was that no more of the powderous ash came to thicken the grief. Nevertheless, it was already thick enough. I pushed my brave hat in front of me through the hole to clear the way and lay on my back to begin the downwards then upwards bend of the hole, head first. The downwards felt unnatural because it is not the way I was designed to see where I am going forwards. Whatever I did to use my hat as a herald to my coming, the grey ash smothered me and fell in my face. This was inevitable I suppose, but I considered it unfortunate that it coincided with the sharp and hard and intrusive Granite stones which wanted to trap me. Altogether it was not a happy experience. It was not a space made for me, even puny me, and never would have been, not even when I used to be punier. Now that my remaining puniness was toughened up, harder and thicker than before, passing through was more difficult. Perhaps the softer me of former days could have squidged without so much harm, but I had never thought of squidging until now, which was ironic. The Granite succeeded three times and I had to hurt myself to escape its grip and I could not be sure that return was possible. I finally pushed my way through the grey grief that my hat had piled outside. I could not breath for several seconds during which time my residual breath depleted itself rapidly due to my throbbing heart. I heard the tinkle of a small falling stone or two behind me that I must have been dislodged by my squeezing, a crumbly dust fell on my legs and I was free. My rough tunic had protected me a great deal and did not tear or wear through but was of such an extreme roughness that it grated me at the same time as preventing laceration. I came out raw, bleeding in new places under my clothes, the red spreading here and there to overcome the grey dustiness on the fabric. I pushed the ashen hat on my head and sat down to gather my courage for the long trip in this monotone land that I had never visited before.

The grey ash was surprising. With tentative steps I advanced toward the grey lump that I was pretty sure was the half-way tree with the old lightning strike. Sometimes the land felt solid below my feet and would try to lull me into a belief in monotonous solidity before it would surprise me by letting me sink deeply or giving way, sending me skidding to the kind of palpitating halt that is easy to imagine in such circumstances. It was light and soft but deceptive, and made the earth and plants and burnt bits and rocks beneath it deceptive as well.

Bothered and not best beautiful, I arrived. At least Uncle Heap would not see me in this state. I made my way towards him and he came into sight as I rounded the house. It was a blow when I saw that the paper had lazily flapped off and was nowhere to be seen but I did not let it affect me until I had tried to get the better of the situation. I walked right up to Uncle Heap in the Fair chair.

'Hello Uncle Heap. It was hard getting here through that small hole,' I whispered habitually, 'and my knife has gone a bit rusty Uncle Heap. It's very bad.'

He was a bit chewed, a bit eaten, but only by the mice and harmless birds who like soft bits, like eyes or the tender parts inside your lips. His body was all there and resting just as he had left it. His cheeks looked pendulous but I guessed that they were like sheets of hanging ice. I marvelled at the bloodless whiteness of the skin of his face that the mice and birds had left. The comforting hands that I had loved so long were swollen and purple and, as I held them, hard and cold. Still, I was extremely pleased to see him almost to the point of forgetting the paper. But I did not.

'Where is the paper Uncle Heap?' I whisperingly demanded in his leathery ear. 'Where has the wind put it? Curse this grey ash that disguises everything as something else.'

In a state of hateful grumbling, resisting the domination of this droning grey, I set out to look for the paper, scuffing with my feet and delving with my hands into the soft tedium thereabouts. It didn't take long before it was there with me, snail-trailed and grief-smeared, but legible enough. In a faint and faltering hand were written the words: BILD A WINDOH.

'Build a window?' I whispered under my astonished breath. 'What a brilliant idea.'

I held the precious paper in my two grey hands, absorbing all its qualities little by little. Considering that it was written by the man who had, with great foresight, taught me to read, it lacked some of the sophistication I would have expected. Sharp memories of some of our reading lessons flew unbidden into my mind: hours spent shuffling on my feet around the giant letter shapes Uncle Heap had drawn on the floor, then trying to find tiny versions of those same letters on the page with the ends of my fingers; of critical discoveries involving delicate but important words like 'secret' or 'marauding' or 'autophonomania'; of the covert suspicion that mother understood nothing of my word world. Clearly Uncle Heap had not been in good shape when he wrote this most astonishing note, but the main thing was that he got his important message across. I know I had begun to write him off as a continuing force for shaping my life, but here he was proving that he was as perceptive and wise as he ever had been and loved me no less. He had answered all the pain that the big dipper had dipped me into. This, his last gesture, proved to me beyond doubt that we were indeed co-stars in the same story.

'Uncle Heap?' I whispered again in the leathery ear, as of old. I gathered myself. 'You're brilliant. Thank you. We're co-stars in the same story. Thank you Uncle Heap.'

A happy skip came to my legs and I flipped away to see Great Uncle Lollo, stuffing the important piece of paper inside my tunic to a place where it would not escape and nor would it be blushed by any of my fresh bleeding.

'Great Uncle Lollo!' my voice burst out as I approached.

He made a question mark out of each dusty

eyebrow as he saw me, then broke into a cheerful, 'Nya nya! Nya nya! Nya nya!' and began conducting the symphony that accompanied my arrival. He stuck out his tongue and wiggled it playfully in time with the birds.

'Hello Great Uncle Lollo,' I said breathlessly, 'I'm going to build my own window.'

'Nya nya!' he enthusiastically replied.

'But I have to go now. It was nice to see you.'

'Nya nya! Nya nya!' his delight rained down on me.

Unfortunately, so did a rain of water from the sky. It was spitting at me as I left Great Uncle Lollo, then it came more plop, plop for a minute and I felt resigned, then large sheets of wetness sliced me for a while before the spitting came back. My bone beaded hat allowed a stream of rain to come through the old hole in the brim from our first expedition, but in general it shooed away much of the water from my head. Needless to say, the rest of me was a sopping blob. My highest hope was that my precious paper was still all right but I dared not pull it out to check lest it should become wet (if, indeed, it was dry). Worse than me being a sopping blob, all the grey ash of Uncle Heap's death turned into a slurry that was at least as slippery as any experience I had ever had with algal clods and brown goo in the wet times of climbing to the tops of my walls. Even worse still, I could sense the first of the darkness approaching.

'The Wuh-Wild Times have subsided, the Wuh-Wild Times have subsided, the Wuh-Wild Times have sub-sub-sided,' I muttered to myself as I slithered and squadged this way and that in the vague direction of the gate. The rain was letting up but the slurry it had left behind began to suction me to the ground as well as send me around in accelerating yelps to sticky landings, one or the other, either, at will. 'The Wuh-Wild Times have subsided, the Wuh-Wild Times have subsided, the Wuh-Wild Times have sub-subsided,' I chanted as my energy waned, along with the light, half way to the half way tree.

I knew I could make it to the tree but judging distances in the dark was not easy with my progress hampered so. My bone beaded hat seemed a hindrance, the beads themselves confusing the marginal impressions I was getting from my environment, but I dared not remove it. The grey paste was climbing up my leggings and up my tunic, up my arms, through my hair. The red blodges on my tunic were obscured and the significance of the wounds I had sustained earlier dimmed as I dragged this weight of stodge, attaching ever more firmly to me, gaspingly arriving at the half way tree. I clawed toward the tree's trunk and hung there, breathing more than my usual three hundred millilitres tidal volume of air and being haunted by memories of the evil strings of great juicy purple flowers that had hung alluringly along stems, curling furtively around this very trunk when I had first visited it with Uncle Heap. I shivered, moved on, breathed and breathed, knew I had to focus, so I started counting, measuring. I was not sure how far I had already come, but it was a lot more than six steps, eleven pants and a gasp already, a lot more. It was not yet completely dark, but it was a dark night and I counted three steps, four hundred and twenty-four slips, eighty-two frightening slips and three falls, all covered by eight hundred and eighty-nine breaths, amounting to nearly two hundred and sixty-seven litres of air, even at my normal tidal volume, before I stumbled headlong into my east-facing rough Granite wall. After that it was just a case of feeling along the wall until I recognised the ventilation ditch. And then feeling the other way as well, as it turned out, until I really found it. There it was, a tiny, gaping blackness in the huge, gaping blackness of the night, more fearful than when I had come through it earlier in the day because, 1) I got hurt on the first passage and knew I could look forward to more of the same, and 2) I couldn't see anything. I had to go head first, upside down again because I knew I would get stuck if I didn't. I felt nearly at the end of my energies before I began and only two things kept me going, 1) Fear of being out in the open, and 2) the excitement of having my letter to read (and read again) when I made it back to cardboard corner.

It was not the nicest thing. The grey paste had sludged into the dip making a suction effect and I am pretty certain that what I felt down there on my face and in my hands were small slimy creatures, which didn't appeal much. (I felt pleased to have killed at least one whose guts I found on my tunic in the morning, orange and white and black, all knit together with incredible slime that I could never completely get rid of.) I also found the tinkling stones that had tumbled due to my squeezing on my previous way through. Unfortunately I found them under my back and they were the cause of more grating and blood spilled outside (blood) and blood spilled inside (bruises). I did not struggle to breathe because of smothering ash this time, the darkness and my fear put together were thick enough to nearly choke me. I almost left my right arm behind, from the shoulder down, because the hole was so tight and the Granite so unfriendly. I thought it was more important to save my ribs and lungs. There was more dusty crumbling and stony falling in the hole as I brought my upper body inside my safe safe house then a bigger crumble rumble and the tiny tunnel collapsed on my legs. I worked to save my feet now and lay at times in a feverish exhaustion with them still buried. My smallness shrank before the size of the day but, obviously, I made it.

It had been a variegated experience. I awoke after untold cold hours with my head full of the fizzing static of all my yet to be explored plans. The big dipper had dipped me, shown me my direction and then dipped off somewhere else. A window, eh. I cleaned myself up as best I could so that I could root out and regard the magic letter which had not only lain intimate with my body since its retrieval from the ash, but had also endured the same trials as I had when coming through the ventilation hole in order to return to my home.

'BILD A WINDOH'

'Build. A. Window,' I whispered, thinkingly.

A window, a window, a window. It was all so simple, so perfect but I knew nothing more than how to build walls, up and up, how to bleed and sweat, how to collapse tunnels, how to breathe and climb without so much fear as to push me off. I wracked my brains but I could not identify any other resources, although I did take out my Granite knife and twiddle with it for inspiration and noted that it had cleaned up its rustiness and was ready for action.

Days of plotting mooched suspiciously past, with a kind of spiral of thoughts stumbling in my mind before I definitely knew that I could build it. Even if I had come no further on the craftsmanship side of things, I had named my last resource: I knew how to adapt to the inevitable. My window's coming into being was written in stone, carved in eternity, a foregone conclusion from the moment Uncle Heap conceived the plan, and therefore I would find the way to make it. I felt calm and purposeful and alone and confident and so did my magical knife, because it had cured itself from its rusty sadness. I knew I would never have a door, but I could make it a very fine window, of course I could, I could. I could illumine the inner darkness of my safety and from it I could look out on the beautiful world, soak up comfort and inspiration together, be seen, paused elegantly there, framed by my own skillfulness.

It was a major project and I had to be inventive. My brain began to work ceaselessly and I obsessed about window craft. Its dimensions relative to me were important so that I would experience its cosiness as well as its liberation from my puny standpoint: I wanted to be able to have that sense of flying without a strong possibility of tumbling out. Its dimensions relative to my safe safe house were important too: it must not compromise the structure or the symmetry of the building and be normal, as windows went, in my view of things. Its aspect was a huge question, of course: which way should it face?

Facing west I would have the full thrill of the deadly drop cliffs and the volatile sea below; I would measure emotions in the relentless aggression of the water against the rock and the infinity of turmoil across to the horizon; the setting sun would count the days and beckon the nights and I could watch the constellation of the bucket leap slowly across the sky heading for the wet smoothness of the distant future.

North would give me a view of land and land that spilled forward and onward, giving a sense of endless possibilities, clambering alongside the never-decided duplicitous yellow scrub whose scent pervaded still; I could look into the pit of stillness as the sky revolved around my view and find stillness within myself; here the crisp secrets of shadows would be distilled for me to spend my days deciphering.

A south facing window would mean I could check on my only fruit tree and swill with happy memories of sweet berries when the season came, breathe its scented blossoms in their time; I would catch the wind and ride on the warmth of the lowering arc of the sun all day long, even in the deepest bleakness; the magic of infinity would touch me as the land dropped eternally away; the power of transformation would be laid out before me as the unbroken, charred earth sprung up soft and green under the sky, new growth making way over the Wild

251

Times history.

Facing east, the rising moon would count my months and I could spy on my neighbours.

Window construction was something I had to invent all by myself. I even took out some of my precious paper and used my pencil to imagine new ways that an upwards of stone wall might leave an elegant hole, despite climbing against the persistent will of gravity. I rediscovered my hank of string (that I had strung from a particularly stringy plant so long ago) from its Granite crevice and used it in various measuring and shaping plans to guide my creative mind. I considered ways to make my window strong and had disturbing recurrences of the ventilation hole collapse come uninvited to my mind. Could extra blood and spit and sweat make a crucial difference? My building knife was sure to play an important role in the coming event and I held it in my other hand as I pencilled my ideas, hoping to make its inspiration leak through, hoping that if ever its rustiness returned it would cure itself or I could cure it.

It took much thought, experimentation and tessellation of information to piece together a picture of how the moonlight would fall at different times and in different seasons. I found this particularly important because of my long held dream that Uncle Heap had helped to keep vivid, that one day I would sleep in moonlight, or gaze at the round ball of it from my sleeping place at very least. This had many implications in reality, first amongst which was the removal of just-for-the-time-being cardboard corner to a higher and brighter domain. This was exceedingly ambitious after so many aeons in the increasingly slimy bowels of darkness, a conceptual leap that would summon courage to manifest. It also meant that anything else that might additionally come through my window was important too, be it rain, sun, wind, insects, birds, spray, darkness, noise, clouds or whatever. So all these things had to be calculated as best I could with the information I had, and noted and borne in mind against what would remain the ever-sturdy protection of my ancestral cardboard.

I contemplated all these notions and never touched my stone, not once, but my blood and spit seemed to flow more than ever, just with the exertion of thinking. They spread on my thinking paper and dripped into my building dirt, followed by the plashing tears that trembled along my jaw, squeezed out by my concentration and rush of daring planning. I lived in constant, dripping gratitude to Uncle Heap for lifting me out of the dipper and I thanked him for dying so conveniently and thoughtfully of me.

'THANK. YOU. UNCLE. HEAP!' I shouted most days while he sat there, then slumped there, absolutely still, on the other Fair chair, looking in worse health as time passed.

I owed my re-built pride to him, my re-found dignity and a brand new lustrous nobility, that were all framed by a beautiful Granite window in my mind. It would never be a door I knew, but I had to lay this thought aside and focus on the perfect window. I would never walk free, but I could assimilate all that my senses desired from this stunning viewpoint. My window was my salve after the blows of bunting and music, the subsidence of the Wild Times, doorlessness and old bitternesses about Ervil Nitzo. It smoothed the climb out of my big dip and shed a radiant light upon the coming journey.

Needless to say, I chose to opt for an east facing window.

Chapter Thirty-One: Crumbling

I came to not mind that my ventilation hole had collapsed: less draughts up my tunic. I forgot the ashen grey journey that I had made, forgot it ever more robustly, as I read and reread my letter from Uncle Heap with a bursting excitement in me. 'BILD A WINDOH,' pencilled in a spidery hand that was so sure it had to write the message that it overcame the cling of spideriness in order to do so. 'BILD A WINDOH.' My forgetting of the journey was a wall that rose between me (with my window building potential, holding the precious paper aloft, kissing it), and the monochrome memory of my one walking freedom, the single day when I had existed outside without the press of danger, safe from the Wild Times. Needless to say, my forgetting was a Granite wall, and in it was a window. I closed my eyes and looked through my window-to-come and watched as the ash blew away, daintily lifted on the westerly winds, and washed away in the plashing rains that ran in grey rivulets towards the deadly drop cliffs, after which the sea itself washed a grey tail out to the writhing line of the horizon. Colour flowed back into the landscape: greens usurped the downtrodden blacks; heavenly blue saturated the sky, flecked by friendly white flying things; flowers sprung up like exploded rainbows that had been scattered in a moment of joy. And all this framed by my window plans and visions. Windows were everything and the only thing that mattered. Windows were the new way. The questions and delays and difficulties of my past tallied in one perfect answer: a window. The ring of truth resounded in a great, wobbling window-ow-ow-ow-ow-

ow-ow-ow-ow-ow-ow-ow-ow-ow-ow-ow-ow-ow,   that repeated itself, a mesmeric call, a bell filling my head like a mist fills an empty valley, settling.   It was all one beautiful, window-shaped, reverberating blur.

Of course Uncle Heap needed to be buried. This knowledge would stab through my reverberations, and make my lip curl with a latent whinge. I didn't have time to think about it and didn't have any ideas about it without thinking about it.   His purpling corpse was shrinking in his tatty, stained overalls and a leakiness seemed to be collecting under the Fair chair in which he was slumping. I wondered if it would be good for sitting on again or if it would rot with Uncle Heap. Still nothing had eaten him, not properly at least, and I considered that nothing would want to now anyway. Maybe he was already being eaten by larvae and small things crawling and slinking through his fibres and wetness, sliding off his bones.

The good thing that came of the situation was that Menith spoke to me for the first time in years.   I wondered if I had understood her wrongly all along, been too seduced by her irritating nail-painting fetish. Maybe I had mangled her in my narrow-mindedness and never seen what she was. The voice with which she spoke to me was not that of a woman. It was a cloth-ripping voice whose source was utterly wild, never to be tamed, and untainted by the constrictions of painted nails. She was a rough animal, an ocean, a sea of waves, waves with red claws one day and purple the next. I saw in her frazzled hair, filled with sticks again, the truth of how she had been living and caught the gleam in her frightened and frightening eyes. Her face was streaked with scratches where she had clawed it and I saw her push back her sleeves, pull up her leggings in order to claw at any other skin she could reach. Her desperation screeched out to me through the gulf between us and I answered through my ringing window blur as best I could.

'Deeeeeeeeeeeeeeeeeeeeeeeeeeeeeeeeeeeeeeeeeead!' she would start up, tearing at her hair. 'Deeeeeeeeeeeeead! Dead! Dead! Dead! Dead-dead! Look! See! Dead! Stinking dead! Get him out of here! Stinking!' And then after a brief pause, 'Deeeeeeeeeeeeeeeead!!'

It was understandable. I hadn't even seen her on the doorstep for a while painting her fingers or toes. He probably didn't smell too nice.

'HAVE. TO. BURY. HIM,' I shouted, practically.

'Can't! I can't! He's rotting! Stinking! He'll fall to pieces in my hands! I can't!' she responded, impractically.

Her voice tore the air and raced at me like a crude, whittled weapon, more lethal because of its rough edges. She had a point: Uncle Heap was no longer in good shape and might be crumbly by now.

'NEXT. TO. MOTHER,' I directed.

'No! Nooooo!' and she broke off into a long, screaming, 'aaaaaeeeiiiiiiyyyyyyeee!', tearing at her clothes, paused, then resumed, 'He stinks! Rotting! Foul! Can't! Noooooooo!'

The 'no' rang on interminably and I sighed before it eventually got blown away in the breeze.

'DRAG. THE. CHAIR. NEXT. TO. MOTHER.'

'Nooooo! Can't! Stinks!' she screamed as she approached the chair and took hold of it, then, 'aaaaaaaaeeeeeeeeeee-ii!' as she began dragging it, swollen arms dangling and dragging feet grating the ground, leaving a deathly trail.

I noted Great Uncle Lollo while this was going on. He emerged, curious, from his shed with his tether behind him and sampled the new sounds with his nose and his fingers, tried the feel of the random, cutting pitch. Somehow it did not blend for him. He tried going inside again, shuffling, but that didn't last long. He was seduced to listen and came out again after a short interval, only to sit down with his head in his hands, swaying, occasionally looking up or shifting to cover his ears. I had never seen him so dumbfounded. He shook his head, got up, shambled and scuffed around, sat down, stood up, hands here, hands there, at a loss. Happy Great Uncle Lollo, no wonder he could not understand.

Menith dropped Uncle Heap and the chair and ran to the side of the house crying, 'Aaaaaaaah! Aaaaaaaaah!' and waving her arms frantically, 'I can't! Stinks!' then bent over to vomit. The vomiting did not quell her tongue and she ran back to Uncle Heap as fast as she had run away, still screaming, 'Deeeeead! Disgusting!' and dragged the chair a little closer to mother's burial plot.

Thus it continued, the dragging, the screaming, the shambling, the scuffing, the smelling, the rotting, the trailing. I offered minimal but, I think, useful support in how to get it done, and before nightfall Uncle Heap was tipped to the floor and covered by a rough pile of Granite rocks just as he fell, then left to rot in peace. Menith had redoubled her frenzy when I told her to cover him in stone. She ran away, clawing her flesh, pulling her hair and crying out in a persistent negative affirmation of her abilities. The Granite was clearly as fearful to her as it had been to me all that time ago before building, before safety, before blurred window plans. I tried to tell her what she needed to do, but I was speaking to someone for whom wisdom meant nothing unless it could be used to refine her nail-painting skills, so there was a strong resistance on her part to my suggestions. I comforted her as best I could, and imparted my Granite knowledge in the softest way that Granite would allow.

She did it anyway, and rather well in the end as far as I could tell. The great tragedy was her nails, of course. They were terribly damaged in the effort and she was most distressed, holding her shaking hands before her face and sobbing. I could hear her sobbing through the night and through the next day and the next, although she disappeared from view and went into the old house to suffer alone, with her nail varnish supplies at hand. The pitch of it was not the same hysteria as when she was burying Uncle Heap, this nail sorrow was more of a deep, fatal emotion whose swelling roar could not find space to live in her body and burgeoned out of her under no control into her lonely, aching world.

After that, the sky crumbled, just as I imagined Uncle Heap crumbling. A set of driving storms rained something pure over all the land and I felt that he must now be well planted in his grave, joined, sludge for sludge with the earth around him. The grey ash was indeed washed away, rivulets of it scampering cliff-wards just like in my window visions. The time was absolutely right for window construction.

Chapter Thirty-Two: Finishing with Negativity

The building force that was now in me was more powerful than ever before, my confidence and will unparalleled. I recognised, with love, the mightiness that was manifesting itself in me, and knew that dear Uncle Heap had bequeathed to me his share of it. I imagined that mightiness flying from Uncle Heap, over the tussocky earth, skirting the halfway tree, glancing off the grey rivulets and streaming up to the heights of my walls that punctured the sky with their loftiness, to enter me without invitation or announcement, a secret army installed with weapons drawn, smiling.

And it was with this new smiling that I began building my window. I had decided to make a negative window, a whole window where there would later be a hole, then build the rim of my beautiful view around it, render it solid and reliable, then push away the negative window, down to the faraway ground where falling things didn't matter. Thus I began, making a smooth, broad shelf to place the first of my negative window's stones upon, only so wide, polished and lovely to touch. I scattered it with a thick layer of dry dust and was at great pains not to allow any blood or spit or sweat or tears or any binding factor touch this dry material so that it might later let the rejected stones slide and fall away easily (I hoped).

I worked carefully, slowly, quietly singingly, no hurry, without anything more than Uncle Heap's smiling army inside me to tell me that it would work, and my flashing knife to make it pretty. I was sure of everything, sure even within all of its uncertainty. If uncertainty led to the wrong thing then I knew I would see, by its side, another right answer that I had not formerly thought of and then rightness would come about as it rightly should.

As I worked, I felt that nothing could touch me or interfere with my purpose. Because of this, a lurking something appeared, to lurkingly test my sureness in an enigmatic and threatening way. All the while there was a lingering seam in the sky above me that tried to pester me, a seam that still threatened to split, to open, and for my mother to reach down from it and take my life away, touch me with her freezing hand and still me in my work, infect my building with failure and smother my happiness. That is what she would have supposed was meant to happen, but I withered that bursting seam's burstiness and deflated its badness with my happy gaze, coughed and did not bow down to any inflated bigness it had. It stayed up there, higher even that me, shivering in the distant sky, lonely in a desert of thin blue air which leached its pressure, sucked away its turgidity and puffed it away as just another dusty cloud scudding on some elevated death plain. I think this lingering seam was mother's last effort to spell her doom on me, and I think it came because something important was happening: my window was under construction.

Happy seasons passed in my window work. I had started with the glamorous smoothness of my sill, but of course there was the wall to build to the same height all the way around my safe safe house, the negative window to build in a future hole, the window to build around the future hole and a roof to put over the top. Years of seasons I suppose. My middle age perhaps.

I loved every day. Clare visited now and then and admired my window spirit, skill and ingenuity as well as telling me about music and bunting events that were happening locally, thus explaining some of the things I saw and heard from the tops of my walls. The death in her face seemed calm and painless and she inquired less after my personal details and talked more of her own.

The bleak season softened and shortened, and the season of unbearable heat tamed itself into a drawn-out perfection of window building weather. Great Uncle Lollo conducted the majestic clouds when he was not conducting me or the birds (more numerous than ever). I noticed that I hadn't seen Toobit Lonkins for a while one day and, in fact, I never saw him again, so I suppose the thing that happens happened, and his fleas must have found another home if they continued to be fleas. Great Uncle Lollo was as happy as ever though.

Menith, when she finally emerged, was much tidier than during the burying time, and she continued to look more relaxed as time went on, sprawled in languishing nail-painting poses on the grass, no sticks in her hair now. I even saw her sleeping there in the sun, her hands laid carefully before her face where she could keep an eye on them at short notice if necessary, half wild animal, half painted sophisticate. She never spoke to me again but did acknowledge me with her eyes, which I valued.

For me, I did not invest everything in the success of my first ever attempted window, but I felt all the years of building and bleeding with the hard-hearted Granite coming to a close, one way or another. I worked with the knowledge of rest ahead of me, reward and enjoyment waiting to be mine when I lived with my new view on the world, now emerging from my dripping hands. No hurry. When first the floor plan of my safe safe house had been laid out so long ago, it seemed enormous. Now my house was many times higher than it was wide or long. More of a safe safe tower, or a safe-against-nothing tower, or a tower of achievement, or a tower of questions, with countless floors that I scrambled through on my little stone steps each day, lost in spinning numbers of how high it could all be measured. I was building the last floor and this would transform my rough Granite beginnings into a complete home, my labours into pride, my lost years into an architectural feature, my past into my present. It was good work, my secret army smiling as they brandished their weapons to the task.

I spiralled upwards with my Granite, one neat layer after the next, right around my whole safe safe house's thick walls, heaving stone from the darkness below in slow and deliberate stages to patiently complete what I now saw was what I had wanted for as long as Uncle Heap had known me (my whole life). On the long way around the south, west and north walls I constantly looked back to where my window was forming, relished the gleam of the burnished stone that peeped out from where my sill would be and drew the arc of window above it in my imagination. That's how I planned it: an arced window, one smooth curve from one end of the sill up over my head then down to the other end, all in burnished stone.

'I thought it was time for a window you see, it's as simple as that,' I shouted down to Clare one day when I was feeling particularly pleased with myself.

'Oh yes, good idea love,' she squeaked in a somewhat distracted way, looking over the scrub at the sky.

Of all the thick, nourishing air I had gulped and all the woinking thickening of my bones and my hair, of all my apparent growing, I could grow no more. I kept gulping in case I became weak for want of it, but I was sure I would get no bigger because the growing had stopped a long time ago. This was most fortunate because it meant I could plan my window for a fully grown me.

The sill was at hip height and, if I spread out my arms as I stood in the middle I could not reach both ends at once. The distance beyond my fingertips was a generous space as long as my forearms on each side, and I judged it enough to lend itself to an attractive arc that would rise well over my head without giving an impression that I was altogether as puny as I used to be. I had made these judgements and plans by laying an arc of stones on the floor and lying down inside it, doing my best to be inside my body lying there to be seen, and outside my body to see me lying there at the same time. It was a good enough strategy and worked, I believe. I'm no esteemed architect, as you know.

In the exciting times when I was building around my whole window/window hole I got to use up all the imaginative force I had generated and stored up while looking that way on my spiral around the rest of the walls. My imagination was profoundly sensual and I had, in this way, already lived the smells and feels and so on of this new invented building technique. It didn't always go as my imagination had seen it, meaning that I had to invent it twice, once when I imagined it, and again when I really had to do it. But there was no hurry. For my negative window I crafted each rock into the ideal shape with my knife then packed it gently around with building dust, constantly wiping the blood from my hands, the sweat from my face, holding back the tears so that the balancing act could all tumble when the time for tumbling came. It seemed extremely untumbleable as I built it, thick and satisfied, but I did not want to test it too severely just in case it tumbled for good, or my hope tumbled for good, one or the other. Things in life were apt to change (I had learned), but some things were worth trying to preserve for a while, if only to test out a theory.

The window itself was a different thing altogether, and different from how I had imagined it also. In the end I chose long, thin stones that would span the whole thickness of the wall, the depth of my sill, and I cut them and finished them and shined them with such a passion before laying them around my negative window, one on top of the other as I went up the side of my arc, then one next to the other as I went over the top, then one on top of the other again on the other side. They glowed with a heavy surety of presence and I loved them, continuously. Placing them was very difficult because I had to combine laying them on the layer of building dust that covered the negative window (and must have no juices added) with placing them in conjunction with their neighbouring window stones (to whom they had to be wholeheartedly and more firmly than ever joined, juices galore). It was tricky, but there was no hurry and the shine was important.

There came a morning when the negative window was finished. Later there was a day when the burnished window of my vision was complete around it. A month rolled in during which the walls reached the ultimate height that I had planned. Some year or other the roof was completed, and shortly after this, my pots were shifted to the new heights where they would stay for good. Everything was ready. It was the tumble day, the day for pushing and falling and seeing the view from my window for the first time.

Chapter Thirty-Three: The View from My Window

There had to be nerves. I worried, for instance, that the building dust or the falling stones might scratch my carefully burnished window. I had planned to make a full inspection from my new roof garden before the big push, but at this point I fretted that perhaps it had been unwise to assume that nobody and nothing could align itself under the path of the falling stone in the time it took me to run below and effect the collapse. How long would the tumble take, after all? It might be too heavy for me and take a long time. Or I might not be able to do it at all. I might have built it much too strongly and would need a Nursten-sized body to throw it out. Perhaps the window would prove to be too big in the end and I would be cold in my safe safe house because of it. Or maybe all my calculations, based on flexible facts, were wrong, subjective, and the moon would never flow through to me.

I sat out in my roof garden with the sun on my hair. I was staring out to the little homesteads and hills to the east, letting these questions and countless other thoughts stream through my mind, crystallising the last pre-window moments in my memory when suddenly I had had enough. The pre-window era had ended and that was that. I took a cursory glance below to make sure Clare wasn't there then ran my body below using my legs, with an excited and smiling army running inside me at the same time.

'Re-Rah!!!' they shouted as a body as I flung myself at my negative window.

Nothing at all happened, not that I could see in the

darkness at least, perhaps a slight movement of dust, not more. There were grumblings and re-groupings and strategy-plannings amongst my army and I gathered myself for a second assault, this time with my shoulder.

'Ho-Ho!!' came the call and I was excited again.

But still nothing happened, apart from maybe the dust again, I couldn't be totally sure. This would need some thought. More thought, I thought. I fought a feeling of the tiredness of thinking and forced thoughts around in my head, rearranging my minimal resources into different configurations around the pushing problem. Height, I needed height. I needed to reach the topmost part of the negative window arc and destroy it first at its weakest spot then work down its resistance elsewhere. A stick, I had none, but my spiked club, although it wasn't very spiky any more was as long as my arm. A chair or something to stand on, I had none, but if I could build walls into the sky I could certainly build a pushing platform.

Days later I was ready and poised on my pushing platform in front of the dark, never-before-open window, my blunted club in my hand, my bone beaded hat on my head for extra confidence and Clare hopefully not running under my east wall (she had never run, and these days she amble-wobbled, followed by her new expanded hips). The smiling army smiled in a whispering huddle and, there in the teetering shadows, I gave an almighty shove with my club at the highest place I could reach on my negative window (pretty high, but not the absolute very top).

There was a definite dusting, this time followed by a crunching sound, a shift of rock on rock and an excited murmur from the huddled army. I shoved again at the same spot which started a trickling, just like when my ventilation tunnel had collapsed, then a rush and the tumble began before I really believed in it at all. A high

266

kick with my left leg swiftly engaged me in the drama but, suddenly, without believing this either, I myself tumbled forwards from my pushing platform, got caught in the rush of stone, my gasp of shock filled with dirt and inaudible in the loudness of this carefully designed apocalypse. As the rock pushed through, I pulled my startled left leg back to safety. I intended to at least. I caught it on my sill, or maybe it got caught in the downward press of panicked Granite. Either way, the flighty stone seized its moment and suddenly clasped my leg, with my body attached to it, in an attempt to drag the whole of me into the roaring chaos of the fall. Struggling in my window hole, I began to be part of the ever downward tumble to the ever below, which would, in my case, have definitely meant forever. I heard the stone falling ahead of me, below me as it were, and knew I could not die, not now, not after all this. I tried to cling to my window to save myself, the gape of descent below my lonely feet, my slippery bleeding hands clinging, and me hoping that I had been right all along and that my fingertips would be much grippier than they appeared now that a crisis had emerged. The tears running down my face were like the rivulets of grey ash that had not so long ago disappeared over the deadly drop cliffs and I gasped the shocking dirt into my lungs, wanting, wanting very hard not to fall.

Finally, it was finished. A dusty and shocked me clambered inside to look outside for the first time. My heart hammered, but this was partly due to the thrill of my window. It was not an arrogant window. I fitted it. The light had burst through and my safe safe house had become a home. I brushed the sill off with my dusty hands and was reassured to see the burnished glow intact. I touched it, and felt myself in it, surrounded by it. I placed the flats of my hands on the sill and looked out to the eastern view, felt myself calming, framed by the

Granite all around me but open and connected at once. I moved about in my room, checking the mood of its presence and how it diminished only slightly as I got further away from it, then I looked back into my room (still full of shattered pushing platform and dusty debris, obviously) and saw for the first time the inside of my Granite safety, caught the three dimensions of my space as the dust particles roamed through the light.

I knew I had the best window within my horizons and I burst with pride. It was so much more than I could have put together just by thinking about it, like poetry I suppose, more than a sum of its parts, it had a contribution of its own that it made spontaneously, a magical quality. I knew that if the world was not already talking about my window they would be soon. They would be very jealous, full of awe, they would question how one puny female could do this, what kind of Granite marvel she must be. I felt marvellous.

The success of my window was not something I got used to for a long time. It could not dim and I bathed in it as though I had never seen light before. I spent some time throwing the remains of my pushing platform that nearly killed me out of the window too. I built it, so it was my prerogative to nearly die when I used it and my prerogative to then throw it out. I cleaned up inside and installed my few belongings, including my ancestral cardboard and kept the whole place beautiful. I pushed some of my few remaining blue and yellow flower seeds into the crevices around my window and they sprung up with alacrity, as proud as me, showing their delicate blooms with a hearty swagger. The wisdom and practicality of my forebears and my own pluck and resourcefulness were thus combined into a perfect living place, a balance.

'THANK. YOU. UNCLE. HEAP!' I shouted gloriously to the sky, leaning out from my sill. 'THANK. YOU. FOR.

268

THE. CARDBOARD. THANK. YOU. FOR. EVERYTHING!'

Thereafter, I took the daily thick air at my window, not getting bigger, but staying strong. I placed the purposeless round things that had come in my youthful bag onto my sill as ornaments to the long past, and donned my smart new tunic, made for a time of rest, never to be bled upon. It was so comfortable to take in the highness from the frame of my window. I had time to reflect on my life, and saw the window outcome as fitting, a sense of just arrival, the shambolic past of flying plates or whispered secrets or secret loves or splattering deaths or bloody building dirt all a memory that I owned still, but lived outside.

Below and around me I witnessed the beautiful world turning over in its seasons and loves. The scorched earth was covered over quickly by a green carpet with smatterings of pink and yellow, and this all matured and grew into shrubby things, which grew into soft trees, which filled with more birds in song than Great Uncle Lollo could ever have dreamt of. Through this wove paths that I discerned people walking along from time to time, couples holding hands, young men whistling or people going about their business moving normally from place to place without worry. The evenings were often flavoured with distant music and I heard laughter a few times that went with it. The weather became so benign and ready to please that it was a joy for me to see each sunrise and look forward to the day, and I believe my potted plants agreed with me.

The best and most satisfying thing, a thing that I discovered slowly over time and cycles of night, was that the moonlight did fall much as I had hoped, where I had placed my cardboard bed, where I lay to soak it up. The eternal song of that speechless light filled cavities of emptinesses in me that not even pain had recognised existed. How had I known? How did it know? It poured its way through that carefully considered path that was my window, for me and because of me.

(Today, Much Later, I Write an Extra Bit You Might Not Like, Sorry.)

(Reading this will depend on your strength of character and your devotion to windows (the first should be big, the second should be small). Read on only if you are brave. Don't be shocked at any of it because, for me, it was all a very long time ago, the window building. I still have my window smile today but it is wrinkled by great age. I can feel, with my now stiff fingers, that crevasses run up and down my cheeks when I am smiling and when the smile leaves me the topographical interest draws around my lips and under my chin, a soft landscape of downy flaccidity. I suspect that I may be even older than Uncle Heap ever got to be, who knows. When I move around my safe safe house my feet are at least as heavy as his ever used to look and my flesh hangs from me everywhere that I can see, my colour changed to a limp purple like that of someone whose blood no longer cares for excitement. On my arms, I witness again the crumpling of thin skin that will never uncrumple until it turns to a buried sludge, just like Uncle Heap had. My new stooped shoulders do not help me manage the care of my toenails, and I fancy that the veins may stand out a little more than they used to on the backs of my hands. I have enjoyed my years of post-building rest, and continue to enjoy them today. I feel love and great pride for my window, not in the sharp, blinding way that I did when it was first pushed through, but they are deep-running sentiments that define me nevertheless.

However, whatever my purplish hue suggests, I do care for excitement. I care for it more and more. There

271

has been ample time to consider and quantify the ferocity of the obstinacy that was in each of my family, that survival demanded, expressed one way or another. I think of mother (I always think of mother), the most obstinate of us all, her obstinacy so dense that she could not even move under its weight. She really lived. Whilst my obstinacy might have been bland at times, it was enough to get me through and to leave me room to grow old with a desire for excitement. Clare and her face died long ago. My snail is long since dry.

It could be said that it is the youthlessness of my youth that is to blame for this bout of senile thrill-seeking, but no, my youth was filled with the rich endlessness of detail and unfettered feelings that all youths have, as certainly as the stones weigh over a grave. It is difficult to pinpoint, but the truth is that today I live in my proud proud house in an increasingly unsettled state. I stumble through spells of unexplainable upset and am buffeted by gusts of grumpiness. I still see mother in my dreams, staring at me through the extinguished coals that were her eyes that she never looked at me with in life. I awake as though soaked by the sound of distant mockery, approaching me with the intent to smash my face with buttoned fists. Even the round laugh of the moon, that has so long swelled me and fed me, occasionally feels sad and puffy.

However pure or powerful my nugget is, there is a part of it that still trembles, a frightened hostage held in sad circumstances, its captors the murky, weeping figures who have all predeceased me, protagonists in the stories told or the stories withheld. There is a torpor that takes hold of me, an apathy which comes from nowhere and I have no patience to describe. It seems a poor match for the voracity of oblivion that I have avoided, and I dispel it as such with all the aged power left to me. Let it have no name. I, a puny person who has loved and overcome and transformed and endured, have no time for it. I want something else.

This wanting of something else is mountainously unforeseen. I never saw it coming at all. Even the softness of the distant trees that has so long wet my throat did not alert me. Perhaps I was just too absorbed in each day as it came, each project or each problem. I don't want to disappoint, I don't, but the raw truth is all I have ever known how to deal with, and this may be more of a disloyalty to windows and window building than you can bear to read. I feel like I am letting my window down, wavering in my window dedication. Age is shrinking me once more. It is hard to keep up the reserves to stay big, inside or outside.

Basically, I am left with a gentle intimacy of Granite, of myself, and a violent irritation of those things too. I hardly know how to say it, but what it comes down to, what I want but don't want to breathe into being with my voice is this: windows are not enough for me anymore.

It began when I found myself whispering to the stars in my dreams and waking wondering who I was. 'Windows are not enough.'

It seeped into the mornings and I whispered it to myself. 'You who are called Moot, your window is not enough for you anymore.'

In the afternoons, the taste of the green-shady trees began rising to my mouth and the pulse in my ears was nothing if not the gentle, rhythmic call of their sappy hearts, who said, 'Beyond windows... more.'

Then I would feel the night-time whispers coming on and it would arouse evening discussions with my window in the twilight as I lay in my ancestral cardboard. 'I'm sorry window, but I don't think you are enough for me anymore, however much I admire you.'

It has grown and grown and pierced me and poked me forward to my window, forced me to make a declaration to all the strange world that has never belonged to me, to shout more loudly than Uncle Heap ever heard me shout, to grate my throat with words grown angry, to puncture the clouds with the sharpened blades of my frustration.

'AWINDOWISNOTENOOOOUGHFORMEEEE!!!'

I tore the sky to ribbons before exhausting my rage and coming back to the blank thought that had seemed so easy years ago: it will never be a door. I regard the towering investment of my life to doorlessness, an investment that now precludes the choice of doors, and I have to fight off the weakness that comes with it, shoo away the blurry, insomniac shadows that are the sad answers to the questions that arise.

I can say to myself in a steady voice now that windows are definitely not enough. They are good, but never enough, not for anyone who aspires to living. I say it reasonably: no, windows will never be enough and should not be, however burnished they are, however elegant. I loved my window, and love it now. It was good in its time, but windows attract cobwebs: stand by them long enough and you will be wrapped in a lacy confinement. That's how it is.

Now I am old and punier again. Even the jungles in my armpits have thinned and gone white. I am old enough to spidery write my own piece of paper for the snails to trail on, search out my own way to answer the problems and difficulties of daily life. I have chipped away at the memories of the Wild Times and undermined them all, tumbling them away like falling rock, and I am left to weigh my doorless choices with fading time.

I decided it would be a good second investment to bring out my magical knife and set about further refining the beautifulness of my home in a profound and visible way with elaborate decorations. It was work I could pour myself into, careful, thoughtful, beautiful work that would have tangible results that would also rationalise my intangible thoughts about existence. I imagined the knife's flashing blades at work by my window in the half-light of the first of the moon and the last of the sun, coloured by the luminous discs and streaks that had so often graced my skies. It seemed a poetic image of persistence, but somehow lacking in love, lacking in spirit. No. It is a response spawned by the old me. Somehow I cannot drag that same old determination out again and trail it around, it has grown too heavy and cumbersome and can only serve to further monumentalise my doorlessness now. What happens to today, after all? It will go the way of all days that have gone and will ever go, slip away to the other side of death where Uncle Heap is roaming for his own obscure and battered reasons (as usual). This day will go, no matter what I do, whether I live and spread my wings or marry the stone where I sit, carving yet more commitment into my tower of unbelievable hopes.

No, it has come to me now. It has come as naturally as daylight, as silently as the savage darkness, as certainly as slow age. Filtering through all the information I have learned, all the words on my pilfered paper, all my surreptitious chats with Uncle Heap, all the feelings I have felt about all of it, finally I sift through my strange chats with Clare (love) and there I find it: knitting. I must knit. My resources are limited but at least I have this departing day, maybe the next, and I still have my wits, I think. I see it clearly and I begin: knitting my ladder that will take me down all the bloody walls of my middle age, of my youth, of my resilience and my stretched hopes. I will climb down my ladder and escape to the wildness that is good. I plan to feel the morning wetness of the new grasses between my toes as I make my way under the green shade of the big, distant trees, to embrace their living pulse; to discover afresh, and yet still sleep under the moonlight. I am knitting it from the cobwebs that my window has attracted, and from those hidden in my safe safe corners. I make my dark daily search through the layers of my tower for more and more cobwebs and stickily bring them back to my knitting. I bind them together with my own hairs, fallen in age. My old scalp no longer has the tenacity to hold onto these strong things, forged of the thick air over years of breathing. So I gather them, and the mouldering remains of my hank of string from my youth, re-weave them into the fabric of me, my present, using my small bony hands. I sit by my window and knit my escape ladder. I admire the view as I knit, knit, slowly knit, and know I will join it: infinity, blooming, beckoning, changing.)

About the Author

Born to an Eastern European émigré family swimming in the debris of a post-traumatic era, Gail Varga has sailed oceans, climbed mountains, pedalled across countries, lost blood sweat and tears over notions of progress, failed, loved, dealt bluntly with necessity, been close by when death was visiting and written this book, which was, at one point, rescued from her shipwrecked vessel in a remote part of the South Pacific and has had quite a life itself.

You can find out more about Gail Varga at gailvarga.com

In hopes that you have enjoyed this book (but even if you did not!), it would be very much appreciated if you left an honest review at amazon.com/author/gailvarga, or amazon.co.uk/author/gailvarga.

Acknowledgements

I would like to thank those who have helped me with editorial advice, including Chris Woolford, Brian Ellwood, Lavender Sansom and Juri Gabriel. The first draft of this novel was mainly written aboard s/v Ri Ri, and I would like to thank captain and owner Frank Conway for that special space to write.

www.ingramcontent.com/pod-product-compliance
Lightning Source LLC
Chambersburg PA
CBHW031703170626
46808CB00005B/1588